CW01096139

PAN

ALSO BY MICHAEL CLUNE

Gamelife: A Memoir

Writing Against Time

A Defense of Judgment

White Out: The Secret Life of Heroin

PAN

Michael Clune

FERN
PRESS

1 3 5 7 9 10 8 6 4 2

Fern Press, an imprint of Vintage, is part of
the Penguin Random House group of companies

Vintage, Penguin Random House UK, One Embassy Gardens,
8 Viaduct Gardens, London SW11 7BW

penguin.co.uk/vintage
global.penguinrandomhouse.com

First published in Great Britain by Fern Press in 2025
First published in the United States of America by Penguin Press,
an imprint of Penguin Random House LLC, in 2025

Designed by Alexis Farabaugh

Printed and bound in Great Britain by Clays Ltd, Elcograf S.p.A.

The authorised representative in the EEA is Penguin Random House Ireland,
Morrison Chambers, 32 Nassau Street, Dublin D02 YH68

A CIP catalogue record for this book is available from the British Library

HB ISBN 9781911717614
TPB ISBN 9781911717621

Penguin Random House is committed to a sustainable future
for our business, our readers and our planet. This book is made
from Forest Stewardship Council® certified paper.

For Aislin

But don’t dig too deeply into your mind . . .
you know we have to glide a little over the surface of thoughts.

MADAME DE SÉVIGNÉ

PAN

1. Light too bright.
2. Something's wrong.
3. Tingling in the fingers and toes.
4. Faster heartbeat.
5. Faster breathing.
6. Eyes moving around a lot.
7. The feeling that everything is strange.
8. The feeling that material objects are strange. And alien. They've always been horribly strange and alien, but only now am I really seeing it. Now is the *first time* I'm really seeing it, and it doesn't feel like it's just me, it doesn't feel like it's just a feeling, it's more than a feeling. These . . . *things*.
9. The conviction that my body is a thing. My hands. My nose.
10. Eyes starting to stick in things.
11. The fringe of body around my looking getting very bright.
12. Very alien.
13. The feeling that I could come out of my body. My head, in particular.
14. That my looking/thinking could pour or leap out.
15. Wonder where thoughts come from.
16. Wonder what looking is.
17. Afraid of what's next.
18. Carl.

PART I

SPRING

1.

Before the Castle of Chaluz, Near Limoges

My mom kicked me out. My behavior was getting out of control. Plus, she said, a teenage boy needed his father. So I went to live with Dad. He had a little town house. There was no town anywhere. I guess it's a polite term for "little house." The kind of house that would be respectable in the city, where land is expensive, but dropped out in the distant suburb of Libertyville, where land is cheap. Very cheap construction.

We lived in a small subdivision of town houses surrounded by empty land waiting to be developed. No sidewalks. No one knew anyone. No one's face held any kind of future for any neighbor, and so you couldn't even remember what the people who lived right next to you looked like. Always surrounded by unfamiliar faces. Just like in the city. But here there were only maybe twenty of us. In this subdivision. Maybe less. The subdivision was called Chariot Courts. We lived at 12A.

In the winter it was almost completely exposed. The raw death of the endless future, which at night in the Midwest in winter is sometimes bare inches above the roofs. Cheap housing's always more or less exposed. There was a housing project in Chicago where they found a four-year-old girl dead of old age. That was the coroner's conclusion, after examining her organs. It happened in the nineties. The coroner's report was supposed to be secret, but Larry's stepdad was a cop and he saw it. He had pictures of Dahmer's apartment too, pictures the newspapers never got. They shut that housing project down, farmed the residents out into town houses.

Chariot Courts wasn't the worst in terms of low-grade housing—far from it. The builders had wrought a few charms against total exposure to time. The name, first of all. And there was a cast-iron gate. If you could call it that. It was an odd gate, perched on an island in the center of the subdivision's entrance. On the right you had the drive going in, and on the left you had the drive going out. In the center was this little grassy island and in the middle was the gate, supported between two brick pillars. The pillars were maybe four feet high. The gate was maybe three feet wide. Real wrought iron. The bars bent into fantasies and curlicues of iron, and in the center the swirls thickened into letters:

CHARIOT COURTS

The gate had a handle, but it never opened. I mean, you could walk around to the other side easy enough. But you couldn't go through the gate. Me and Ty tried to open it one time when we were drunk.

"This fucking thing," he panted, pulling on the handle.

"It's closed," I said stupidly.

He stopped pulling, stumbled back. Looked at it.

"It's like they knew they couldn't really close this place."

I knew what he was thinking. Half the time we knew what the other was thinking.

"There's no way to really close a place like this," I said.

"It's so cheap," Ty said. "Squirrels could probably afford it."

"Wind could afford it," I said. "Trash."

"Remember that Styrofoam cup we found in your living room?" Ty said. "And no one knew how it got there?"

"Anything can come in," I said.

"If it wants to," he said.

"But they made sure no one could go through the gate," I said.

"They closed what they could," Ty finished.

The gate was the second charm. The third charm was the mailboxes. They were made out of wrought iron like the gate. There was no place to put your name. I mean, people were moving in and out of Chariot Courts all the time. Some of the unfamiliar faces were actually new, in the sense of not being here yesterday. Most places like that, the mailboxes have a little window where you can stick a scrap of paper or an index card or something with your name on it. But these mailboxes were above that kind of thing. They came from the eternal motionless past. You had to write your featherlight name on a piece of paper and tape it next to the box. Your name written on wind. Your squirrel name. The mailbox itself wouldn't acknowledge the possibility that a resident's name could change.

I was fifteen when Mom kicked me out and I moved into Chariot Courts with Dad. Those three charms meant a lot to me. I associated them with money. When there's nothing solid behind the present moment, when there's no real past, no tradition, when everything's basically exposed to the future, everything's constantly flying away into the hole of the future, money is the next best thing. The gate and the mailboxes and the name were like pieces dropped off of real houses. In a spiritual sense they were the heaviest objects around. They helped to weigh the place down, on nights when the future hung its open mouth above us, and the years burned like paper in our dreams.

*

It happened in the middle of January, when I was sitting in geometry class. Winter in Illinois, the flesh comes off the bones, what did we need geometry for? We could look at the naked angles of the trees, the circles in the sky at night. At noon we could look at our own faces. All the basic shapes were there, in bone. Bright winter sun turns kids skinless. Skins them. But there we were in geometry class. The teacher also taught physics. He was grotesquely tall. Thin. He'd demonstrate the angles on his bones.

This was Catholic school. The blackboard was useless. A gray swamp dense with half-drowned numbers. Mr. Streeling would bend a leg in midair: ninety degrees, cleaner than a protractor. He'd stand and tilt his impossibly flat torso: forty-five degrees. He could lift his pants leg, unbundle new levels of bone like a spider: fifteen degrees, fifty-five, one hundred . . .

"So this is an acute angle"—he lifts his leg. The girls turn away. The guys stare in mute fascination. Mr. Streeling graded girls' tests on a curve.

I was sitting in geometry class under the fluorescents when it happened. The first time, technically. Though I could only tell it was the first time in retrospect, looking back from the third time. This must have been in early January. My right hand on my desk, my left hand fiddling with a pencil in the air.

Mr. Streeling's voice booms out, "Open the textbook, page ninety-six." The textbook lies next to my hand on the desk. Next to the textbook is a large blue rubber eraser. Hand, textbook, eraser. Desktop bright in the fake light.

My hand, I realize slowly, it's a . . . *thing*.

My hand is a thing too. Hand, textbook, eraser. Three things.

Oh.

That's when I forgot how to breathe. Ty saw it happen. He was sitting across the room. The teacher didn't allow us to sit together, no teacher did. But he saw me, and he gave me a look like *what the hell*. Watching me trying to remember how to breathe. It wasn't going well. I was sucking in too much air, or I wasn't breathing enough out. The rhythm was all wrong.

Darkness at the edge of vision . . .

Two seconds blotted out . . . when I came back my lungs had picked up the tune. The old in-and-out, the tune you hear all the time. If it ever stops, try to remember it. You can't. Breathe in, breathe out, breathe in, breathe out. It never stops. But if it does, it's hard to remember how it goes. Ask dead people. Ask me. I gave Ty a shaky smile, like I'd been joking, my face probably red or maybe white or even a little blue. Ty turned slowly back to his textbook, shaking his head, like I was crazy. The idea that I was crazy and he was evil was the background joke of our friendship. It didn't bother him to see me like that. He didn't mention it.

The second time, it happened in a movie theater. My dad had

taken me to see *The Godfather III.* It was a Tuesday night. Late January. The theater was basically deserted. Kind of depressing, this father-son outing on a school night. Kind of cool too. Like we didn't give a fuck about school nights.

I think the show started around ten p.m. Everything was fine. The film was pretty good. Until halfway through when the Al Pacino character gets diabetes. As they said that word, *diabetes,* I could feel gas rising in my blood. The gas started to rise maybe a minute before *diabetes.* Like I knew they were going to say it. Like I prophesied it.

This time what I forgot was how to move blood through my body. My blood stopped. When your blood stops, the gas rises. That's my experience. Gas rising in the blood. Dad snored beside me. I woke him up, said we have to go. He looked at me. Ok.

As soon as we got up my blood started to move again. I was still in shock or something. Walking like I was about to fall over. When we got to the car I lay back in the passenger seat and pressed my forehead to the cold glass and Dad asked me if I was ok and I said yes, which he knew was a lie, but there was nothing else I could say.

I couldn't tell him that my blood had stopped. I couldn't tell him about the gas in my blood. Those were inside symptoms, not outside symptoms. I knew on some intuitive level that my blood stopping at the word *diabetes* wasn't a symptom Dad could work with. There'd be questions. Plus my blood actually stopped about a minute before the word that caused it. Hard to explain.

In fact there was nothing that could be said between myself and Dad about what happened to me in the theater. So it was the same as nothing happening. That was the second time.

The third time occurred two weeks later. A Sunday night in February. I was in my bed. 12A Chariot Courts. Typically my bedtime on school nights was ten thirty. I had to get up at six thirty to eat breakfast and shower. The bus came at seven. Dad went to bed at nine. When he was home. Which wasn't every night. He got up at an absurd, legendary hour. Four a.m., a time that no fifteen-year-old has ever seen. Until then.

On that Sunday night I climbed into my narrow bed in my narrow room at Dad's place. If you want to imagine what's on the walls of my bedroom, you can picture nothing. Just bare white paint. In reality there probably was something on the walls, but I can't see it from the angle I'm looking at it, coming from the future.

It's possible there was nothing on the walls. Divorced guys have a limited range of wall covering options when furnishing a town house for their kid who unexpectedly comes to live with them. One of those options, maybe the only option, is nothing.

I wonder sometimes if there had been something on the wall, whether the third time would have happened. If the third time didn't happen, the first two would have vanished on their own. Then who would I be?

If the wall of my bedroom had a picture of a sailboat, for instance. Or a picture of a castle. What if there had been a piece of wrought iron fixed to the wall? An old, ornate knocker. Maybe a fourth charm would have been enough.

*

I was reading *Ivanhoe*. The old Signet Classics paperback edition. There was a painting of a joust on the cover. A lot of red in the painting, I remember that. But not from bleeding knights like you'd expect. The knights were whole. The red was in the atmosphere. I sat up in my bed with my pillow propped against the wall and opened the book and started to read. It was probably ten fifteen or so. I usually read for a little while before falling asleep.

At a certain point early in the first chapter I became aware that I was having or was about to have a heart attack. As long as I kept reading I didn't have to think about this too much. When you're reading, the words of the book borrow the voice in your head. Words need a voice. The voice they use when you read is your voice. It's the voice your thoughts talk in. So if you give the voice to the book, your thoughts have no voice. They have to wait for the ends of paragraphs. They have to hold their breath until the chapter breaks.

So the lords and the ladies went to the joust, and the Saxon guy threw meat to his dog in his hall, and the other Saxon guy ran away, and the Jewish guy spoke to his daughter, and I was having a heart attack, and the Knight Templar looked down from atop his warhorse. He had an evil gleam in his eye.

I read at a medium pace. Too fast and the voice in your head can't keep up with the words. That's what your thoughts are waiting for. They catch the voice and flood your head with news of the catastrophe unfolding in your body.

But if you read too slow, then it's not just the chapter breaks you have to watch out for. Now you've got holes and gaps between the words. Maybe in some situations that's a good thing. You can savor the words. The words come swaddled with silence, like expensive truffles come swaddled, each one separate, while cheap chocolates are packed next to each other with their sides touching.

In a reading situation like mine you want the words packed next to each other with their sides touching. Because silence isn't delicate truffle-swaddling in that situation. It's heart attack holes. It's not even silence. Every second the book isn't talking, your thoughts are talking, urgently, telling you about this heart attack you're either having or about to have.

So I read at a medium pace. A constant, medium pace. I developed a technique where I'd read over the chapter breaks, and run the paragraphs together. I didn't pause. Sometimes I'd feel myself speeding up—the voice in my head began slipping on words. But I didn't lose it. I slowed down. Not too much. I kept the pace medium.

By chapter three I had it cold. I was a genius at reading *Ivanhoe* by chapter three. I doubt it's ever been read so well. It had a voice all to itself, with no interruptions, and no breaks, for the entire length of the book. How often has that happened in the history of *Ivanhoe*? The whole time I was reading I never even found out whether I was actually having the heart attack or just about to have it. That's how good an *Ivanhoe*-reader I got to be. The very next thought would have told me. But the next thought never came.

I suspended the heart attack in *Ivanhoe*. Like when you shake a bottle of oil-and-vinegar salad dressing. As long as you shake the bottle, the oil is suspended in the vinegar. When you stop shaking it, the oil comes out. So long as I read *Ivanhoe* my heart attack stayed suspended in the story.

I didn't stop reading. I didn't go to the bathroom. I didn't change my position. I didn't look at the clock. We went through the hours like that. Me, the Saxon lord, the Jewish guy, the heart attack, and the Knight Templar. We moved through eleven p.m. like that. In suspension. Midnight. One a.m. Two a.m. Three a.m. And then the legendary, unseen hour. Four a.m.

I heard Dad get up. The end of the story was very close now. Richard Coeur de Lion has come home. The news of his return spreads. Dad moves behind the thin wall that separates my room from his. Ivanhoe, Rowena. The sound of the shower. Rebecca! Rebecca . . . Dad goes down the stairs and I can hear the clink of silverware. The sound of the fridge opening . . .

"Ivanhoe distinguished himself in the service of Richard, and was graced with farther marks of the royal favour. He might have risen still higher, but for the premature death of the heroic Coeur-de-Lion, before the Castle of Chaluz, near Limoges."

At 4:35 a.m. *Ivanhoe* ended. I put down the book. I put on my pants and pulled on my sweater. Then I walked downstairs and told Dad that I was having a heart attack.

2.

Spring Starts Inside

At the emergency room they told me I was having a panic attack.

"Panic attack?" I repeated.

The bright fluorescence of the hospital room shone on red and black medical devices. Shone on my hands, crossed on my lap. They looked more like things than ever.

Dad welcomed the news.

"A panic attack," he said. "Nothing to worry about, thank God."

The emergency room doctor nodded.

"People often think they're having a heart attack when they first have a panic attack."

Actually it was the third time, I realized. It took three tries for it to learn how to mimic recognizable symptoms, to make itself public.

"What am I panicking about?" I asked.

They didn't find it easy to answer that question. To tell the truth they didn't find it a very compelling question. In the emergency room they deal with organ failure, stab wounds. Things of that nature. Philosophical questions about quasi diseases give way to the urgency of actual, vivid, outside-the-body blood, in large amounts. Pulseless wrists, severed legs. Prestigious, respectable conditions with absolutely unfakeable symptoms.

"Probably nothing," Dad ventured after a few seconds, looking hesitantly at the doctor.

"Could be anything," said the doctor. "If it happens again, breathe into a paper bag."

"What?"

"A paper bag," he repeated.

He explained that what happens when you have a panic attack is you hyperventilate. You breathe in more than you breathe out. So you don't have enough carbon dioxide, and your blood vessels contract, which causes you to feel lightheaded. You get tingling in the extremities, and other symptoms that can easily mimic an ignorant person's impression of what a heart attack is like.

He looked at me compassionately.

"But if you breathe into a paper bag, that will restore the carbon dioxide."

"So a paper bag cures panic attacks?" Dad asked.

The doctor paused. His beeper started to go off.

"Yes," he said. "Please excuse me now."

On the way back from the hospital, Dad stopped at the grocery store to buy some paper bags. He gave me two to stuff into my backpack. Then he dropped me off at school.

"Wait," he yelled from the car as I was walking away.

I hurried back. He thrust something at me through the open window.

"Better take one more bag," he said. "In case one of them gets wet."

"My mouth's dry," I said.

"What," he said.

"It's not wet," I said. "There's no way the bag can get wet."

"What," he said.

"Ok," I said, taking the bag.

"Have a good day," he said, rolling up the window and driving off.

*

The regular entrance, where the bus dropped you off, was locked. So I had to go in through the main entrance. I'd never used it before. Plainly it was designed for adults. The door swung open into a corridor with what looked like real marble on the floor. Expensive-looking dark-green tiles on the walls.

I crept through silently. The right side of the wall had about a hundred framed black-and-white photographs hung on it. Priests. All smiling. Facing the camera with the confidence of men who know they won't have faces for long. Now they'd all stepped out of their faces. That's what black-and-white photographs mean.

The faces hung there like rows of empty sneakers in a shop window. The priests had stepped out. Into the air, I thought. Breathing out, never breathing in. Maybe that's what it's like when you step out of your face at the end. Like the opposite of a panic attack. You breathe out more than you breathe in. Then you're out. Free.

I fingered my paper bag. What had the doctor said? A paper bag is a device for breathing out more than you breathe in. I wondered if other people used them. I stared at the wall of priests. Huffing their own CO_2 in a paper bag right before the shutter clicked. Maybe that's how they practiced for not having a face anymore.

I was sweating in my winter coat.

Pull yourself together, I thought. I hurried down the corridor.

When I was about ten feet away from the end, the door swung open. A nun I'd never seen stepped through glaring.

"What are you doing here?"

I blinked guiltily. Sweating in my coat, still holding the empty paper bag Dad had given me. I hadn't had a shower that morning. Greasy hair plastered my forehead.

"Get to class," she said.

She held the door open, pointing. I stuffed the bag in my pocket and shuffled forward. When I got close she stopped me. Put her long white hand on my shoulder.

"What's in your pocket?"

I gulped.

"Nothing," I said.

"Show me."

I dug the bags out.

"Just some paper bags," I said.

She squinted down her spectacles.

"That's trash," she observed. "What are you carrying trash around in your pockets for? Throw it out."

She pointed. For a second I didn't realize what she was pointing at. It looked like a model of a spaceship. That opening on top . . . A garbage can! I clutched my bags tighter.

"I can't *throw them out*," I said. "The doctor gave them to me. I mean he prescribed them."

The nun opened her mouth. She stared at me incredulously. Then she closed her mouth.

"You're planning to steal something," she said at last.

"No!" I said.

"Those bags won't be empty when you leave," she said. "Because you're going to steal something to put in them."

"No way," I said.

"I'm right, aren't I?"

"No."

"What are you going to steal?"

I didn't know how to respond.

"Three items," mused the nun. "Three items smaller than a paper lunch bag . . ."

"They aren't lunch bags," I insisted. "They're medical bags."

She ignored this.

"When you leave today," she said, stepping aside, still holding the door open, "come this way. I want to see you before you try to leave."

She made a brushing motion with her free hand, moving me along.

I walked through the door.

"Actually," she snapped at the last second before the door swung shut, "don't come this way when you leave. Don't come through here again."

The door swung shut. I looked down at the bags, clutched in my sweating hand.

They were wet. They were soaking wet.

*

I went into the first bathroom I saw and tried to dry out one of the bags under a hand dryer.

Dry, I thought. Dry, you bastard.

An attack could spring at any second. The damned bag felt like it was shrinking under the heat. When the dryer sound died I looked at what remained in my hand. A soft, warm, wrinkled, tan skin. Like a monkey's nut sack, I thought. I held it up. The neck was all ragged. It was going to be really difficult to get a good seal on it.

I began to experience a strong sensation that my body was a thing. Suddenly I felt very strongly that I had no more in common with my own body than with the gray walls of the bathroom.

Panic attack.

As soon as I put the bag to my mouth it started blowing in and out like an accordion, making an incredible sound, like a monkey was standing up and crouching down and standing up in it.

This is my breath, I thought. This invisible spastic monkey, it's my breath.

I got you in the bag, I thought. Trapped you. I see you now, you little monkey. Look at you jump.

After a while the monkey started to jump a little less frantically. This is what the phrase *got it in the bag* means, I reflected.

I got it in the bag.

I looked at my hand, wrapped around the neck of the bag. It had ceased to resemble the hand of a mannequin. It felt like mine again.

Another thirty seconds and my breath was bobbing gently in the bag, as tame as you please.

Gingerly, I took the bag away from my lips. It went limp. My breath, out of the bag. Free.

I waited to see what it would do.

I took in a big gulp of air and tensed, feeling the air expanding my chest, wondering if the exhale would be normal, or whether it would be just a constipated little gasp.

A good, long, slow breath out. I felt my shoulders relax. Looked at the deflated bag in my palm with relief, and something like affection.

It works, I thought. It's no problem.

The winter ended right then.

When you're fifteen, your body and mind are still tied to nature. The seasons start inside you. God fashions the new season out of interior materials. You discover the season, now you're performing it. You're winter, you're spring. And the things around start to mimic you.

It's why the change in seasons feels like prophecy.

It's why, when you grow older and the link between you and nature snaps, you get nostalgic when the seasons change.

That easy breath—the one I discovered stretched out and warm inside the paper bag—that was the first breeze of spring. Spring is panic's season. That surprises a lot of people. But panic, as I was to learn, isn't a disease of death. It's a disease of life.

*

I had to go to the dean's office to get a pass. I was a little nervous about it. Ty had called in a few times putting on a deep voice and pretending to be my dad so we could skip class. He loved imitating white people. He was really good at it. But now I was worried, because I knew my dad would've called in about my hospital visit from his car phone. Would the secretary notice the difference? Would she say something?

But she had the pass all written out when I entered the office. She looked up from her paperwork briefly and pushed it across her desk. A lot of things you worry about turn out to be nothing. And then you start having panic attacks for no reason.

When I opened the door to geometry class everyone turned smirking. I walked in and dropped the pass onto Mr. Streeling's desk. He screwed up his face to examine it, like a drug dealer looking at a worn twenty.

Waste of time. Everyone knew you couldn't fake those passes, they were on this special paper, kept locked in the dean's office. No one even knew where in the dean's office they kept the stuff, not even Caitlin, whose mom was one of the secretaries. There was simply no way to get your hands on it. And it's not like you could just xerox the letterhead. The paper itself had this thickness and quality that was impossible to imitate. But still Streeling would scrutinize every pass for occult signs of forgery.

Eventually he nodded at me. A bunch of the kids grinned like

I'd put something over. When you do enough bad-ass stuff, I reflected, you get credit even when you're following the rules.

Most of my social standing came from a vague perception that I did bad-ass stuff. Once in a while I'd get a detention for some little thing, like asking the biology teacher if you could get AIDS from eating used toilet paper. But my social prestige, such as it was, depended on the idea that bigger things happened out of sight.

Ty and I never wanted to get in real trouble. We never worked with marquee-level acts, the kind of spectacular violation that would instantly proclaim our rebel coolness to everyone. So it came down to a bunch of little things, properly framed. Like skipping school. What were we really doing when we skipped school? Watching daytime TV on my dad's couch and maybe drinking a little vermouth out of his liquor cabinet. Mixed with Gatorade.

But when people asked what you did when you skipped, you could talk about it in ways that, without lying exactly, would give people the impression of significant crime. The baseball-card thing came later. That was actually criminal. It was like four different felonies, so we had to stay quiet about it. Which was too bad, because it was a marquee-level act for sure. But then we didn't do the baseball-card scam for status. We did it for money.

Leaving the baseball-card thing aside, the usual game was how to play mildly bad-ass acts for full bad-ass prestige. Me and Ty had no aspiration of reaching the social summit. But in high school you have to be aware of your popularity. It's like your credit rating in adulthood, except that falling below a certain level means that anyone can attack you at any time, for any reason or for no reason.

Maybe a better analogy is temperature. You're made out of ice, and if your temperature rises too high, you melt. Keep cool. Minor popularity calculations were just part of the background hum of high school consciousness.

"Where were you?" Tony whispered to me.

Tony was an Italian kid of solid and unexceptional popularity, roughly the same level as me and Ty, though he'd gotten there by a different route. His strategy was total normality. Always effective, never impressive. I'd become friendly with him due to the more-than-faintly-bizarre circumstance of us being assigned seats next to each other in all of our classes. There was nothing alphabetical about it. His last name started with *S*.

"I was busy," I said, to buy time.

I hadn't figured out whether what I'd been through that morning was shareable. It was weird, for sure. Sometimes weird could go over. Matt Deck, for example, performed a dance routine to "Stayin' Alive" in front of the entire school. He'd somehow convinced the teacher running the pep rally to let him do it. I remember the moment in the stands when we realized that what Matt was doing down there all alone with everyone watching him was preparing to dance. Then the music came on. And he started to dance.

Everyone went quiet. The gym with its packed bleachers, "Stayin' Alive" blaring, Matt does his thing. His thing was a long slide, then a clap, then a long slide the other way. A jump in the air—a full turn. The turn was impressive in purely athletic terms. Then the long slide again.

Everyone motionless. Nothing in our experience had prepared us for this. You had the sense that anything could happen. Normally, in high school, the social meaning of every possible act is settled far in advance. But there we all were, waiting in real time to find out what Matt's dancing meant.

About halfway through his routine a kid started to laugh. That was ambiguous. A little later someone clapped. Just once, a single clap, after the full turn. But it was enough. The whole gym started clapping and laughing.

It ended as a total triumph. Legendary, in fact. But then Matt was an intrinsically cool guy. He genuinely didn't care what anyone else thought about him. He didn't even seem to know. If you had that quality, you could do a dance routine to "Stayin' Alive" in front of everyone at Carmel Catholic High School and it would go over great.

I didn't have that quality. Weird was generally risky.

Plus, I thought. Mental illness.

I realized that people would have access to one concept that would make sense of the weird thing that had happened to me. A concept that would quickly dispel the cloud of mystery that clung to the morning's events. This was the concept of mental illness.

Not that the idea that I might be mentally ill bothered me. I had the paper bags. I was fine. But I was thinking about *them*. There was nothing cool about mental illness in my high school. Maybe things are different now. But I don't think so. A guy comes into a room. He's obviously panicking. There's nothing wrong. He's freaking out by himself for no reason. Hard to imagine anyone looking at that and thinking, how cool.

Panic is the opposite of cool. Cool is the relative absence of consciousness. Which is why not caring is cool. The coolest eyes are dead eyes. Sunglasses are perennially cool. I believe that sunglasses have a different origin than other forms of eyewear. Sunglasses, I believe, have nothing genetically in common with regular glasses. Sunglasses are descended directly from the opaque visors of knights.

Military violence is the root of all social prestige. The knights attack with the coolness of metal. With opaque metal where their eyes should be. Hit me all you want, say their visored eyes. I won't feel a thing.

Cool is minimal consciousness. Approximation of the smooth, unblinking surface of polished stone or metal. Cool is alliance with the endless strength of the inorganic.

Panic, on the other hand, is excess of consciousness. Your consciousness gets so strong it actually leaps out of your mind entirely. It starts vibrating your body. It shakes meat and bone. When you're cool you feel a kind of identification with inanimate objects. When you're in a state of panic you feel completely alienated from the object world. Panic shakes the thing that you are in horror. Panic belongs to the air.

I whispered a couple words to Tony that artfully conveyed the impression that I had skipped class to do something cool.

While I whispered to Tony I watched Ty.

Ty watched me.

Ty knew for a fact that I was incapable of doing anything cool without him. He would have no scruples about embarrassing me in front of the whole school. Me being mentally ill might strike Ty as very, very funny.

If he found out about the hospital and the panic attacks, two things might happen. The first is that he would be sympathetic and maybe a little bored. His gaze might start to wander while I was talking. That would be a good sign.

The second possibility is that his eyes would spark as soon as I said the word *hospital*. Before I was done talking he'd be smiling, and when I was trying to backtrack, having realized my mistake, he'd be shouting: "Nick is mentally ill!" Shouting it to anyone within earshot, pointing at me and laughing, while I tried in a low voice to shut him up, to explain, to lie. A dead giveaway. Person A laughing and yelling while person B tries in a low voice to shut them up—kids can detect that from across a crowded room. They can spot that from an airplane. Soon there'd be a dozen of them laughing at me.

Ty would be totally oblivious of the fact that because he was my best friend, this embarrassing revelation about me was also socially damaging to him. He wouldn't care. Getting the maximum fun out of the materials at hand without being arrested or expelled was Ty's job. No other considerations applied when he was working.

A few minutes later Tony passed me a note, which I knew was from Ty before I even opened it.

"Where were you?"

I quickly scrawled my message below his, refolded it, and passed it back to Tony.

"Diarrhea."

In my experience, when someone asks you where you were and you tell them you had diarrhea, they never ask you about it again. To them, it's like it never happened.

"You were supposed to be there. You promised. Where the hell were you?"

"I had diarrhea."

And that's the end. If you're absent when you should have been present, the diarrhea excuse is the best. It simply annihilates your absence. There's literally nothing left to be excused once you say those four syllables. Plus, unlike other excuses, you can use it more than once, with very minor consequences, if any. If you fall into the habit of not being where you should be, it's a good word to know.

You have to be above a certain age, of course, for it to be effective. At age twelve, people still think diarrhea is funny. By fifteen, most people have matured into the adult relation to that word.

I watched Ty unfold my note. A faint wrinkle of disgust crossed his face when he read it. Then he crumpled it into a ball.

The clock said 10:21. I fingered the paper bag in my pocket with satisfaction.

Streeling droned. Now I could really feel my lack of sleep. The room seemed dim; the kids looked ghostly. 10:22. I yawned.

At 10:23 I turned to my left and looked out the window at the end of my row.

The window showed the same scene it always did: a brick path, thirty or forty feet long, terminating in the middle of a broad field. Back in the fall when school started I'd sometimes lazily wondered about this path. Maybe there'd been another building planned, and they built the path, then ran out of money.

Sometimes I imagined that the path's present form was intended from the beginning. A path that led into the middle of an empty field. I wondered what motive could lie behind such a path. Perhaps it had a religious significance. Catholic school, after all. They put you on the path. You start to walk, then the path ends. There you are. Nowhere. Now you have to rely on God. I could kind of imagine it. Part of some ritual, something you did in senior year religion class.

The thought of standing there at the end of the path, waiting for some kind of guidance from God, while the teacher and the rest of the class observed me from the window, made me nervous. Not that I disbelieved in guidance from God. Quite the contrary. But I felt sure that divine guidance wouldn't be forthcoming for me in that kind of situation. I felt that Tony would do fine with that kind of thing. Not me.

Gradually, over many hours of class-time boredom, and as a partial solution to my discomfort with the path outside the window, I'd come to see it as a pier. I began to see the field as a lake. This took some concentration at first. When it got to the point where I could see the lake as soon as I looked out the window, I started to try to see it as a part of the ocean. Finally, I was able to see the field as the whole ocean. This last step was made easier when the field was covered with snow, and I could experience the leafless trees not as marking the end of a field, but as black birds hovering over the ocean.

I'd been looking out the window this way more or less since January.

It was a relaxing way to look. Your mind inevitably starts to imagine departures when you look at a path or a sidewalk or a road or a highway. When you think about departing, you have to think about where you'd go and why. These aren't soothing thoughts. They have a tendency to make you feel as if you have to do something or go somewhere in real life.

Plus, if you're departing, you have to have an idea of where you're going, what you'll find. There's no magic in that. Depart for Chicago, arrive in Chicago. Two plus two equals four. Departure is a fundamentally rational, future-oriented state of mind.

But if you look at a pier, you think of arrivals. God typically communicated with me through arrivals.

At 10:23 in February on Panic Attack Monday, I saw that spring had arrived on the pier.

The sun had lost its winter quality. In winter the sunlight stands apart from things. When the winter sun touches the brick of the path, it's like a hand touching a cheek. But when the spring sun touches brick, it goes into it.

The brick begins to glow. The sun doesn't stay on the skin of things. It enters like food and water. The borders between things, as they begin to glow in the spring sun, become less distinct.

The sun outside the window was the spring sun. The prophecy I'd experienced in the bathroom with my paper bag was coming to fruition.

I tore off a corner of a page from my notebook, scribbled,

SPRING HAS STARTED

I folded the bit of paper, and tossed it over the shoulder of the auburn-haired girl seated in the desk in front of mine.

Sarah.

All semester I'd been wondering about something to tell her. Or ask her. I'd been waiting for some kind of opening. And now I had it. An inspiration. An arrival. I tossed the note onto her desk—

—and immediately asked myself what demon had possessed

me. As soon as I saw the square of paper bounce on her desk, I thought, What the fuck did I just do?

I dug my nails into my palms. My breath sped up.

I saw her look down at her desk. Maybe she'll think it's a mistake, I thought. Maybe I should lean forward and whisper, *Please pass that note to Ty.*

I should do that right now, I thought.

Do it now. Do it. Right now.

But it was too late. She picked up the note in one of her slender hands, unpicked it in a flowing motion.

I couldn't actually see her hands. I imagined them. All I could see was the grace of her shoulders' infinitesimal movements as her hands and arms worked, the slight inclination of her head. I heard the tiny gasps of unfolding paper.

In the front of the class Mr. Streeling was slowly rolling his pants leg up over his bony shin.

I watched Sarah's head turn to the left, saw her profile.

She looked out the window. The corner of her mouth turned up.

Twelve seconds later the paper square bounced on my desk. I unpicked it with sweating hands.

Below my message, she'd written a single word.

YES.

3.

Openings

I prophesied spring's early arrival. I prophesied the word *diabetes* in the movie theater, a whole minute before it happened. Is that improbable? Science fictional? No. At age fifteen, I still had a living connection with one element of the childhood world: prophecy. Most people remember nothing of this childhood power. I have a few theories about why.

First, the prophecies have a very short time horizon—somewhere between two seconds and one minute. That's not enough time for most kids to put the prophecy into words. And since we tend to remember events that have become entangled in words, it's not surprising that we forget most or all of our prophetic experiences.

Second, and related to the first, the prophecies tend to concern things with minimal social relevance—an acorn about to fall, the imminence of a blue car, a word someone will speak. Such things are of little interest to adults, who act as the gatekeepers for what children will remember, by selecting what internal and external events they ask the child to put into words.

You remember when you had a fever when you were four, because Mom noticed you were flushed and asked you how you were feeling. Then she took your temperature and told you it was a fever. But a lot of the other strange things that happened in your body—things much more intense and unusual than a fever's mild hallucinations—entirely escape the sieve of memory.

Yet some circumstances lead kids to both put the prophecy into words and to speak the words to an adult. If this happens, you remember. When I was five, I practiced prophecy as a way of impressing my babysitter, who I was in love with.

"Courtney," I said. "I love you."

She looked down at me irritably.

"You need to hold on to my hand, Nicholas," she said. "Why do I have to tell you every time?"

We were in the middle of the street. I'd wriggled out of her grip. Courtney's sense of danger seemed to me to be misplaced. Ours was a very quiet street—whole hours could pass without seeing a car. I also frankly doubted that being physically tied to a large, lumbering, slow-moving adult would help me avoid being hit by a car. The opposite seemed to be true. I had privately resolved that if a speeding car should ever unexpectedly round the corner and bear down on us, I would immediately slip free of whatever adult was holding my hand. But holding hands in the street was the Rule. My little brother held tightly on to Courtney's other hand.

"You *have* to hold hands," Alex said primly, earning him a smile.

Nothing would have pleased me better than to hold Courtney's hand in mine. But not the way we held hands crossing the street. That wasn't my idea of holding hands. *She* was holding *my* hand—more than my hand, in fact. She had a good portion of my arm in her grip. It was the kind of grip people used on luggage, or on bags of trash.

"I can walk across the street fine," I said. "I'm not like Alex. You don't have to make me."

I demonstrated my competence by matching Courtney step for step, not straying an inch. I kept the arm closest to hers tucked behind my back, in case she should try to snatch it. She sighed.

On the far side of the street lay the park, a wide, grassy expanse where no one had ever seen a car. Alex, released from Courtney's grip, ran off to play in the sandbox.

"What a beautiful day," I said.

Courtney looked at me strangely.

"Don't you want to go play in the sandbox?"

For a moment I was tempted. The sandbox was a magical place. Four wooden planks separated the earth of the sandbox from the earth of the ordinary world. The actual contents of the sandbox were not, despite its name, all that distinctive. Over the years grass and dirt had migrated into the box, and sand had crossed the border going the other direction. But within the frame, matter became meaningful. Outside the sandbox a pile of dirt was just a pile of dirt. Inside, it was a real pyramid, with priests and pharaohs.

I tore my gaze away from it.

"No," I said, resolutely. "I am enjoying the beautiful day."

This was a formula I'd heard my mother use when she didn't want to move. Courtney shrugged and sat down on the bench, digging her book out of her bag.

The March day may or may not have been beautiful, a word whose meaning I wasn't entirely sure about. But it did hold rare, wild energies. Big white clouds scudded across the blue sky, visible signs of the wind, which was invisible like God, cold, and marvelous.

There would be an interval of stillness. Suddenly the dead air moved, the bare tree branches danced, shivers of excitement passed across the stray pools left from the morning's rains. The silent solid world began to *breathe*. Stray pieces of matter—dead leaves or bits of newspaper—rose into the middle air and whirled.

Alex, sitting in the sandbox, threw back his head and raised both of his arms. I bit my lip to keep from grinning, stood into the wind like a soldier.

Then it vanished. The world grew ordinary and unmagical again. But you could sense the half-visible feelers, like the torn bit of newspaper, now trapped in the brambles of a bush, spread like a sail, waiting . . .

"Hey, Courtney," I said.

"What," she said without looking up from her book.

"I know when the wind is going to come."

That made her look up. Amusement curled her lip.

"Oh yeah?" she said.

"Yes."

I stood with my arms crossed over my chest, looking back at her. I waited a few seconds, until I felt it. I raised my right hand.

"Now," I said.

Instantly the wind blew out of nowhere. Wild excitement filled the world. Alex, sitting in the sandbox, raised both his arms.

The wind died.

Alex and I lowered our arms.

Courtney blinked.

"Whoa," she said. She was looking at me quizzically now. "That was a coincidence."

"What's a coincidence?" I asked.

"A coincidence," she said, "is when something happens for no reason."

I considered.

"What is it called when you know something is going to happen and then it does?"

She thought for a moment.

"Prophecy," she said.

"That's what I can do," I said. "Prophecy."

She smiled at me. I raised my hand. The air stood up and rushed around, the white clouds sped, the scrap of newspaper rose into the sky and disappeared in a flash of sun.

The wind died. Courtney's mouth opened, surprise and the start of belief in her eyes. She was seventeen. Maybe she was remembering how this worked. All afternoon I prophesied the wind.

When we were ready to cross the street again, she grabbed Alex's hand. Then she waited until I took her hand in mine.

*

Now I was fifteen, and prophecy had mostly decayed into coincidence. I could still prophesy the seasons, a little. And occasionally other things. Like the word *diabetes*, which I had prophesied a minute before its appearance in *The Godfather III*.

It was a word of dark magic, of poisoned time. I'd first encountered it in a book I'd read at age eight, in which a minor character—a child—gets thirsty, is diagnosed with diabetes, and dies within two pages. Since then I'd occasionally recognize in an otherwise blank hour the smile of an old enemy. The word would appear.

I also experienced false prophecies. At lunch period, two days and one and a half hours after Sarah had passed me the note that said "YES," I sat at my usual table with Ty and Nicole and the others. I was intensely aware of Sarah, who was sitting three tables behind me. I wondered if she was watching my back, guessing the movements of my hands as I ate my sandwich. I sat straight, tried to give my motions a studied insouciance.

"You have food on your face," Nicole observed.

That was when I had the false prophecy. I suddenly felt absolutely certain that Nicole was about to say "diabetes." I stared at her. The air went into prediabetic stillness. The seconds flattened and stretched. I felt Sarah's gaze on the back of my head.

I stared straight at Nicole's face, waiting.

"What," she said. "The fuck. Are you staring at?"

Misfire. No diabetes. But I couldn't blink. Neither did she. A feeling of unbearable intimacy developed. Staring at each other, our intertwined gazes like a sliver of ice, sliced off the social glacier, floating.

"Staring contest," Ty said.

I somehow unscrewed my gaze from Nicole's spiral eyes. We both blinked. She looked back at me with quick, darting glances, like her eyes were sore.

"Weirdo," she said.

"I'm zoned out," I said. "I haven't been sleeping too good."

"You should drink cough syrup for that," Ty said.

"That's your answer for everything," Nicole said.

"My dad's a doctor."

"Does he prescribe cough syrup for everything?"

"No," he said.

Nicole laughed.

"He's a bad doctor," Ty finished.

Ty was covering for me. He'd noticed the weirdness, and he was spraying the table with the small-arms fire of a stupid joke to provide cover for me to pull it together. That was the kind of thing that made you love him. On the one hand, he'd humiliate you in public if the mood took him. But that was strictly between me and him, the other people were just amplifiers, devices used to enhance a victory entirely contained within the walls of our friendship.

But when it came to other people attacking on their own initiative, to Nicole calling me "weirdo," for example, Ty had utter, instinctive loyalty. He'd covered for me countless times. Soon I was able to smile again.

"Ty's right," I told Nicole. "Cough syrup will cure any disease."

"It's just a question," he said, "of the right dosage."

"Two tablespoons to fall asleep," I said.

"Half a bottle cures fever," Ty said.

"And ten bottles," said Nicole, joining in, "cures diabetes."

My smile vanished.

"Cures it permanent," said Ty.

I put the smile back on my face. I got up and walked across the cafeteria toward the bathroom. The fluorescent lights were too bright. I was having trouble with my eyes. They would get stuck, as I was walking. Looking at a spot of tiled wall in front of me, I got stuck in it. Like staring at Nicole, but generalized. Inorganic surfaces became porous to my looking.

I felt my gaze vibrating inside my face. I became excruciatingly aware of the socket of my face, the socket that held my looking: the little fringe of my long hair, the faint brown circles of the frames of my glasses, the flesh-colored shadow of my nose.

My gaze turned in its socket. I couldn't control it. It spiraled into that circle of yellow tile wall. Blinking didn't cut it off. The blinks passed through it like bullets through a column of water.

It started to affect my walk. I was being pulled toward the spot of wall, while I was aiming for the door twenty feet to the right. My head was turned one way, my body another. People will notice, I thought.

I fumbled for the paper bag in my pocket. Somehow I got my gaze free and pointed the right way. Quick glances, I thought. That's the key. That's the secret. Quick, fast glances and the serious stare doesn't develop, the gaze doesn't get stuck.

And now I was worrying about whether it was real, whether the gaze-getting-stuck thing was even real, whether anything real had happened between me and Nicole, whether it was a weirdness that had a name, or whether it didn't have a name and would disappear on its own.

Fuck diabetes, I thought.

I got into the bathroom. Dull mirror and drab metal passed sickly fluorescence between them. Thankfully there was an empty stall. I kicked the seat down, then kicked the toilet paper roller hard with my foot so it sounded like I was getting a whole lot of toilet paper, effectively masking the sound of me unwrinkling my paper bag. If people were listening, I thought, they could think I needed a lot of toilet paper. They could think I had diarrhea. The word would go into their heads and disappear. It was a self-erasing word. The opposite of *diabetes*.

Then I had the bag to my face and the carbon dioxide was expanding my lungs and my thoughts were slowing. I forgot that my gaze was lodged in a socket of flesh, a socket of thingly substance. The frames of my glasses no longer stood out against my vision as alien.

It's just a reaction, I thought. Everyone has words that are bad for them.

My breath came slower now. The bag de- and re-flated calmly and regularly, with the unurgency of a domestic machine. A lawnmower, a vacuum cleaner. I lowered the bag.

I sat on the closed toilet seat with the paper bag loose in my right hand, breathing slowly, a smile growing on my face. I was thinking about Sarah. I was thinking how easy it would be. I could just walk up to her, take a few hits from the paper bag, and then ask her for her phone number. Or where she lived. Maybe I could ride the bus over there, if it was too far to bike. I had a feeling she didn't live close to me. We could go to a park, if the weather was nice. I could ask her what kind of music she liked.

*

After a few weeks I'd learned how to deal with the panic attacks pretty well. Just having a paper bag—knowing it was the ten-bottles-of-cough-syrup cure for panic—gave me confidence. Plus I began to learn some little tricks. When I felt the looking getting heavy and bright in my head—when I felt the first sudden flicker of awareness at the *weirdness* of my face and skull being a *thing* that had somehow trapped this thinking-looking that was thinking *this very thought* that was burrowing *out* of my head *into* something else—when I felt that, I started to move my look around.

Quick, fast glances, not lingering on any object—and especially not any face. Linger for no more than a second. That was my rule. Keep it moving. The panic would dissipate after a few minutes of that.

I wondered a little about why and how it worked. I'd wonder—what the hell is wrong with me, anyway? Who or what am I? Why, in certain moods, when my gaze rested too long on a single object, did I physically feel as if I was starting to come out of my head? Like my head and face were a diving board. My thinking and looking standing on the diving board. Starting to bounce a little. Blue water below. Or yellow tile wall. Or Nicole's eyes. Or a carpet, or the dull metal of a bathroom stall. The diving board: a stray strand of my dark hair, the flesh-colored shadow of my nose, the frames of my glasses. My looking stood on this, started to bounce a little, testing . . .

Like I could dive out of my face, leave the empty vibrating board of my head behind. Like my looking could drip onto the porous yellow tile of the lunchroom wall, or pour into Nicole's eyes, into the capacious strangeness of her thoughts, the rooms she knew, her instinctive movements. And I'd be out there in that, gone.

I wondered if the panic was my head clenching down on my looking. The way you bite down to keep from throwing up. I wondered—but not for long, because some thoughts could start the panic. Thinking about panic could turn into panic. I wasn't even sure if thinking about panic was actually different from panic. A philosophical question. I was a pragmatist. I kept my eyes moving. I kept a paper bag in my pocket. I was good. The majority of the time I felt fine. Better than fine.

Because spring was really working now. I'd wake up on my bed at Dad's with this unbelievable color all over my chest and hands. The sun streaming through my window—it was more than a color. It had shapes like clouds in it, the kind of clouds on which angels reclined in tall paintings at the Art Institute downtown.

And when I got outside there'd be this incredible lightness to the air. It was mostly the absence of cold, but it made the air buoyant, like very salty water. Your steps would get bigger, longer, your gestures unfurled from your body like an emperor's. It wasn't just me, everyone felt it. I saw little kids down at the bus stop throwing their hands up in grandiose gestures of victory and success.

Everyone on the bus was happy. Kids would have the bus windows down the two-inch maximum, and put everything out that would fit. Winter was over, we'd won, the bus was a float in our victory parade, trailing streamers of tissues, gum wrappers, gnawed pencil bits, gloves, cigarette butts, nickels, buttons, petals.

Just moving through air and light made you feel rich. And condescending. Geometry class was just blown completely open.

I sat in geometry class and stared out the window at my pier, the spring light lapping at it, the spring light of orange and blue and pink and gold. I imagined ships arriving at the pier, ships covered with climbing vines, with grass, with orchids.

I no longer allowed myself to understand a single word Mr. Streeling spoke. I was way above that now.

"Nicholas," Streeling said, leaning his long, thin frame on a cloud of brilliant gold light spilling in from the window. The sunlight made the fluorescent cave of the classroom look cheap and unreal, fabricated out of cardboard and masking tape.

I looked at the teacher like I'd never seen him before, like he'd just arrived, stepped off a phantom ship. The watery light from the window soaked the flimsy cardboard construction of the room. It was getting translucent in places. Streeling stirred impatiently.

"The answer to number four, Nicholas," he said.

I replayed my look of surprise and astonishment.

"The area of the isosceles triangle . . ." He looked at me expectantly.

I looked at him like I'd never heard a human voice before. After about three seconds he called on someone else.

That was the thing with Streeling. He felt uncomfortable in a position of authority. He never liked to come down on a kid. Plus he was nervous. You had the feeling in any given verbal exchange that he was never one hundred percent sure he was doing ok. If things broke down, maybe it was his fault. Maybe it was no one's fault. A lot of math guys are like that.

I didn't mean to be a jerk. But what the sunlight was doing to the classroom was real. There were places in the wall now that had become practically see-through. The light was just rubbing out bits of the classroom. It was impossible to concentrate. And geometry, come on. I just couldn't take geometry seriously anymore. The whole point of spring is that it ruins geometry. All the angles get pushed out or covered up, shapes grow over shapes.

Plus this was the part of spring when nothing is green. It was the two-week period of the flowering trees. The world goes white and red and gold and blue and orange. It's the time when you understand where the idea of royalty comes from. This idea of natural and intrinsic superiority. When you're fifteen you look down at the adults. In the springtime especially, you look down at anyone who has a job. Every adult seems like a loser.

Maybe I was being a little bit of a jerk to Streeling, but that's the idea of royalty, and it's the most natural idea in the world for a fifteen-year-old in the spring. It literally grows from the earth. The idea that I was a thousand times more important and better than any possible adult wasn't an idea. It was like breathing. Ty dug it.

"I just need to say," he said. "The way you handled Streeling. That's hardcore."

We were messing around on the basketball court a few blocks from his house, playing horse. Wearing sweatshirts, no coats. Fifty degrees, going up.

"It's just natural to me," I said truthfully.

Ty nodded. He was holding the basketball, pausing before his shot.

"Yeah, that's what I say to motherfuckers, like that motherfucker Jason, said you was a pussy."

Ty was on the basketball team; Jason was a senior jock.

"Jason said I was a pussy?"

Ty shook his head.

"Said you looked like a pussy. Whatever. I told him you were true hardcore, inside. Outside there's a layer of pussy. Then a layer of hardcore. Then another layer of pussy. Then a heart of pure. Hard. Core."

Ty took the shot and made it. I reflected that his analysis of my character was basically accurate. I resolved to ask Sarah for her phone number the next day in class. I'd do it natural, like the way I looked out of the heart of new light at Streeling. Pure hardcore.

*

When the words come from my core, they are powerful and they compel adults and children. But when I talk to other people in real time I have to use my face and mouth, and those are fundamentally exterior parts. The layer of pussy, as Ty would put it.

This isn't going to be anything like dealing with Streeling, I thought, staring at the back of Sarah's head, her unreal auburn hair. The sunlight didn't do anything to her hair. It wrecked the rest of the classroom; it did brutal things to Streeling. But it didn't hurt her hair at all.

I moved my lips around a little. That's where the words would have to come out from. Inside words, thinking words, only get you so far in this type of situation.

Where do thoughts come from, anyway? Who am I?

I put that line of thinking firmly aside.

The truth, I told myself, getting back on track, is that I'd exchanged maybe a dozen spoken words with Sarah in my life, and none of them were particularly memorable. The note was the sole source of my confidence. "YES."

I thought about that YES all the time. She put it in all caps. Like it was the answer to more than one question. A meta-yes.

Maybe she already answered my question. YES. Like a long-distance, multievent prophecy. YES I can have her phone number, YES she would go out with me, YES I could kiss her.

This concept of the meta-yes comforted me. It meant maybe I didn't have to ask her anything. It was already done. Complete. Successful.

Often in my life, when certain of success in an encounter, I've felt a nearly irresistible impulse not to go through with it. To walk away, maintaining success in its pure, virtual state.

It's as if the prospect of relationship with others offers me two games. In one game, the result of asking a girl out, doing a job interview, trying to get away with something, is plotted along a VICTORY/DEFEAT axis.

In the other game, the results are scored differently. Getting a job means you have to go work for someone. Getting away with something means you must pretend to be someone else. Getting a girl to say she'd go out with you . . . at fifteen, who even knew what that meant? In each case, the positive outcome involves a kind of surrender, an opening to something unknown.

Call this the OPEN/CLOSED axis.

So when certain of success in a social encounter, I was tempted to walk away without going through with it. Tempted to keep my VICTORY pure and free.

But life didn't work that way. You can't actually choose one game over the other. The VICTORY/DEFEAT axis is connected to the OPEN/CLOSED axis. There's an inverse relationship between the two games. DEFEAT and OPEN are mysteriously related. VICTORY and CLOSED are uncanny twins. The two games were tied end to end, like a snake swallowing its tail.

Panic showed me this. It was one of its first lessons.

When I stared too long at a person or thing, the panic shock of

DEFEAT coincided with the raising sluices, the tingling release, the exciting movement *out*. OPEN.

When I thought about Sarah's "YES," when I thought only of the YES, with my eyes moving swiftly over the sun colors of my bedroom ceiling, the joy-pulse of VICTORY carried with it the cool, inorganic, deathly invulnerability of CLOSED.

I was pretty sure Sarah would give me her phone number if I asked her. But reflecting on this lesson of panic, I felt that this would hardly constitute an unalloyed success. Victory leads to openness, which is a kind of defeat. If she said yes, there would be good and bad aspects of it, that's all one could say with confidence, that's all anyone could say about anything with confidence.

This made me less nervous about asking her. And more reluctant.

Enough thinking, I thought finally. I'm going to ask her. No matter what I think, sitting here while the minutes left in class tick down, watching the back of her head like it's a clock, like when the hour strikes, the head will swivel around with its good/bad, opening/defeating YES, sitting here thinking of what I'm going to do or not do, it doesn't matter. It won't change anything.

I'm going to ask her. I was always going to ask her.

When the bell rang, I timed my rising to happen a split second before hers. I was on my feet and passing her desk just as she was getting up.

"Hey," I said, my heart racing.

She turned her face to me. Her look had the coolness of sunlight on water. The look of a liquid that regularly evaporates into bright air.

"I was, um, wondering," I began.

I'd thought of strong prefatory material, a good excuse, a particular, ordinary, just-friends reason why I needed her phone number.

Suddenly all that was impossible to remember.

"Could I get your phone number?"

One corner of her mouth turned up. A fraction of the coolness in her look evaporated; the air brightened by a fraction.

"Sure," she said.

4.

Salome

That happened on Wednesday. I was planning to wait a couple days to call her. Play it cool. Dad was on a business trip again. He'd left me forty dollars, a huge sum, and told me to get my own dinner. I didn't know how he expected me to do that, at age fifteen, with no car, stranded amid the vast suburban distances.

But I had a tried-and-true plan for these occasions. I called Ty, and while he was riding his bike over, I called a cab. Then I had about twenty minutes to wait. So I sat on the couch with the lights off, with the spring sunset coming through the slats of the blinds, spilling thin bars of sun onto the white carpet.

At no other time was the interior of the town house worth looking at. Whether lit by the lamps inside, by the television, by the streetlamps outside, by daylight, or winter or autumn sunsets, the atmosphere at Chariot Courts was generally spiritually inert.

But when I was alone, at fifteen, with the spring sunset on the carpet . . .

It was like looking at life from somewhere far outside. There are mystical places and times of the year in the American suburbs. Just like there are mystical places and times of the year in ancient Egypt, in Antarctica, in the Soviet Union.

When the sunset was almost gone, I turned on the lights. I dug Sarah's number out of my pocket and looked at it. Ty knocked on the door. I opened it and he brought his bike inside. Chariot Courts didn't seem like a high crime area, but no one really knew anything about it. Ty always left his bike in the house when he came over.

When the cab got there the driver seemed a little surprised, like the drivers always did. He drove off with Ty talking maniacally to him about sports.

"What about the Bulls, huh? Fucking Jordan, right?"

The cabbie made a noncommittal sound.

"Michael Jordan is unbelievable. Isn't he unbelievable? Come on. Forget about it. What did you say your name was?"

"Shut up," I whispered to Ty. "You sound demented."

"*You* shut up," he whispered back. "This is how you talk in a cab, faggot."

"So," he said loudly, talking to the cabbie again. "Are we going to win it all this year or what?"

The cabbie said nothing.

"Talking 'bout the Bulls!" Ty yelled.

I hid my face in my hands.

When we arrived at Ruby Tuesday, I got the exact change from the driver. He made a disgusted sound and drove off, like the drivers always did.

"You see," I told Ty.

"*You* see," he said. "It was your creepy whispering."

Neither of us knew about the custom of giving tips to cab drivers.

Ruby Tuesday was always almost deserted on weeknights. They did their big business on the weekends, with the mall shoppers. To us the lack of other customers just added to the glamour of the place. Eating out in a real sit-down restaurant with your friend and no parents when you're fifteen. Glamour. They had stained-glass light shades. The booths had seats that felt like real leather.

"Is this real leather?" Ty asked the waitress.

"No," she said.

Ty stopped stroking his seat.

"You kids waiting for someone?"

We looked at each other. This was always one of the highlights.

"No," I said.

We always tried to keep from grinning at this moment, and we always failed.

"We're ready to order," said Ty.

After she left, he turned to me.

"I bet I could get a beer."

"No way," I said. "They'd never serve you."

"White people can't tell how old I am."

I looked at him.

"No way," I said.

He never had the guts. Once in a while he'd ask for the drink menu, which they would give him with a certain look that dissuaded him from going any further.

I always got a hamburger, which came on a real plate, with

thick fries that were nothing like McDonald's fries. They didn't taste better. To tell the truth, they tasted worse. But that wasn't the point. They were restaurant fries, heavy with the prestige of a sit-down restaurant. Ty ordered something different every time. This time he had some kind of fish with fruit on it.

"I asked Sarah out," I said. "In class."

"Cool," he said absently. "Hey check it out, I'm going to try to talk to Tod tomorrow."

"Tod?" I asked, irritated at his lack of interest in my news.

"Yeah," he said. "You know. The dude in health class. In the back."

I realized who he was talking about. Tod had pale white skin and long black hair. He sat in the back and said nothing to anyone. He appeared to be possessed by a level of coolness that was totally unique in our high school.

There was nothing to compare him to. We couldn't even be sure that he was cool, though we couldn't see what else it could be. There was a vague sense that he hung out with people who didn't go to our high school. Maybe who didn't go to high school at all. Ty was sure he could get us weed.

When I realized who Ty was talking about, I remembered that I'd seen Sarah and Tod talking together.

"What are you going to say?"

"I don't know," Ty said. "I'll think of something."

"Not sports," I said.

"Fuck you."

"You think he'll talk to you?"

Ty considered.

"I don't know," he confessed.

"That dude," I said.

"I know," he said.

"You can tell just by looking at him."

"I asked Jason about him."

"What did Jason say?"

Ty shook his head.

"He said that dude's into something."

"His exact words?"

Ty nodded.

"That dude's *into* something," Ty said, imitating Jason's deep voice. "That dude's *into* some *stuff*."

I paused.

"Well, which was it?"

"What?"

"Did he say Tod was into *something*, or into *some stuff*."

"The fuck does it matter?"

"*Stuff* is a word that doesn't typically refer to anything very cool," I said. "Short stuff. Gay stuff. Kid stuff. Fun stuff."

Ty held up his fork.

"I'm going to stuff this fork up your big white asshole," he said. "Isn't that cool?"

"Gentlemen," said the waitress. "I'm going to have to ask you to watch your language."

We both fell silent, embarrassed. She put down our plates, gave us each a reproving glance, and then walked away.

"She's supposed to be working for us," Ty said. "We're paying her salary."

"No," I said. "If you say anything in a place like this about putting something in someone's asshole, they don't have to treat you good anymore."

"Not something," Ty said. "Stuff."

We started giggling. Eating out at a real restaurant was awesome. When we were done we had the bartender call us a cab.

Back at Chariot Courts the sunset was long gone. The carpet was clean and meaningless in the artificial light. I was feeling pretty good.

I realized that if I waited a couple days to call Sarah, I'd have the problem of what to say to her in class. Just totally ignore her? That seemed fucked up. But if I talked to her in class, then what would I save for over the phone? And if I was just going to say something I could say to her face, then what was the significance of her phone number?

So when Ty left I called her. It was kind of late, but I was feeling confident. Ruby Tuesday had that effect. Sarah picked up after three rings. She must have her own line, I figured. Kids who didn't have their own line either picked up on the first ring or not at all.

I said hi, it's Nick, and she said hey, I know, and then there was silence. I started to talk about Tod. I said I had the feeling he was into some cool stuff. I said me and Ty were going to talk to him, together, maybe do some fun stuff with him.

I couldn't believe what I was saying. It was like a nightmare.

At some point Sarah interrupted me to say that she knew Tod. They'd gone to the same private grade school. They were friends. She said her parents would be gone on Saturday. Why didn't I come over?

She told me where she lived. I'd calmed down by then. I wrote out her address. I knew the subdivision; it was maybe five miles from Chariot Courts. No problem on my bike.

*

By the time I got to Sarah's I felt pretty good. The bike ride burned off most of the nerves. Sarah's subdivision was called River's Grove. It didn't have a wrought iron gate that you couldn't open, and the houses didn't have wrought iron mailboxes. They didn't need them. They were big, long houses, set back on their own grassy hills, with regular metal mailboxes way down at the end of their own private driveways.

Sarah's house was a tawny-colored ranch, surrounded by big trees. As I rode up the driveway she walked out of the open garage. There were no cars inside.

"Hey," she said.

I got off my bike and rested it against the side of the garage.

"What's up," I said.

She was wearing tight jeans of a very light blue color, and a green sweater.

"The p's are gone," she said. "Visiting my brother. He lives downtown. He's like thirty."

"Whoa," I said.

"Yeah."

She led me through the garage.

"Have you guys lived here long?" I asked.

"My whole life," she answered.

I wondered what it would be like to live in the same house your whole life. My mom once calculated that we'd moved eight times before we even came to America.

When Sarah opened the door from the garage into the house, I saw what it was like. All around me were things she knew so intimately that she didn't see them. The polished wood floor of the hallway. Plants in ornate pots. The late-morning light coming in through big windows, illuminating the giant living room.

I could tell by the way she moved. This house is a place she looks out from, I thought, it's not a place she sees. I'd never lived in a place long enough for that to happen. The furniture in the town houses and apartments we lived in maintained their obtrusive, alien quality until we moved again.

There were two long leather couches in her living room, plus five or six chairs. Still the room didn't look crowded. A number of paintings on the wall, some of them were even abstract. All these expensive things had passed into her and become a part of her. She didn't realize it. She was too close to them. Looking at these things, I thought, was like looking at her when she thought she was alone.

Her eyes had developed in these rooms. The spaciousness of the way she looked at you, like there was more room in her looking than you could take up. It was one of the things that made her beauty intimidating. But there was nothing personal in it, I realized, nothing about me. It's just the way a person looks at things when they grow up in a house like this, I thought.

She was standing in the middle of the living room biting her thumb. It became clear that neither of us had any idea what to do.

"Your brother's thirty, huh," I said, to say something.

Sarah brightened.

"Want to see his room?"

I nodded desperately.

She led me down the hallway, opening a door that led to a staircase going down. Into the basement, I thought, but at the landing was a window. I stopped and looked out at a ravine full of trees, with a little stream glinting in the sun at the bottom.

"I don't get this house at all," I said.

Sarah laughed. It was the first time I'd ever heard her laugh. Like bells, each note distinct. She put her hand over her mouth.

"It's built into the hillside," she said. "The house, I mean."

I was smiling too.

When we got to the bottom of the stairs the air smelled faintly musty.

"This is it," she said, opening a door. "He hasn't lived here for years, but it's basically the same as ever. Supposedly when he's done with grad school he's going to move his stuff out."

The large room contained a low bed, which I tried not to look at, and an old, beat-up, dull red fabric couch, somewhat surprising in the elegant surroundings. No windows—we were now truly underground—but two paintings of mountains, spaced apart like windows, with a color in them that worked like light. Tall, narrow chrome speakers flanked a stereo and turntable.

"What kind of music do you like?" she asked, already on her knees before a sheaf of records.

"All kinds, I guess," I said. "Except for country."

She laughed. I sat down on the sagging couch. It seemed to want me to lean back. I didn't know what to do with my hands. Sarah turned around, holding up *Faith* by George Michael, one eyebrow cocked ironically.

"Terrible," I agreed.

She made a face, kept flipping through the records.

"What about this?"

And held up Eurythmics, the one with Annie Lennox wearing some kind of black mask, otherwise naked. I nodded and gulped, but she went digging through the records again.

"Oh *shit*!"

She turned and displayed the cover: the famous pinball machine lettering. The blue-and-orange UFO guitar. It was from the seventies—ancient. But also somehow new. It made George Michael seem old in comparison.

"My brother says that lots of people like Boston, but no one *loves* Boston." Sarah looked at me solemnly. "I love Boston."

"They're magic!" I blurted out, leaning forward excitedly. "The first time I heard 'More Than a Feeling' . . . "

I stopped, becoming self-conscious. Sarah picked it up.

"That song," she said. "It's not, like, *solid*."

She closed her eyes, concentrating. Shook her head in wonder.

"The song has like literally got a door in the middle of it. When the guitars go up—dum dum dee dee dum—ok? The whole song like *opens* in the middle. It's a door, right in the middle of the song, like the door on a UFO, right?"

"That's why you can never get tired of it," I interjected.

"Because the door, like, goes up," she continued. "Every time that part comes around, the door like slides up and there's this space, ok? It's like the *inside* of a UFO. It's like another universe. The cover is *so* perfect."

"Yes," I said. "I mean, I understand."

We were both smiling by now, like little kids sharing a secret.

Her smile had that intensity. Maybe I'm too cautious with my smiles, I thought.

"You know about the thing with volume?" she whispered. "My brother showed me."

"What thing?"

"When the volume is like really low," Sarah said, smiling almost like she was afraid now. "When it's *really* low—you can, like, hear the *inside* of the UFO."

She looked directly into my eyes when she said this—her smile trembled.

I reached over and took her hand in mine. I didn't think about it.

Her eyes dropped to the album cover. We both looked at it silently.

"I don't think I can really listen to this right now," she murmured.

"I know what you mean."

We laughed nervously. I dropped her hand. She got up and slid the album back into the sheaf. Her fingers danced along the spines. She withdrew one showing a man with glasses and a blank look.

"This," she said.

She put the vinyl disk delicately on the turntable. Crackling came through the speakers. Slow piano music started to play. She turned back to me.

"It's not that I'm tired of 'More Than a Feeling,' ok. You can *never* get tired of that song."

I nodded.

"But sometimes it's too much," she finished.

I nodded again. She sat down on the couch next to me. There was a distance between us now. It didn't feel bad—it wasn't a cold distance. A quiet, thoughtful distance. I could tell she was thinking about something. At last she spoke.

"I think things that are open inside stay beautiful for longer than things that are solid."

She looked at me.

"I wrote a poem about that," she said hesitantly.

"Tell me."

"Not like the whole thing," she said. "Maybe part."

"What?"

"No."

"Come on."

She sat straight up, closed her eyes.

"*Beauty is a shape open to feeling*," she recited.

I didn't know what to say. She opened her eyes.

"You hate it," she said.

"No!" I said. "I like it. Really. I never understand what people mean when they say something is beautiful. But I think I understand what you mean."

"It's like 'More Than a Feeling,'" she explained. "A lot of my friends, they hate that song. They're like so sick of it. It's on the radio all the time, it's dad rock, whatever. But I like things with spaces inside them, like where you can go."

I nodded. My tongue flicked nervously along the roof of my mouth.

"Sometimes," I said, "I think I can go into things."

She looked at me.

"I mean, literally, go out of my head into something," I said. "Like if I look at something or someone long enough I start feeling like, like . . ."

"Like what part of you could go?"

"Like my thoughts," I said. I swallowed. "And my . . . looking."

Sarah blinked.

"I went to the hospital one time because of it. They said it was a panic attack."

I looked at her, a quick glance.

"Has that ever happened to you?"

She watched me for what felt like a long time.

"No," she said. "But have you ever gone out?"

I shook my head.

"When I feel like it's about to happen," I said, "I stop myself."

I thought about telling her about the paper bags. I had one in my pocket. I've said too much already, I thought.

I was trying not to look at her face.

"Why do you stop?" she asked.

I took a deep breath. Her face, I thought. *A shape open to feeling.* I could feel the pressure rising.

She's sitting right next to me, I thought. She's thinking something. Right now, I thought, she's thinking something. I can tell by the way she's looking at me. I can feel her looking at me, she's *staring* at me, I know she is, I can't stare at her, but she's *staring* at me, she's staring at me and she's not afraid, she is not afraid that any part of her will *come out.* She doesn't feel her *thinking* and *looking* standing on her face like on a diving board—she doesn't feel as if she could *pour out of her own face*!

What's it like inside her?

I thought of the sun, sliding across an astronaut's black visor . . .

"I never told anyone any of that before," I said finally.

Suddenly I wanted to get the hell out of there.

*

I took a deep breath. Chill out, I thought.

Sarah was touching my shoulder.

"What about that painting?" she asked.

I looked up. She was gesturing at the painting of the mountain nearest to us.

I examined it. Quick glances at first, but the painting was so interesting I soon forgot. Light appeared to be coming from inside it. There were no wires or anything, it was just a flat piece of canvas. How did they do that? I wondered. Light—and a kind of shadow . . .

"It's weird," I said. "I mean, it's cool."

"It's *beautiful*," Sarah replied. "*Everyone* thinks that painting is beautiful. But what does it feel like when *you* see it?"

Like it's something I shouldn't look at too long, I thought.

"I don't know," I said.

"You're not even looking at it."

"I can't."

"Why?"

"I told you." My voice came out in a whisper. "My thoughts, they . . ." I cleared my throat.

"When I look at it, it's like my thoughts . . . They push up to my eyes, like they want to touch it. There's a lot of them now—they're coming heavy now—it kind of hurts—and—I can see their, um"—I was whispering again—"their shadow."

That's the best way I could put it. I risked a glance back at the painting. Something on the canvas, a kind of warp. *The shadow of my thinking.* My shadow. The shadow of whatever is standing right now on the diving board of my face.

I looked away, blinking. *Dangerous to stare.* Now I knew why. It's not just superstition. A shiver ran along the back of my neck.

I darted a glance at Sarah. Her green eyes full of fascination.

"What do you think would happen if you kept staring?"

I shook my head.

She curled her legs under her on the couch, leaned close to me, smiling in excitement.

"Would your head like suddenly be empty? Would I like be sitting here with you, and suddenly your head would like—roll back—and your tongue would loll out? Would you be in the painting? Would you be out there in the air . . . *headless*?"

I couldn't wait any longer.

"Hey, Sarah?"

"Yes?"

"Can I ask you something?"

"Ok."

"I have a paper bag in my pocket. Can I take it out?"

The excitement and humor vanished from her face. She uncurled her legs, straightened on the couch. Moved a little way away from me.

"Ok," she said.

As I was taking out the bag, I explained about hyperventilation. I was talking pretty fast. Then I breathed into the bag for a bit. Sarah turned off the stereo. *This is an emergency situation*, her posture seemed to say. All you could hear was the papery wheezing of my breath in the bag.

When I felt normal again, I put the bag back in my pocket. I felt embarrassed. But there was nothing else I could have done.

"It's called panic attack?" she asked.

"I guess," I said.

"And they said to use the bag or you'll like come out of your head?"

"Oh," I said. "No, they didn't say anything about that. I mean, I haven't talked to anyone about that part of it."

"We could go to the library," she said. "We could see what they say about it. In a medical book. We could see if it's really a danger. I mean, you leaving your head."

"It doesn't really seem like something that would be in a medical book," I said.

"No," she said. "I guess not."

We were both quiet for a while.

"Do you think it's real?" she asked.

I thought about it a little.

"I don't know," I said. "I think probably it's not real. Just a feeling."

"More than a feeling," she said, smiling a little.

"Maybe."

"You could be the same as other people," she said, "and it's nothing. Or you could like, ok, *really* be different."

"Or," I said, "I could be the same as other people, and just panic at things that other people don't."

"Like what?" she asked. "What's there to panic about? Right here, I mean?"

I shrugged.

"The whole thing, I guess."

She slowly started to smile. At first I tried being cool, but then I let myself smile a little, and then I let myself smile as much as I felt I needed to. My smile was really big by then. Like I was five years old. But it was ok, Sarah's smile was huge too.

"The whole thing," she said, making a gesture that included the world. "The whole fucking thing."

We laughed our asses off.

*

The next day I went to the library to find out about panic attacks. I rode my bike all the way into downtown Libertyville, a thirty-minute trip. When I got inside, I found that, as usual, the library was mostly inhabited by little kids and their mothers. They were concentrated in the children's book section, which was separated from the rest of the library by soundproof glass.

As I walked by the children's book section, kids pressed against the glass, making horrific faces, showing what they'd do to me if they ever got loose. Their mothers hovered in the background, dim, harassed figures. Once in a while a really little kid would streak by, half naked, waving a book, a stick, or a diaper.

I watched for a little while. It was strangely soothing. Viewed from the outside, the children's book section was more like an aquarium than a zoo, with the soupy undersea light and the differing velocities, altitudes, and sizes of the inhabitants. Also like an aquarium, it was totally silent.

Inside the children's book section, as you were reminded whenever the door opened, it was more like a zoo.

I walked into the adult section. The rare inhabitants intrigued me. Furtive, awkward individuals, carrying books. I didn't know any adults who read books, except for Ty's mom, who was a feminist. I certainly didn't know any adults who went to the library.

What did the adults who came here do? What did they read? Where did they come from?

There were never more than two or three of them in the library at a time. Often there were none. Once I caught a fake. A few months before, I'd seen a man walking briskly out of the stacks carrying a book. He looked like he could be one of my friends' dads. He wore a dress suit, and expensive-looking shoes. He had a look of determination on his face.

And then he passed me, and I saw the book he was carrying was suspiciously large and thin. When he turned toward the checkout counter, I recognized the garish colors of a children's book.

For a while afterward, I believed there must be a shelf of children's books hidden in the adult section. An outpost for the creeping pollution of ordinary domestic suburban family life, infiltrating the austere quarter of books without pictures.

On the Sunday after going over to Sarah's for the first time, I saw one adult. A medium-sized woman, of middle age, with glasses. Someone who would have been unremarkable if she'd appeared at the supermarket, or in the children's book section. But here she was carrying what appeared to be an adult book, of appropriate size and thickness, through the adult section of the Libertyville library on a Sunday.

I wondered if she was a feminist like Ty's mom. I wasn't entirely sure what feminism was. Ty's mom's feminism seemed to be a kind of deep magic, one that left no discernible effect on the surface of her life. There was a general feeling that Ty's dad beat her. Ty sometimes dropped hints along those lines. I would get very embarrassed at such moments, and quickly try to forget. I mostly succeeded. But I noticed, when I was at Ty's house, how quickly his mother obeyed his dad.

I'd see her feminist books in the back of her minivan when she drove us home from school. I was curious about what the books said, though not enough to risk opening one. They were mostly paperbacks of a medium thickness, with images of red and black shadows on the covers. I wondered how our lives looked from the perspective of those books. Sometimes I'd catch a distant, refracted glimpse.

One day, driving us home from school, she heard us talking about a play that school was putting on. It had been described by the teachers as a "classic."

"That play is not a classic," she said. "It's trash."

I thought of Ty's mom as the woman in the adult section of the library took her book and sat down in one of the comfortable armchairs at the ends of the stacks.

I went to the card catalog to look up "panic." There were four subjects starting with that word:

Panic Attacks Prevention
Panic Disorders Chemotherapy
Panic Political Aspects
Panic Finance

I wrote down the numbers for the books and began searching the stacks. The single book the catalog listed under the first heading was missing, perhaps checked out.

The single book under the second heading was very technical, and concerned panic disorders as a side effect of cancer chemotherapy. It didn't really say much more about panic attacks themselves than the ER doctor had told me. It was mostly about different medications that seemed to prevent cancer patients from getting panic attacks, plus speculation about the parts of the brain affected. It didn't mention paper bags, oddly, which made me think that maybe chemotherapy panic attacks were different from the ones I had.

There were no books at all under the third heading.

There were six books under the last heading, about financial panics.

I read a little from the introductions to the two least thick financial panic books. Maybe, I thought, they called them financial panics because they're somehow like panic attacks. Or maybe the financial panics came first, and they named the other kind, the kind I had, after the financial panics, because of how they resembled them.

These books turned out to be much more illuminating and relevant than the chemotherapy book. The basic idea of a financial panic is that the stock market starts to fall, and then people start to panic. In an extraordinary passage, the author of the second book seemed to suggest that sometimes people just *thought* that the stock market was about to fall, so they panicked, and only *then* did the stock market actually fall.

This seemed to have potential application to my own case.

Perhaps when I felt the possibility of leaving my face and head—the possibility of falling out of my head, so to speak—I started to panic. Or was it the panic itself that caused me to feel like I was about to fall out of my head?

I couldn't be sure.

Regardless, there was one important difference between my condition and financial panics. The stock market did in fact fall. But I had never fallen out of my head and face.

So far, I reminded myself. I hadn't fallen out *so far.* In the financial panics, the stock market always fell. "The bottom dropped out" is how one author put it. The market fell catastrophically. This was how you knew it was a panic. It was how you diagnosed the panic.

Perhaps, I thought, I hadn't actually had a real panic attack yet. Maybe I was just continually being brought to the edge of panic, suspended at a prepanic stage. Maybe the paper bags, and the other tricks I'd found—like moving my eyes around—prevented the actual panic. Real panic was falling. Catastrophic falling.

All this was suggestive, and more than a little anxiety producing, but it left me with more questions than answers. I needed to find information about my specific kind of panic, but I didn't know where to find it. I had the vague sense that the Libertyville public library had significant gaps.

I scoured the medical section of the stacks. It wasn't easy. There was *diabetes* everywhere in those books. Every page was like a minefield potentially hiding the word. Plus *cancer,* a word that was making me increasingly uncomfortable.

I didn't want to ask the librarian for help. Due to the nature of the library's customer base, the librarians were mainly children's book people. Young adult people at best. When visitors checked out children's or young adult titles, the librarians would be full of chatter, recommendations, effusions, general interest. On the rare occasions when I'd observed someone check out an adult title, the librarians were totally silent.

The librarian now at the checkout would certainly assume that I was looking up panic attacks because I had them. Librarians were the kind of people who spread rumors, who gossip. The kind of people who never steal. The kind of people who lie.

I was tired of standing in the stacks holding heavy reference volumes, tired of avoiding the word *diabetes*, cringing at the word *cancer*. I was about to call it a day, when the nondescript woman suddenly got up from her chair.

She'd been reading from two different books. I'd surreptitiously observed her from time to time. Now she got up, gathered her things, and prepared to leave. I risked a searching glance as she passed me. She was holding only one of the two books she'd been reading. I waited, pretending to peruse the medical book in my hand, until she'd passed through the checkout line, under the unsmiling eyes of the librarian, and out the front door.

Then I slowly, casually made my way to the chair she'd vacated. Making sure the librarian wasn't watching, I picked up the book the woman had left lying there.

The book was very old. On the spine was the title:

The Collected Plays of Oscar Wilde

The author's name meant nothing to me. I opened the book. The print font was a style I'd never seen before. It was quite legible, but it had a certain airy quality. The book smelled ancient. Not ancient like old-people smell. But not the scentless timelessness of a rock or a stone either. A third kind of oldness.

I looked at the table of contents. Then I picked a title in the middle: *Salome*. I turned to its page. Under the play's name was an ornate image of a thin woman holding a man's head on a plate.

I began to read.

The language was like nothing I'd ever encountered. A little like the Bible, maybe. But only a little. By the end of the first page, I felt excitement rising in me.

Or was it panic?

I stopped reading. I looked around—the stacks, the white walls, the lights, the distant checkout counter with the librarian, laughing gaily with a patron.

Panic, I thought. Or prepanic. Whatever it was, I felt it clearly now. On the diving board . . .

I looked back down at the book, and now I could see the shadow of my thought . . . the warp across the page. But then the part of the page I was looking at resolved into a word, the word dissolved into a sentence. Then I was inside the book:

> You are always looking at her. You look at her too much. It is dangerous to look at people in such fashion. Something terrible may happen.

My scalp started to tingle. *Dangerous to look at people too much.* I understood! I kept reading.

> Ah! I have kissed thy mouth, Jokanaan, I have kissed thy mouth. There was a bitter taste on thy lips. Is it the taste of blood? But perchance it is the taste of love!

I read. I didn't stop. The play wasn't very long, but it was long enough. When I looked up again, the lights in the children's section were off. The librarian was standing behind the checkout counter, glaring at me. The clock read ten to four. The library closed at four on Sundays.

I couldn't think about that.

I thought about *Ivanhoe*, about how I'd suspended a panic attack in that book too.

I thought about Sarah: "*Beauty is a shape open to feeling.*"

Salome's sentences were open to feeling. But they were also closed. OPEN/CLOSED. They opened, then they closed behind what had entered.

Feeling would keep the shape those sentences gave them, I thought.

I thought about Salome. Salome dancing. I thought about Herod. I thought about Jokanaan. The man. Her lover. The headless lover.

The meaning of the play was completely clear to me. It wasn't clear to Herod, who sees Salome kissing the decapitated head and orders her killed. He thinks she's a pervert. The play's meaning probably, I thought, wasn't clear to other people who read the play.

Today I am older, I have done the research, and I know that none of the many people who have written about that play have understood it.

I understood it at once.

Salome had committed no crime by having Jokanaan's head cut off. Jokanaan wasn't in that head. The play wasn't the story of a beautiful woman and a man who dies. It's the story of the love between a beautiful woman and a living, headless man. A true story.

I remembered what Sarah had said, yesterday, talking about my panic.

"Would your head suddenly be empty? Would I be sitting here with you, and suddenly your head would like—roll back—and your tongue would loll out? Would you be out there in the air . . . *headless*?"

Prophecy, I thought.

My mouth was dry.

I went into the stacks and didn't come out until I had every book by Oscar Wilde the library possessed. I even found a biography of him.

5.

The Presence of the God

The biography of Oscar Wilde was mostly useless. The author didn't understand *Salome*. Not one mention of panic.

But it wasn't entirely useless. It described Oscar Wilde's fascination with ancient Greece. When I mentioned this to Sarah at school, she grew thoughtful. She wondered if the word *panic* had anything to do with the Greek god Pan. Then she conceived the idea of going to the school library during lunch and looking up both "Pan" and "panic" in the encyclopedia, something that had never occurred to me.

The very first sentence of the encyclopedia entry on "panic" confirmed Sarah's intuition.

> The word panic is derived from the god Pan, and originally referred to the sudden fear aroused by the presence of a god.

We thought about this in silence.

The day was overcast; the high library windows held thin blocks of undifferentiated light. I leaned against a shelf, looking absently at the solemn, terse titles of reference works. On the spine of the *L* volume of the encyclopedia, an enormous fly moved slowly.

Sarah sat cross-legged on the narrow tile floor between the stacks, the big *P* volume spread open in her lap. Now she was reading the entry for "Pan." Her lips moved silently.

Her eyes widened.

"*What*?" I asked.

Disturbed by the unintentionally high volume of my voice, I peeked out nervously, glancing down the central hall to confirm what I knew I'd find: the nun at the checkout glowering in our direction. We were the only kids in the library. It was technically legal for students to be there during lunch. But it was strange. The nun's suspicions had been aroused.

"What," I whispered.

Sarah gestured at the page.

"It says here that Pan was generally a happy and playful god. But sometimes, when he was woken from a deep sleep, he would like let out a great *yell* that would scare everyone."

"Everyone?" I asked.

She looked up blinking.

"The shepherds, I guess, or the animals. Pan is the god of the wild."

"The wild?" I whispered.

That's when she grinned. Years later, when I was in college, I saw in a history book I was reading for class a picture of Stalin's daughter, Svetlana, sitting on Beria's lap and grinning exactly like Sarah did then.

Look it up. Google "Stalin's daughter Beria photograph."

Beria's eyes are obscured by the glare of the flash on his round glasses. His face is expressionless. Stalin works at a table in the background. Only Svetlana shows emotion.

She's grinning. And it's as if the entire horror and mystery of that scene—literally millions of people being killed for no reason, Stalin working on a list of enemies in the background, Beria, the head of the secret police, Stalin's chief executioner—the entire emotional range of that terrifying world is compressed into Svetlana's grin. A thousand tons of pressure per inch.

That grin is the only expression of human emotion from the heart of Stalinist Russia ever captured on film.

Human?

The look in Svetlana's eyes—it's not *in* her eyes, the look leaps *out* of her eyes. It's loose, free, in the air.

The expression of a wild animal. Her grin is the expression of a wild animal. Wild animals, when trapped, when caged, often frown, sometimes grin. All animals grin, if they have the right lips. The ones with the right lips grin constantly. Tigers. Apes. Hippos.

The wildness of Svetlana's grin is . . . obscene. No one could ever understand it. That's what *wild* means. I first saw that image almost exactly seven years after that afternoon with Sarah in the Carmel High School library. And I recognized it. When I said the word *wild*, Sarah lifted her head from the entry on Pan and grinned at me like Svetlana.

"Pan is the god," she whispered grinning, "of the wild. Of, like, shepherds. Of wild music, and . . ." Her grin opened wider. "The Greeks considered him also to be the god of *theatrical criticism*."

I literally fell down. I fell against the stacks and then slid to the ground, knocking half a dozen volumes down with me.

"No," I said. "Fucking way."

"Look," she said. She was laughing now. I was laughing. She held the *P* volume to me, finger pointing. I was collapsed on the floor amid a heap of books. When she lifted the *P* volume from her lap I saw her white panties, a curl of dark hair at the edge.

I tore my eyes away, stared at the sentence she pointed to, not understanding. Over a slow second it resolved.

"In addition, the Greeks considered Pan to be the patron god of theatrical criticism."

"*Salome*'s a *play*," Sarah said slowly. "You interpreted the *meaning* of the play, which is the meaning of *panic*. You did *theatrical criticism* on *Salome* to understand *panic*, which comes from the god *Pan*, and *Pan* is the *god* of *theatrical criticism*."

"What are you two doing on the floor?" said the nun.

We looked up, into the light. The camera clicked. Sarah, with her wild smile and open legs. Me, with my round glasses full of blank light, with my face like a mask.

*

The nun didn't do anything to us. She made me clean up the books I'd spilled, of course. But she didn't report us to the dean or anything. She did say that we weren't allowed in the library anymore, but I don't think she meant it. I think she was just expressing her feelings.

I don't know if Sarah had the same sense I did that the nun, in looking at us, had taken a photograph of us on behalf of the future. I didn't ask her because the idea didn't occur to me until years later, when I saw the picture of Svetlana and remembered that afternoon in every detail.

On the way back to the lunchroom from the library I sobered, struggling with the feeling that Sarah was perhaps giving more significance to all this than it deserved. I confessed to her that my efforts at what I now knew to be *theatrical criticism* were by no means uniformly successful. I'd tried reading some of Wilde's other plays, but they were totally different from *Salome*. They were about rich English people who ate cucumber sandwiches and did things like threaten to leave the room.

But Sarah said there was now no reason to look for the answer in books. I experienced the true panic myself. What did I need more books for?

"You are your own book," she said.

She suggested that *Salome* had given me the confidence to take what I felt seriously. In our lives we're constantly looking outside, she implied, to other people, to books, for the meaning of the experiences that occur inside our own body and mind.

Sarah said it was obvious to her that most experiences fitted poorly or not at all into the words and categories everyday people used. She actually used the example of the word *sex*, which made me lose track of what she was saying for the rest of the long walk back to the cafeteria.

But I think I got the gist, which was that my theatrical criticism of *Salome*, which led to the discovery of the Pan/panic connection, confirmed something Sarah had suspected since that first day at her house. Since that day, she'd believed that my panic—and in particular my feeling that I was about to *come out of my own head*—was strange, even magical, something that couldn't be accounted for in the everyday adult language of medicine and psychology. That's why she hadn't bothered to read more of the encyclopedia entry on panic after that first sentence about Pan.

"You are your own book," she said again, breaking the spell that the spoken word *sex* had cast over me.

The bell ending lunch rang as soon as we stepped into the cafeteria. Neither of us had eaten, but I didn't feel hungry. Eating seemed superfluous to me. I never felt hungry with Sarah.

If we lived together, I thought irrelevantly, my body would gradually cease to exist.

I stood in the fluorescent light of the cafeteria looking at the line of kids waiting to throw the detritus of their lunches into the garbage cans. Maybe Sarah wasn't giving too much weight to *Salome*, I thought. It seemed to me that the thought was only accidently inside my head. It could be out. I could be out. Jokanaan, I thought.

I resolved to write out the characteristics of panic that night, like she'd suggested.

Ty had basketball practice, so I wouldn't be getting a ride home from school with him and his mom. There was nothing for it but the bus, which I hated. The special humiliation of having to ride the Catholic high school bus at fifteen was that the same bus serviced all the Catholic school kids who lived along a certain route. When my bus pulled up in front of the glass doors at Carmel, it had already stopped at the Catholic middle school, Saint Norbert's. The bus was full of children as young as nine.

The middle school kids were horrible. Everything from their

basic shape to their spasmodic gestures to their constant use of "cool" words like *fuck* and *shit* made them an obscene caricature of high schoolers like me.

The worst was that they were constantly trying to befriend you. I knew some kids in my class—kids who had already accepted total social defeat—actually welcomed this attention. Keith Sadowsky, for instance, rode the same bus as me. As soon as he got on, his face lost the sullen mask of the terminally bullied and took on a new life and confidence. A swarm of nine-year-old boys—even a girl—would crowd around his seat.

If you listened, you could hear him telling them outrageous lies about his lifestyle and popularity. Their little faces were Keith's own personal high school, where he reigned for thirty minutes each school-day afternoon.

But this apparently harmless indulgence came at a terrible price. Keith had no real idea what cool kids in high school did, what kind of music they listened to, what drugs they took, what they did with girls, how they talked about it, what words they used.

He was dependent on his audience for the vocabulary of his fantasy. They would suggest things—Hey, Keith, did you ever yell *fuck* in physics class? Did you ever drink a daiquiri? Hey, Keith, did you ever French-kiss a cheerleader? Hey, Keith, did you do it doggy style? In the gym locker room? Did you ever steal a bus? Did you shit on the seats?

And he would say yes, filling in the details, his deep voice, his endless use of *fuck* and *shit*, his cartoonish expressions lifting him higher and higher in the eyes of his nine-year-old audience. In their eyes he learned how high he could rise.

In this manner, by a slow and surreptitious process, his mind became deranged. The fantasies of a group of nine-year-olds colonized his inner life.

This affected his posture. It affected everything. You'd see Keith slinking along the halls in Carmel, walking like a cartoon villain. Suddenly a ludicrous cocky expression would steal over his features. Then Jason or Ty or someone would turn the corner, and he'd droop into the blank, mute submission that provided him partial protection from their fists, their stares, their laughter.

One time I was in the bathroom, using a paper bag in a stall, when I heard Keith come in. I could tell it was him by the shuffle of his feet. I drew my legs up. The panic attack was over. I was curious what Keith would do. After a few seconds, I heard him talking to himself.

"Doggystyle," he whispered. "I do it doggystyle."

A very low whisper. I could tell he was looking at himself in the mirror. It wasn't him inside his head anymore. It was five or six nine-year-old boys and maybe one girl. They'd infected his head. Keith was gone.

When I was done, I banged the bathroom-stall door so loud that he jumped. I could see the ghost of the old Keith in his wide, frightened eyes.

"You made a bad mistake here today, Keith," I told him.

I left it at that. It was the fashion to make enigmatic threats to people like Keith. People who shamed everyone by proclaiming through their every movement, in full daylight, just how low a human being could sink.

"Please don't tell anyone," he pleaded as I walked out.

By the time you're twenty-five, people like that are gone.

But I had little time for philosophical reflections of this kind on the bus. I had my own private nine-year-old demon. So when I climbed up the rubber-covered stairs the day Sarah and I discovered the origin of the word *panic* in the library, I grimly surveyed the scene. Pushing past Keith's audience of pint-sized vampires, I went straight to the back of the bus. Chariot Courts was the last stop. But that's not why I walked all the way to the back.

I did it so I could check each row to see if Carl was there. If I saw him, I ignored him. If he wasn't there, I relaxed.

Ignoring Carl reduced the likelihood of his trying to sit next to me by approximately ten percent. Anything else—hostility, derision, any form of attention at all—guaranteed that he'd follow me back and try to sit next to me.

I'd tried violence once. I'd sat down next to him, and before he could open his mouth I had his sleeve up and was giving him a raw snake bite burn on his forearm. That had worked pretty well, but I got nervous that his mom would see the mark. Within a week he was in the back row with me again.

I'd gotten so I could see if he was in a row without turning my head. That day, somewhere in the middle rows I got a bad feeling. It got worse. I didn't have to turn around to know he was following me.

I sat in the rear right seat, like always. I stared out the window, looking at the trees much harder than they could really stand to be looked at. They splintered in my gaze. I lost touch with their whole shape. Vivid fragments of bark and leaf.

"Hey," said Carl.

I said nothing.

"Keith is a fucktard," he said.

Carl always had a hook.

"How do *you* know," I said, without turning to face him.

Carl snorted.

"I'm not stupid like those fucktards up there who worship him."

Carl and I had never spoken about Keith. I had no idea how he knew that I'd been thinking about Keith, how he'd managed to stumble on perhaps the only thing he could have said that would get my attention that afternoon.

But I wasn't really surprised. Carl always had a hook.

"It's good you know that about Keith," I said. "Now leave me alone."

The bus started to move. A long period of silence, punctuated by the distant sound of Keith's voice uttering obscenities. I'm already too old to get away with violence against a nine-year-old, I thought. I'm turning into my father.

"Hey," said Carl finally.

His timing was unsettling.

"I drew something kind of cool today," he said.

I didn't say anything. I continued to stare out the window.

"Here," he said.

I felt him push something against my shoulder.

"Here," he said again.

Angry at myself, I turned around. Carl was holding out his notebook. He was wearing an entirely red outfit—even his corduroys were red—with a blue bow tie. I told you I could see him when I walked by without turning my head.

I grabbed the notebook. There was a folded candy wrapper in the middle, like a bookmark. I opened up to the marked page and stared down at Carl's drawing.

It was a large, erect, red penis.

I had a panic attack. Right there on the bus. I had to use the paper bag and everything, with Carl watching.

Carl watching was the worst part. I'm feeling like I'm about to come out of my eyes, and Carl's right there, staring at me. No smile, no expression. His eyes open wide, like he's trying to catch me in them.

*

When I got home, I got out my unused geometry notebook and began to write down the characteristics of panic. They were fresh in my mind.

1. Light too bright.
2. Something's wrong.
3. Tingling in the fingers and toes.
4. Faster heartbeat.
5. Faster breathing.
6. Eyes moving around a lot.
7. The feeling that everything is strange.
8. The feeling that material objects are strange. And alien. They've always been horribly strange and alien, but only now am I really seeing it. Now is the *first time* I'm really seeing it, and it doesn't feel like it's just me, it doesn't feel like it's just a feeling, it's more than a feeling. These . . . *things*.
9. The conviction that my body is a thing. My hands. My nose.

10. Eyes starting to stick in things.

11. The fringe of body around my looking getting very bright.

12. Very alien.

13. The feeling that I could come out of my body. My head, in particular.

14. That my looking/thinking could pour or leap out.

15. Wonder where thoughts come from.

16. Wonder what looking is.

17. Afraid of what's next.

18. Carl.

I crossed out Carl. I remembered in religion class Father Snow talking about the contingent and essential properties of Jesus. The holiness of His blood was essential. The color of His hair contingent.

Carl, I thought, is a contingent property of panic. He just happened to be there during my most recent attack.

But then I put a circle around the crossed-out Carl. It might not be easy to sort out the essential from the contingent. Because each panic attack gave me the very clear sense that I was *seeing* and *understanding* things for the *first time*, things I'd never seen or understood before. This was symptom number 7 on my list.

Of course, part of me always knew this was wrong, *I've felt this way before*, part of me knew, *this is just another panic attack*, *time to get out the paper bag*. With déjà vu, you feel like this has happened before, but you rationally know it hasn't. A panic attack is the opposite. When one struck, I rationally knew it had happened before, but it didn't feel like it. It took a little while, and sometimes a long while, for me to accept that what was happening wasn't happening for the first time.

Because a panic attack doesn't feel like a panic attack. It feels like insight.

*

The phone rang. I pulled myself together and looked around. The microwave clock read 4:30 p.m. I was still wearing my school clothes. They were still burning on my body, so to speak. Light-blue shirt, dark-blue pants. Regulation Catholic school uniform. Everyone had to buy them from the same store.

Something about the fabric. It seemed to hold on to the smells of the lunchroom. I'd barely passed through the lunchroom today. I'd been in there for maybe two minutes. Sarah and I'd gotten back from the library just as the bell rang.

Yet my shirt smelled intensely of the fats, oils, and cold sweats of the cafeteria. If you put my shirt in a large, empty space, I thought, that space would *be* the cafeteria. All you'd need were the tables and chairs. The smells would be completely taken care of.

The phone continued to ring. I shook my head a little to clear it, and picked up the phone.

"Hello," I said.

This was a landline. No one back then had cell phones, except for some kids' fathers, in their cars, attached to their cars. They were called "car phones." Very few people I knew even had caller

ID. When you answered the phone, you had to say, "Hello," in a voice appropriate for everyone and anyone.

"Hello."

You were speaking to a being with a face to come, with an age to come, with unknown thoughts, attitudes, predilections, memories. Answering the phone back then was a little like writing.

"Hello," I said.

The voice on the line uttered a crude and insulting imitation of my voice saying, "Hello."

It was Ty.

"Fuck you," I said.

"I got kicked off the team," he said.

"For what?"

"My dad kicked me off."

"That's not getting kicked off," I said. "That's your parents not letting you play."

"Whatever," he said. "Tod wants to hang out."

I was speechless.

First it was the news itself. This was big. The unexpected fruition of something we'd been plotting and speculating for months. And then it was the coolness, the casualness with which Ty delivered it.

Ty always opened phone conversations with a bang, with some exciting, crazy thing, news that turned out to be either wildly exaggerated or completely invented. I doubted, for example, that he'd be off the team for long. His dad was always punishing him in random ways and then forgetting about the punishments just as randomly.

I'd been prepared for Ty's opening news, and I'd shot it down expertly, with a vocabulary correction, no less. But now I realized that was just a feint. Ty had saved the really big news until my defenses were down, when I thought the danger of his impressing me and rendering me speechless was over.

"Damn," I said finally.

"Keep it cool," Ty said.

"I am," I said.

"Don't embarrass yourself."

"How'd it happen anyway? Tod suddenly wanting to hang out."

Ty paused for a second, to yell something at his mom.

"What were you saying?" he said.

The break had given me enough time to cool down a little.

"When," I said.

"Tomorrow," he said. "They'll pick us up at your place."

They. Don't ask. Don't give him the satisfaction. Play it cool.

"Tomorrow? School night?"

Ty laughed into the phone.

"Don't be a pussy."

My dad would be home late. It should be ok if I got in before him. And anyway, it was worth the risk.

I hung up on Ty without saying goodbye. If his strength was openings, mine was endings. I never said goodbye before I hung up. It drove him crazy. He never had any idea when I'd do it. Sometimes I'd do it in the middle of a sentence. Once I called him and hung up as soon as he said, "Hello."

I chuckled a little after I hung up on him.

And then I thought about Tod and got serious. *Pick us up at your place.* That meant a car. Tod's own car, probably. For a second I got nervous. I didn't like people to see where I lived. Chariot

Courts was basically the cheapest place in all of Libertyville. Ty's house was at least three times the size of our tiny town house. And what if Sarah was with him? She'd said they were friends.

But then I got excited again. This would be the first time I would enter a car driven by someone who wasn't a parent or a taxi driver. And that was just the beginning. Tod represented a level of coolness unprecedented, unique. *They.* There could be adults in the car, I realized. Tod was the sort of person you could imagine hanging out with actual adults. Dangerous, unparentlike adults.

This was a major breakthrough for us. I had no idea how Ty had cracked the code. The scale of our triumph built over the remainder of the afternoon, as I sat on the couch in jeans and a Bulls T-shirt, watching *Head of the Class* and then *Who's the Boss?*

I felt like things were really starting to happen for me. During the commercials I'd think about Tod, wonder what the other kids at Carmel would say when they heard me and Ty were hanging out with him, driving around with him, with *them.*

Then I'd think about Sarah, about how she was friends with Tod, about how we'd have that in common soon too, about how beautiful she was, how we seemed to be heading in a definite romantic direction. I should try to kiss her.

Then the commercials would be over and *Head of the Class* would come on and I'd drop into oblivion and the ads would come back and I'd think about Tod again. Sometimes I'd think a little about the panic. Not a lot, just a little. There was still relatively little seepage between the attacks and the rest of the time. So little in fact it sometimes surprised me.

I'd tell myself, Hey, wake up, you've got these panic attacks! But then *Head of the Class* was back on, the fat guy was saying something funny, or maybe there'd be a romantic tangle, people getting together or breaking up, and when the ads came on I'd think about Sarah again.

It gradually grew dark in the room. Soon the blue flicker of television light was the only illumination. My thoughts darkened too.

I started to think about Carl's drawing.

At first it was just a little shiver, a red lightning bolt that cut through my thought of Tod and his car for a split second and was gone.

Then it was there for longer. Soon I found I couldn't remember Tod's face very clearly. Carl's drawing was there when I tried to remember Sarah's face.

Where do thoughts come from?

Carl's drawing.

Carl. His red suit. His drawing.

Tod. Just a name now. Sarah. Only a name. Seventeen essential characteristics of panic. One contingent characteristic.

Or eighteen essential characteristics of panic.

Carl.

His drawing.

After *Head of the Class* was *Who's the Boss?* After *Who's the Boss?* was *Roseanne*.

It was almost nine when Dad got home. We had microwave pasta for dinner.

I had microwave lasagna.

Dad had microwave pasta primavera.

6.

The Barn

One hour before sunset the next night Tod pulled up in the Chariot Courts parking lot in a black car. I learned later it was a Pontiac Grand Prix. The late light flared in its panels. It was like watching the sun on a black television.

Ty and I were waiting at my window. As soon as the car pulled up we knew who it was.

Tod looked back when we got in and kind of nodded. The car smelled like cigarette smoke. There was someone in the passenger seat. She turned around and smiled at us.

"I'm Steph," she said.

Ty and I said our names. Steph nodded. As soon as we pulled onto the street, Tod switched on the stereo and the music came on so loud I couldn't tell whether I knew the song or not. Like holding a book too close to read.

Dazed, I peered up at the front seat. Tod and Steph actually appeared to be talking. Steph had her face turned and her lips moved and Tod looked at the road, nodding from time to time. There's no way they can hear each other, I thought. Every time the drums came down, I blacked out a little.

When we reached Route 176 Tod hit the gas and the music's volume started to make sense. Cool wind blew through the windows. Tod pointed the car directly at the giant sunset, flaking red and orange in the speed. Pieces of the song whipped through the air like shards of the sun, rushed deafening into our ears, disappeared.

If I look in the rearview mirror, my pupils might be red, I thought. Like in a bad photograph. I didn't look. Tod turned the volume up. Ty hit my shoulder, *This song is awesome.* His lips made the words. The volume seemed to lessen a little near the crater of his open mouth.

Then the walls of the song rose up—it got quiet—I floated in a valley between towering waves of music—craning my neck, staring at the words on the waves:

When I'm tired and thinking cold
I hide in my music, forget the day

I was floating in the open space at the center of "More Than a Feeling."

The tickle of the thought in the last instant before the waves of guitar came down—*this song is so beautiful*—guitar coming down so hard I lost my place in the song and I lost my thought too but it didn't matter. When the next open space came I felt around in my head for the thought—found it—I hope this song never ends.

Tod's lips moved in the rearview. Steph nodded. The speedometer jumped. Outside, the deserted sidewalks of Libertyville turned into the empty fields of Wauconda. Libertyville was still a distant suburb of Chicago. No one knew what Wauconda was.

At last the car turned and began to slow, stopping with a screech. The song cut off, leaving my eardrums grasping at the air like tiny, dumb hands.

"Ok," said Steph.

I stumbled out. Head ringing, numb. And there was Sarah, leaning against the red paint of an old barn. Tod opened his door and stepped out, blocking her. When he shut the door I saw her again. She was talking to Steph. Ty got out of the car, stretched, and yawned theatrically.

Spaciousness in her expression, I thought, looking at Sarah laughing at something Steph was saying. When she laughed, her eyes seemed to hang back and marvel at her laughter. It was as if part of her face was always saying, *Check out this crazy thing my face is doing.*

"Hey!" she said suddenly, looking at me. Her lips quirked in a smile; her eyes went up.

"Hey," I said stupidly. I looked at her as long as I dared, then looked away.

Now that everyone was out in the open, I saw what they were wearing. I'd never seen Tod outside his Catholic school uniform. He wore an extremely cool T-shirt. The two girls wore extremely cool T-shirts too. Bright and dark with images of flattened cars, unpronounceable words, insects, burning telephones, yellow trees.

Ty and I looked down at our clothes self-consciously. He was wearing a Bulls jersey. I had a Guns N' Roses T-shirt on. My shirt had a skull on it, which I thought was cool. But next to them and their shirts I looked like something out of a black-and-white TV show.

"Who's this?" someone asked.

A tall guy with light-blond hair down to his shoulders walked into view. He was wearing an untucked blue dress shirt, black slacks, and dress shoes.

"Nick," Tod said, slamming the car door and jerking a thumb at me. "That's Ty. From school. They're like the only kids in the place who aren't narcs."

The formally dressed individual advanced toward me, hand out.

"Ian," he said. "Tod's brother. I'm a junior at Penn."

A college junior. Ty and I were very careful not to look at each other.

Ian shook hands with each of us. I'd never shaken hands with someone in a social setting before. With another kid, I mean. If you could call Ian a kid, which I guess you couldn't. I did the math in my head for how old a college junior was.

"We've been waiting for you guys," Ian said.

"Barn time," said Steph.

"About time," said Tod, already moving.

*

Inside the barn, silence, and a pound of dust in each long sunbeam. It was starting to get cool outside, but the barn retained the heat of the late-spring day. Steph bent before the slant of a chest-level ray, then limbo'd entirely under it, the flash just cutting her chin. Tod laughed. Ian ascended the wooden stairs in the corner.

Sarah tramped up after him. I followed. Her hand swung back as mine swung forward, and our fingers brushed. In that slow half second, I felt every cell of the warm quarter inch of her finger against mine. Time stretched—the cells beat and breathed and moved—I wondered at how feeling comes and goes in the body—how feeling breathes and moves in a shape of the body, like dust in a sunbeam—then her hand swung forward again and she ducked through the low door and we were there.

It was an old hayloft. They'd turned it into a sort of room by nailing up drywall to close it off from the barn below. A single high window opened on the sky. The paraphernalia of a higher existence lay tumbled around the room. Tie-dyed throws over the couches and chairs. An ornate Turkish carpet on the floor. Wax candles in long silver candlesticks. A portable record player, with an orange extension cord snaking out the window. Even a toaster oven.

And the stunner. A broken fluted column of what looked like real marble. Maybe four feet high.

"This place is crazy," Ty said, awe in his eyes.

Steph smiled at him.

Tod was the last up, shutting the door behind him. He turned on the record player, and soft, tinkling music out of the nineteen sixties came through the tiny speakers. Steph took out a tall purple cylinder from the bag she was carrying. I recognized it from pictures in the backs of Ty's rap magazines. A bong.

Ty and I carefully didn't stare at the bong.

Tod told us to relax. We sat down on couches that made two angles of a triangle, the wall with its single window making the long third. I eased back against the cushions and looked around.

Steph was fumbling in her bag. I didn't want to appear to be watching her. I didn't want to look at Sarah either. If I looked at Ty we'd start grinning like idiots. I was afraid to look at Ian or Tod. So I looked out the window.

Sky. The music tinkled. A bee stumbled among the rafters.

Anytime you look at something you can see a little fringe of yourself—your nose, a bit of your hair. Staring into the blue sky, I noticed the fringe of my body around my vision—the flesh of my eye sockets, strands of my dark hair, the shadow of my nose. Nothing out of the ordinary.

But suddenly I realized how strange and even terrible it is that a person looks out from inside their face. *Realize* is the wrong word. I *felt* the weirdness of it. Like my vision was standing with its feet in my face. Like my face is a diving board, I thought. Like when you're about to jump from the high dive and you look and you can see the edge of the board dark against the blue . . . My nose dark against the sky like that.

Then a certain horrible familiarity crept out on the raw angles of the feeling that my face was a diving board. I've felt this way before.

A quick glance at the others assured me no one was watching.

I'm having a panic attack, I thought. Right now. And for some reason I felt calm inside it. The panic attack unfolding—I could feel my heart accelerate, the tingling in my fingers and toes—but so long as I kept staring at the sky, panic's knifepoint hung suspended. My breathing, relatively calm. No emergency. I didn't need a paper bag. Yet.

Because I didn't want to look at the others, because I didn't want them to know, I stared at the sky—and now it seemed to me there was a dark spot in the center. Like a bruise. Still calm inside the suspended panic, I examined it. Its color seemed oddly insubstantial. Like a shadow—a shadow cast by something behind my head. Something heavy and dark, so heavy it cast a shadow through my flesh . . . I felt Ty start to shift on the couch next to me.

Don't look away—the thought came through my head hard and slow, like a finger pushed through the back of my skull straight to my eyes.

The bruise in the sky deepened. My eyes wouldn't close—I couldn't even feel the lids. The fringe of flesh around my vision vanished—

Ian spoke and my eyelids worked again. I squeezed them shut.

"This may be the only window in the whole low-built county," Ian said loudly. "Where there aren't trees or power lines. No interference at all. Just pure sky."

When I opened my eyes again, the fringe of my face had snapped back around my vision like a frame. I could see a few wisps of my hair, the edge of my nose. I took a deep breath, rubbing my eyes. My heart rate, still elevated. My fingers tingling. The window shone a clear, uniform blue.

Holy shit, I thought.

I breathed out slowly. I hadn't said anything. Not a sound. Thank God. I turned away from the window, and in the corner of my eye I saw Tod quickly move his head.

Had he been watching me?

Steph was packing the bowl of the tall purple bong with light-green buds. Finished, she took a deep breath and hit it, holding the lighter until the flame-veined bud wheezed and grumbled like a limbless demon. Exhaled coughing. Passed it to Ty.

"We call this shit Mola Ram," Tod said.

"You know?" said Steph. "The high priest in *Indiana Jones and the Temple of Doom*?"

Ty, bong in his mouth, nodded his head, bong swaying, water sloshing.

"Careful!" said Steph.

Tod laughed.

"Mole . . . er . . . *am*," said Sarah.

Nothing terrible has happened, I thought. My heart rate was already beginning to slow. No one seemed to notice what had happened to me.

That bruise in the sky, I thought.

Chill out! If you stare long enough at anything it'll look weird.

"What is this place?" Ty asked.

"Just an old barn," Tod said, shrugging. "We've got five hundred acres or something. Our house is up the driveway."

The smoke put a translucent figure in the air, irradiated by the window's blue light. Ty passed the bong to me. I lit it, holding the smoke in my mouth, then blew it out, pretending to cough, careful not to meet anyone's eyes. I passed it to Sarah.

"It was Tod's idea," Ian said. "A year ago, right after he got his license, he called me at my dorm and told me about it. About his vision. What do you think?"

"It's perfect," said Ty quietly—Ty, who never said anything quietly.

I sat there with a smile frozen on my face, sweeping four-second glances across the only pure square of sky in the county. Fast glances, panic prevention. To further calm my thoughts, I focused on Sarah, sitting next to me. Listening carefully, I could sift the sound of her breathing from the music—find the slow, calming rhythm of her breath, tidal under the minor chaos of the room's sonics.

She shifted in her seat—her hand brushed mine. I didn't move. She didn't either. I wondered if she was going out with someone. We'd never actually said anything about us. For all I knew she already had a boyfriend. The sunbeam of my hand lay crossed in the beam of hers. Feeling swirled in it like dust.

A flame spurted in Tod's hand, and I realized how dim the room had gotten. The light had slowly gone out of the sky's color, like a hand withdrawn from a glove, leaving the empty blue sagging in the room like darkness.

"Why are you pretending to smoke?" Tod asked.

I whipped my hand away from Sarah's.

"What are you, the weed police?" she said.

But now the others were looking at me. The long burble of the bong sounded accusingly under Tod's sucking mouth. His eyes, lit from below by the lighter he held at the bowl, shone like wet stone in a face made indefinite by shadow.

He took his thumb off the lighter and his eyes vanished. A shapeless dark figure on the dim couch across from me. Watching. Ty, Ian, all of them. All of them shapeless, looking out at me from rough heads made of shadow.

"You don't have Solid Mind, do you, Nick?" Tod said at last.

My mouth opened and closed in the dark.

"Can't you tell?" said Ian excitedly, turning to the others. "Did you *see* how he stared at the window?"

"Um, yeah," Steph said slowly. Without light, her face and body had lost shape. Her voice carried a new tone—low and serious.

Tod's form rocked back and forth at the bong. Panic clawed up my rib cage. Steph got up, her shadow unfurling into spectral thinness. She moved toward the wall, bent, and sparked the lighter. One by one, the tall candles standing on the floor flickered to life.

The faces came back in the dim, moving light. Their eyes—set in teeming pools of shadow—looked like they were running down their cheeks. Their gaze seeped into the walls, the couches, the floor. Watching me. Waiting.

"What's solid mind?" Ty asked.

"Solid Mind," Ian replied, "is when your head is solid."

Ty raised his eyebrows. The pools of his eye sockets widened.

Solid Mind, the thought skittered through my head. Is that a reference to a movie? A book? I tried to sit as still as possible, while my open mouth sucked in deep, panicked breaths. It's too dark to see my face. If I keep still, I'll look calm.

"Solid Mind," Ian continued, "is when your thoughts flow in grooves, built deep into your brain. You don't even notice them. The thoughts you need are always there, and the thoughts you don't need aren't."

"Hey, Nick," Tod asked, "what do your thoughts feel like?"

"Do you have just the ones you need?" asked Steph.

Play along, I told myself. This is just how stoned people talk. We read about this in health class.

I closed my eyes. The thoughts came faster, rustling through my head like a crowd of wings.

But they *saw*, I thought. They saw the panic attack. They *know* . . .

Why else would they ask me what my thoughts feel like? They

didn't ask anyone else, just me. *They caught me.* I tried to be careful, I'm always careful . . . Sarah—did she tell them?

The thoughts blew through my head like a torrent of flies.

*

When I opened my eyes they were all staring at me.

"Go on," Tod said. "Tell us what your thoughts feel like."

"Feel like?" I repeated, turning to Tod with a jerk. My syllables sounded wet, deformed, as if I'd just woken up. It's hard to turn thoughts into sound on the edge of panic. On the edge of panic, you see that thoughts maybe aren't *meant* for speaking.

I pulled myself together.

"They just . . . I mean . . . You know."

"No, I don't know," he said. "That's why I asked."

They're testing me. To see if I'm stoned. Stoned people love to talk about this kind of shit. They don't know about the panic. They can't see inside me. Play along.

"Thoughts kind of," I began, "I don't know . . . they just kind of buzz around. Like there's a . . . window in your head and they get in. Like flies. You know, like that nursery rhyme."

I cleared my throat.

"*Three little flies, buzzing in my head.*"

It was so quiet I could hear my heart beating.

"You know that song?"

Suddenly the forms crumpled like balled-up sheets of paper. Ty laugh-wheezing, sounding like Axl Rose. Steph, her head buried in her hands, shoulders shaking. Even Sarah, doubled over beside me, her breath shredded into ribbons of quiet laughter.

"No," Tod said at last, wiping his eyes. "We never heard that one."

I could hear my mother's voice, singing it to me in her heavily accented English. Could it be possible I'd never talked about it before? Never tested it? What a fuckup, to say it now! But so what. A surge of anger tightened my stomach. So it's a strange song, maybe it's Russian. Who cares!

"Just forget about the fucking song," I said.

Sarah sat up straight next to me.

"Jeez. Don't yell at us, man."

"I'm not yelling."

"Yes, you are. You just yelled again."

Ty grinned, bloodshot eyes in the grim light. For the first time, I didn't know how to read him.

"You guys are trying to freak me out," I said.

"No one's trying to freak you out," said Steph. "You're freaking *us* out."

I didn't reply. The situation had gone to hell. I was stunned by how fast it had happened.

"Don't be mad at *us*," Steph said. "There aren't any flies buzzing in *our* heads."

That started everyone laughing again. I put my hands to my temples and looked at the floor, gritting my teeth.

"Ok that's enough," Tod said loudly. "Stop fucking with him. Nick, let's end this shit. Just go ahead and tell us one more time what your thoughts feel like and that'll be it. You don't even have to tell us *what* you're thinking. Just tell us how it feels."

I closed my eyes.

"I'm not saying it again," I muttered.

Steph whispered something.

"Shut it, Steph!" Tod said. "Go on, Nick. You said flies, right? Thoughts feel like flies?"

"No," I said in a low, liquid tone, word barely formed.

What kind of torture was this? Like being asked what sweating feels like, or swallowing. Who talked about this stuff?

Some kind of punishment. For pretending to smoke. All through high school, I thought bitterly, the other kids constantly suspicious, you can't wait to get out. And then you finally meet actual college kids and they're a thousand times more suspicious, suspicious of everything. Asking what it feels like for you to think!

"How am I supposed to explain it?" I burst out. "Why don't *you* say how thinking feels?"

"You first."

I stared at the floor, digging my nails into my palms.

"Listen, Nick," Tod said gently. "I know it was just a saying, that thing you said. Different families have different sayings, I know that. But Steph thinks you're weird. She thinks you're kind of crazy, to be honest. And if I go first, and say what it's like, then she'll think whatever *you* say will just be copying me and SHUT THE FUCK UP, STEPH!"

My head snapped up. Steph, who'd been whispering something, now looked down at her bare knees. The music had stopped.

Ian got up in the heavy silence and changed the record. The needle hit the groove and the music began to tinkle and shimmer. It sounded like a ghost, wheeling a glass bicycle.

"Come on, Nick," Tod prodded. "Thoughts feel like flies. Ok. Where do the thoughts come from?"

I closed my eyes. They weren't going to let this go.

"The thoughts," I said warily. "They come from . . ."

I can't believe I'm explaining this, I thought.

"From where?"

"From nowhere," I blurted, made suddenly furious by his insane pretense that he didn't know what *thinking* felt like.

"All right," Tod said quietly, surprising me. "Now I'll tell you where my thoughts come from."

He closed his eyes. He opened them.

"My thoughts today come from yesterday."

I stared at him.

"And my thoughts don't have any feeling to them," Tod continued. "You got all flustered when I asked you what thoughts feel like. But if you ask me that, I don't get flustered. I tell you straight. They feel like nothing."

"Could your head ever just fill up with a bunch of random thoughts from nowhere, Tod?" Ian asked quietly.

"No way," Tod said, looking at me. "My thoughts are solid, built-in, habitual."

He tapped his head with his forefinger.

"Solid."

"I can't even tell if you're joking right now," I said.

"I'm not joking," Tod said.

"Well, people say thoughts pop into their head," I said. "Where do they come from? They're not already there."

"It's a figure of speech."

I could feel sweat pricking the back of my neck. My hands were ice-cold.

"What?"

"*The thought popped into my head*," Tod said. "It's just a figure of speech, Nick. Thoughts don't come from outside. They're built-in."

"Everyone," said Steph, "has the same basic thoughts, built-in from when you're a baby. Like the inside of your mouth or the sound of your voice when you talk. It's not surprising. No one thinks they come from nowhere."

"No one with Solid Mind," Tod added.

"Right," said Steph.

"I can't tell if you're joking right now," I said.

I stared at them.

"No one here is joking," Ian said.

Sarah let out a long breath.

"Whoa," she said. "Just. Whoa."

"Nick doesn't have Solid Mind," Ian said. "So don't ask him why he doesn't smoke. He could literally lose his mind."

"Thoughts really feel like flies to Nick?" Steph whispered to Tod.

"Ssshhh," he said.

7.

The Gate

Calm down, I told myself. They're just messing with me. If they see I'm nervous it'll be worse.

They whispered to each other. The music shimmered. After a while Steph got up and lit more candles.

Sarah's face swam out of the darkness.

"Hey," she said.

I swallowed and looked around. Ty and Ian and Steph were now standing by the record player, talking about music, looking at album covers. Tod was in the far corner, fiddling with the toaster oven.

"You told them," I said.

She looked confused.

"Told them what?"

"You know what," I said. "About the . . ." I checked to see no one was watching. "The *panic*," I whispered.

Sarah shook her head slowly.

"No," she said. "No way."

I took a deep breath and closed my eyes.

"You just . . ." she began.

"What?"

"You were just saying some tripped-out shit, ok?"

I didn't say anything.

Sarah rolled her eyes.

"Tod's always trying to, like, start something," she said. "You don't know him."

She's trying to make me feel better, I thought. I didn't know exactly how things had gotten so bad. I didn't know why Tod had decided to attack me, or what kind of joke he was trying to make with his thoughts-feel-like-this bullshit. Maybe he was just disgusted by me pretending to smoke. Maybe he thought I was hitting on Sarah. Wanted to punish me.

I looked at the broken column of marble, the candlelight flowing over it like water. Five hundred acres, I thought.

Rich kids. Rich kids with their knickknacks. The bronze candle holders. This marble column. The oriental rug. Knickknacks. Like the ones on the mantels in the houses my mother cleaned. I'd worked with her every summer since middle school. Hating every second, dreading seeing one of my friends' mothers or, even worse, one of my school friends, coming into a bathroom where I sat on the floor in cleaning gloves, the automatic apology on their lips giving way to the slow smile.

I remembered my mother holding up a knickknack in some rich person's living room. A little ebony dog, two yellow jewels for eyes.

"This is what they love, Nicholas," she'd told me. "This is what is in their hearts. Don't ever you be ashamed before these things."

She sometimes called other people that, *things*. Elsa, the black woman who was the first person Mom hired when she started her own cleaning business, asked about it one day. Mom told her it was from thinking in Russian. "Russians use same word for people and things." Elsa nodded. But I asked my aunt about it and she laughed and said Russia had different words for people and things, Russia was a poor country but not *that* poor . . .

And now, sitting in the barn with this pretty, rich girl trying to make me feel better, sitting there staring at that marble column, I remembered my mother dusting the tiny, grotesque ebony dog. I remember how she wiped each of its perfectly carved legs with a special soft cloth.

This marble column, I thought, is a *knickknack*. Their weird T-shirts are *knickknacks*. Their statues, their candles, their sky window, their weed, even their jokes: *knickknacks*.

"Want me to tell you something?" Sarah asked.

I took a deep breath.

"What," I managed to say, still staring at the marble column.

"They fucked with you, ok?" she said. "But they only fuck with people they like."

"Whatever."

"You're a strange kid, Nick," she said. "But this isn't high school."

I looked at her, searching her face in the trembling candlelight. She seemed serious.

"We like you," she said. "I thought you knew, I thought we'd talked about it, ok? If you're not like other people, it's cool with us. We don't *like* other people."

Candlelight caught in her long brown hair; her green eyes shone.

"You told me what you're like and I didn't freak," she said. "Did I? Tod's the same. Steph's the same. Ian's freakier than you. You think people here get mad because you said some freaky shit? Look around."

This *isn't* high school, I thought, wondering now.

The toaster-oven alarm began to ring.

"Pizza!" Steph yelled out.

Sarah got up and walked over to where Ty was hitting the bong. I watched as he passed it to her. She threw an unanalyzable glance back at me as she prepared to hit it. Ty wandered over.

"I think there's pizza, man," he said.

"Go ahead. I'm not hungry."

He lingered.

"What?"

"They were saying you were pretending to smoke," he said. "Are you a pussy or something?"

I didn't say anything. He walked away. I sat there with the thought of what Sarah had said electric in my skull. I remembered something I'd read in one of Dad's magazines, about college fraternities and hazing. Was this how stoners did their hazing? *What do your thoughts feel like?* Could that have been some kind of test—a test I'd somehow . . . passed?

Steph came up and touched my shoulder. "Tod needs you," she said.

I got up stiffly, anxiety coursing through my legs. I walked over to where Ian and Ty stood looking with concern at Tod, who sat cross-legged on the floor with a plate of toaster-oven pizza in his hands.

"Tod's sick," Ty said.

"I don't know if you should eat anything," Ian said. "You look ill."

"If I eat it *right* I'll be ok," Tod mumbled.

"Here's Nick," Steph announced.

Tod looked up at me. His eyes were bloodshot.

"The pizza is hot," he said.

"What do you want?"

He looked at me with wide red eyes.

"I need you to feed me."

Steph, Ian, and Sarah, who'd just walked up, all erupted in laughter.

"Fuck you, Tod," I said.

His mouth went down in pathetic disappointment and his face sagged like a clown's.

"*Please,* Nick," he said. "I need you to feed me this hot pizza."

Steph clapped. Ian shook his head, smiling. Was this the sign Sarah was talking about? Tod's expression didn't change. He didn't move his pleading eyes from mine.

"Help me, Nick," he said. "I got a problem."

I turned my head away so he wouldn't see me smile.

"Look at me," he said in a low, slow, heavy tone. "Look at my mouth. I can only open my lips *this much.*"

I looked at him and his lips were just barely pursed, hardly open, maybe a quarter inch of space between them.

"I can't open my lips any wider," he said. "I tried but I can't."

I bit the inside of my cheek to keep from laughing.

"Feed me the hot pizza, Nick," Tod said through his tiny baby mouth. "Please don't burn my lips."

Even Ty was laughing now.

"Please," Tod said. "*Don't burn my lips, Nick.*"

Everyone bent in half with laughter. The idea of pushing a giant slice of hot pizza into Tod's baby mouth and burning the shit out of his lips was just too funny for them. And then it was too funny for me. I laughed—I couldn't stop. Like I was throwing coils of tension up from my stomach, my spine. I gagged on laughter. Tod broke out of his baby mouth and began to bellow.

This is his way of apologizing, I realized. For freaking me out earlier. The tone of laughter shifted. Our laughs blew out like long, effusive, hilariously sentimental words. *You're ok, man!* said the long, gasping laughs. *Everything is fine!*

We stood with our faces close, laughing into and through each other, laughing till we got hoarse, and I knew it was ok to leave.

I'm learning, I thought. High school situations are like a car accident. Adult situations are like a story. In high school, you just tried to get out before the accident happened. Here you had to stay till the end.

Life might actually be great, I thought. The thought excited me, a fly bumping along the underside of my scalp.

*

"These guys rock," Ty whispered from the back of Tod's car as we drove home.

"Don't tell those narcs at school none of this shit," Tod called back to us.

Ty turned to look out the window, pleasantly stoned. Smiling. He'd gotten weed. Just like he'd said, Tod could get us high. Or at least Ty. And he would have gotten me high, if I didn't know pot was bad for panic attacks. I'd gone back to the library in school earlier in the day and read the rest of the encyclopedia entry on panic. Most of it was stuff I already knew, but it did say that drugs like marijuana and LSD could trigger panic attacks and make them worse. They were bad enough without drugs.

Empty fields flew by in the dark.

"I thought you were going to say something," Tod called back.

"What?" I said, startled. "When?"

"When you were staring out the window. Back at the barn. I was watching you. You looked like you had something to say."

My mood flipped. I remembered the blue window, the floating spot of darkness, the *bruise*.

"What do you mean?"

"Nothing," he said.

I squinted in the dark car, trying to see if he was smiling.

Streetlights started to flare past. We were back in Libertyville now.

"I've always got the same thoughts," Tod had said. *"My thoughts today come from yesterday."*

That didn't sound like a joke. I felt suddenly cold in the wind whipping through the window. If that was some kind of stoner joke—it didn't sound like it.

"My thoughts are solid, built into my head."

Imagine it. Thinking that feels like nothing. No surprises. Tod would never feel like he could come out of his head and face. He would never look out of his face at all this *stuff* and think—all this *stuff* is *alien*. He never felt like he had something in him that didn't belong with the *stuff*, something that sometimes seized up and tried to *get out* . . .

If Tod had solid mind, I had loose mind. I didn't know where my thoughts came from. I didn't know how they got in. There was an opening somewhere, an entrance. And my eyes were an exit. Panic was how I clenched down on it. On what? On my mind.

And now I remembered what Sarah had said, about how there were two possibilities. Either I was like other people, but just felt strange about the things that other people didn't feel any way in particular about. Or I was different from other people.

I'd never taken the second option seriously. But I started to now. I realized I didn't know anything about what other people were like. Tod for instance. Tod was ultracool. Solid all the way through. He said it himself. Maybe he didn't have anything that I'd call *thoughts* at all.

There he was in the front seat, driving, maybe with *replicas* of thoughts in his head. Like a line of print scrolling across a computer screen. Just the thoughts he needed.

Not solid, I thought. Empty. Empty people. With none of the wildness of true thinking. The true thoughts and feelings that blow through your mind from nowhere. Empty people, exiled from *the presence of the god*.

I shivered. This is crazy, I told myself. Seepage from the panic attacks. I'm starting to get seepage, I'm letting it in. Stop.

The blank note of the wind blew through the windows. In the front seat, Steph pushed in the power button on the stereo and music started. The volume was so low that almost nothing of it survived the engine sound.

It's the same song they were playing in the barn, I realized after a while. At the end. It was so soft I wondered if I was imagining it. Just a quiet glitter of melody, a whisper of rhythm. Like a glass man, striding alongside the car, bones tinkling.

I listened through the wind, down into the pores of the faint music. Lulls of something like silence, tiny shudders where it got louder—almost as loud as a spoken voice. As loud as the echo of a voice.

I could make out the words now.

It's more than a feeling

*

They dropped us off in front of my house. I opened the door very quietly, but Dad wasn't home yet. It was only nine. Under the lights of the town house, Ty looked very young. His eyes were bloodshot and he was grinning.

"I'm fucking stoned," he said.

"Get out of here," I said. "Before my dad comes back."

After he left I stood there in the cheap kitchen light thinking about everything. Then I heard Dad's key turning in the door, heard the lock tumbling through the thin walls, and I raced up the short flight of stairs, turned off my light, and climbed into bed, still wearing my Guns N' Roses T-shirt.

They'd seen something in my face, I thought. When we first sat down, when I was looking out at the sky. *What* had they seen?

I remembered the fringe of my face, like a frame around my vision . . . Had that somehow been *visible* to others? Could they see it?

I needed to test it. I needed to see what they'd seen.

I waited until I heard Dad lumber up the stairs. I could tell by how he walked that he'd been drinking. As soon as I heard his bedroom door slam I knew it was safe. He'd be out cold in minutes.

I waited a little longer, then crept out of bed and opened the door very quietly. I slunk down the hallway to the bathroom, flipped on the fluorescent lights. And there it was: the mirror above the sink. My own private sky window.

I stared at my face in the mirror. My pale face, sweaty hair plastered against my forehead. I stared into that mirror like I'd stared into the sky window. Stared until my eyes hurt, unblinking.

I became aware of the fringe of body stuff around my looking—the flesh of my eye sockets, stray strands of hair, the shadow of my nose. The tingling started. My heartbeat—already fast—accelerated. *I'm on the diving board*, I thought . . .

The bruise appeared. Darkening my mirrored face like a shadow. I could see the skin of my forehead under it, as if it lay in the shadow of a small, invisible fist.

Keep looking.

The thought surged forward in my head and the dark spot swelled, as if the form casting the shadow drew closer . . . My shocked face entirely covered by shadow now.

The frame of flesh around my looking vanished.

An indescribable sensation—my vision went funny—loose. Eyesight slipped, it was hard to focus, like trying to grip an eel. A flash of the floor, the white walls blazing in fluorescent light. I somehow brought my slippery gaze back to my face in the mirror and held it there.

The shadows were gone. It was me, but I looked different. My hair, my cheeks were the same. Pale, sweating neck. *My eyes.* The pupils . . . they looked like the heads of cold snakes.

My eyes in the mirror blinked.

My eyes blinked in the mirror and for a fraction of a second, I saw my closed eyelids.

I saw my closed eyelids.

The eyes opened again.

I'm not in that face.

*

When I came to, I was lying on the bathroom floor. My back hurt, my hands. I drew myself painfully into a sitting position. Closed my eyes. My heart pounded in my ears.

What just happened? I wondered if I should call for help. The hospital?—No. Don't say anything. Don't say anything to anyone.

Tod is right. The thought stumbled through my head like a spooked fly. People can tell. They can tell just by looking at me. My thinking, maybe it really does go outside my head sometimes. My head *empties of me* and people can look at me and see it!

They can see something going out of my eyes. And then they know. The ones who know what to look for. Who know when to look. They can find out. They can find out there's something in me that's not in them. Something that can go in and out of me.

What am I?

I scrambled off the floor, pushed open the bathroom door, and burst into the grateful soft light of the hallway. Walked fast toward the stairs. *Mom.*

Mom will be asleep, I thought, racing down the stairs. But she'll wake up. She was always afraid of getting calls at night. She listened for them, a light sleeper. She'd wake up. She'd know what to do.

Aquatic shadows cast by the lights of the parking lot slid through the tall, thin window of the stairwell and down the walls. The echoing space multiplied my steps, scattered them rhythmically.

Then I was in the kitchen, my hand on the phone . . .

Wait, I thought. My mind raced back to that encyclopedia entry, the one I'd read by myself in the library, the one Sarah had stopped reading after the reference to the god Pan.

I tried to recall the official list of symptoms.

Dizziness, lightheadedness. I was sure those were among the symptoms. Was there something about vision?

Mom would call 911. It would be like *Ivanhoe* all over again. The doctor calmly explaining that this was just another panic attack, but now Mom would be involved. *Crazy.* That's what she'd think.

A shard of memory, clear and sharp as glass: Mom, hunched over the apartment's scuffed secondhand kitchen table, her face hidden in her arms. Dad slams the front door as he leaves. The windows shake in their frames. The plates jump on the table. Half-eaten dinners—red beets, pale dumplings.

She snaps her head up, at the same time streaking a hand across her eyes. Staring at me. I step back. Nothing in her mouth to indicate she'd been crying, nothing in her look, in the set of her neck, the straightness of her spine. Just a redness in her eyes, like sleeplessness.

"I am not crazy," she says, looking at me. "Maybe it is you, maybe it is *you* who are crazy. Yes, Nicholas, I think maybe it is you . . ."

In the dark kitchen of Chariot Courts, I took my hand off the phone.

I'm not thinking straight, I thought.

I opened the cupboard and got a paper bag out. Breathed into it. After a while the tingling in my hands stopped.

Just a panic attack, I thought, dropping the bag.

I saw my closed eyelids.

I huffed the bag again. Not thinking, just listening to the comforting wheeze and crackle of my breath in the bag. My breath gradually slowed, my shoulders relaxed. When I put the bag down I felt . . . strong. In control. A sudden smile welled up from my body, my muscles, the hard, solid bone.

Ok, I thought. I have a choice. There are things I don't know about my mind. There are things no one knows. No one can see inside someone else's head.

The symptoms of panic are like a gate in my mind, I thought. If I leave the gate shut, it's just a panic attack. But if I open the gate—I'm inside my mind, a place no one else can see, looking at things no one else can find, with a flashlight of raw panic.

But I don't have to open the gate.

Identify the symptom, diagnose the attack, use the bag, leave the gate closed.

Even at the time, this discovery had the feel of revelation. Like

Saint Paul, on the road to Damascus. The kind of revelation that starts a church. A church is a building made to conceal a god. The simplest church is just a building with a box inside with a little door. A tabernacle. On one side of the little door is one or more people, on the other side is the god. When the door is closed, the god is the god, and the people are the people. But if the door opens, no one knows who they are. Or what they are.

My revelation was the foundation of the First Church of Pan. The service was simple: Identify the symptom, diagnose Pan's presence, use the bag, keep the door closed. If my Catholic upbringing had taught me nothing else, it was that churches aren't institutions for bringing the god close, but for keeping him distant.

The gate was closed. I carefully rolled up the paper bag and put it away in its cupboard.

I went upstairs and got back into bed.

I thought about cars, about castles, about summer, about Sarah, about a car as long as the rays of the sun, a car that had already arrived wherever you decided to go.

I thought about the ocean, and rivers. I thought until there were no spaces between the thoughts, until each thought resembled the one before. I thought until my thoughts turned the color of the darkness behind my eyelids, until they sounded like breathing.

8.

The First Church of Pan

About a week later I told Sarah. We were standing in the hallway outside the cafeteria after lunch. For some reason that seemed the best and easiest place for us to talk. It symbolized, to me, the ambiguous status of our relationship. We now sat at the same lunch table, but not right next to each other. And while we never spoke directly to each other there, it seemed she'd laugh a little longer at my jokes than Ty's. I felt she could sense the effort it took for me not to look at her constantly.

After lunch we'd talk, standing up, on either side of the hallway. With our backs against the green tile, kids rushing past between us, dragging our eyes with them, so we didn't have to look directly at each other for too long. We'd talk about how classes were going, or she'd tell me something funny Steph had said. And then we'd kind of move off a few minutes before the bell rang, with a goodbye that always sounded oddly formal.

I was looking for a breakthrough, a way to get back to the Svetlana moment in the library, open it up—see where it went. Or the moment on the couch in her brother's room just before I'd had to take out the paper bag. Or the way her eyes shone in the barn.

"We like you," she'd said. *"I thought you knew."*

"I think I might have found a cure," I said now, leaning against the green tile wall.

She leaned with one leg straight down, one leg braced against the tile, her jeans tight against her thigh.

"Oh yeah?" And her smile exploded. That's what it seemed like. Like a detonation—the curious, quasi-formal reserve she'd worn for the whole lunch period, scattered—her beautiful face growing heart-shaped, ecstatic.

"Yeah," I said, smiling too now. "I mean, not a cure, maybe. But a way to . . . keep it inside."

"To keep your head inside . . . your head?"

She laughed. I had to look away.

"I mean, I still feel it. I still feel like it could happen."

"You felt it right then?" she asked. "When you looked away?"

A little stab of adrenaline in my chest.

"Yes," I said, brushing my glance across her face, blur of ecstatic substance across the tile. "But if I don't think about it. If I don't get, um, panicked about the panic?"

I stopped as a knot of kids walked between us.

"Yeah? If you don't think about it?"

"Then, um. It goes away. Or it stays inside. I mean it's cool."

Another knot of kids. When they were gone and the air between us empty, her smile had changed, gone out of her mouth, just a light dancing in her eyes.

"There's a party this weekend," she said. "You should come."

Another stab of adrenaline. I looked at a chipped tile above her head, kept my voice steady.

"Where?"

"It's at the barn. It's a . . . it's going to be fun. It's for this old holiday. Belt Day. Or something. On Saturday. We did it last year, it was fun! Plus Ian's going to do something that . . ."

"Ian?" I asked.

Nick doesn't have Solid Mind.

"Something that could help you maybe."

Help? I thought, confused now.

And then she pushed herself off the wall, lightly, and came to me. She was so small up close, her head turned up toward me, her collarbones delicate, tiny dust of freckles across her nose . . .

"It's going to be fun," she said.

Her voice was low. Svetlana low. And burred with the fur of wild animals.

*

It had been a cold April, but Saturday dawned bright and weirdly warm. The sun dissolved in the sky—a uniform white glow—you could see each blade of the bare grass, still brown after the late frosts.

The white sun, I called it to myself. It brought a level of visibility to the earth that you couldn't get even on cloudless days. There was nothing to look at in the sky, for one thing. Your gaze slid off the curved, featureless white dome, rained down on things you normally wouldn't notice: bent twigs, a bird's clawprint in a stretch of grassless dirt, half a plastic fork at the base of the curb.

I waited for Ty by the Chariot Courts gates. Belt Day, I thought. An old holiday? My skin prickled with sweat under my light coat. There was an animal smell in the air. I looked at the dead grass at my feet. When you first look at dead grass in the white sun you know what color it is. But after a few seconds you don't know anymore. Ty's mom's minivan careened around the corner, skidded to a stop. I climbed in.

This was the first time we'd driven to the barn by ourselves. I'd never have remembered how to get there from just the one time in Tod's car but Ty said he knew the way. I believed it. He loved maps. It was the kind of thing you'd never know to look at him, that he was obsessed with maps. Every drawer of the desk in his room was stuffed with them. And not exotic maps, either. Not maps of Italy or Africa, but cheap road maps from gas stations of nearby suburbs. Libertyville. Mundelein. Vernon Hills.

Ty said once that when he was moving along the earth and then switched to map mode, seeing his position from a perspective where the chaos of nature turned into clean lines and dots, he felt like a god. *Like a god.* Those were his actual words.

He'd said it when we were drunk off vermouth from his father's liquor cabinet. Ty said that to be able to switch seamlessly, from anywhere, directly into map mode, was the goal. "The goal of what?" I'd asked. "The goal of life," he said.

But you really had to study a map to do that. He estimated it took three hours of map study per square mile to achieve that seamless switch. And you couldn't go outside of a certain area, maybe three suburbs, that was the limit, more than that wasn't really possible to know completely, not so you could switch anywhere, at any time.

Now, driving on 176, the buildings of Mundelein ceding to open fields, Ty had a certain look on his face, and so I said,

"You got a map of Wauconda."

It wasn't a question. He grinned like a kid. God mode.

And he pushed the minivan down the straight lines, then into a sharp, precise turn at a road I didn't even see coming, and then we were slowing, moving down Tod and Ian's driveway, Ty's shoulders relaxing, his eyes blinking, his mind settling back down into his earthbound skull as the van moved farther into territory that the gas station map didn't cover. A hundred yards, two hundred yards, the sticks and trunks of still-bare Midwestern spring woods close on either side, and then the driveway widened, and there was the barn. Its faded red paint turned the color of dead grass in the white sun.

It was May 1.

*

Four other cars parked along the driveway. One was Tod's, one Sarah's. I figured the other two were Ian's and Steph's. I felt a little better, only seeing four cars. The thought of a large party, with a bunch of people I didn't know, for an event I didn't understand, made me nervous.

Ty turned the engine off. We sat there for a little while.

"Guess they're all upstairs," he said finally.

When we got out, the air had grown even warmer. It had to be nearly seventy, I thought. I felt a looseness in the air—the boundaries of my body, after months of freezing, months of constriction at the bone, loosened. There was a little blur at the edges of my limbs, at the back of my neck, a little give.

When Ty opened the barn door, we heard music. Electronic beats, laced with synths, voiceless. It was a kind of music that had just started to reach the suburbs—it reminded me of magic, of early Nintendo games, of pixel gemstones. We climbed up the steps, the music growing louder, ducked our head at the low doorway, and walked out into the loft.

Sarah and Steph, on the couch, turned their heads smiling. Ian held up a labelless, brown, long-necked glass bottle, scrutinizing the liquid within. Tod knelt on the floor, going through the sheaf of records. Neither of them looked up as we entered. But a third guy, long and lean, with curly blond hair and wide blue eyes, moved toward us.

"I'm Larry," he said. His hands were in his pockets. He didn't plan to shake hands.

"Ty," said Ty, nodding.

"I know," said the guy.

Weird silence for a second.

"I know everything," he added.

Steph and Sarah giggled from the couch.

"Ask me something," Larry said. "I know everything, come on ask me something."

He looked like a star out of a movie. His face, his body had that kind of a shape.

"Ok," said Ty. "What am I thinking?"

And Ty just stood there. He could seem menacing when he wanted, just by the way he stood there, the way he breathed, slower than normal people. His eyes half-open.

Larry looked blank for a second. Then he smiled.

"Nothing."

Ty nodded slowly, smiling slower.

"Nothing at all."

The girls laughed, delighted.

"Shut up!"

It was Tod, standing now at the sky window, pointing out. We all went over, crowding together, looking where he pointed.

The white sky was breaking apart. The clouds now full of snaky lines, a heavy gold light leaking out.

"Belt Day," said Tod softly.

"Belt Day!" Steph breathed.

I looked at her. Her mouth was open, her eyes exultant.

*

Everyone took off their shirts. The sun pouring into the barn now, through the sky window, and through a million lesser apertures that the gold light revealed. Spaces between the boards, tiny gaps in the walls, pinprick holes in the roof.

The few shadows that remained in the space swelled—not absences of light, but concentrations, amassings of golden sunlight, coil upon coil of it, until the light turned black. Black is the concentration of light and heat, we learned that in physics class. I discovered its truth now in the corners of the barn, in the shadow cast by Ian's chin on his chest. In the eyebrows of the girls. In Ty's dark skin as he stripped off his shirt grinning.

Tod shrugged out of his hoodie, thin arms and visible ribs. Larry stood lean and muscled. Even the girls took their shirts off—shocking sight of bare breasts—then I was pulling my own shirt off, self-conscious at first, then conscious only of the feel of the warm air, the glad smoothness of my bare skin, my biceps. And the *give* I'd noticed when we first got out of Ty's mom's minivan, the blurred boundaries between the edges of my body's angles and the air.

I cut my arms rapidly through space. I'd never felt movement so fluid, so easy. Sarah watching me laughed and imitated my weird swift movement, like a karate chop. Her high breasts shook, her mouth opened, showing gold light coiled, piled into shadow in her throat.

"What's happening?" I asked, grinning.

"It's Belt Day," she said.

"What's Belt Day?"

But Ian now came up to her holding a long, thin brush in his right hand, the handle of a paint can hanging down from his left. And between her breasts, in a quick, slashing movement he painted a long, twisted sign. The red paint dripped down from its curves.

"Don't touch it!" he said as her hands went up. "Let it dry like that, let it smear where it falls!"

And then he was in front of me, and the brush moved over my chest, furry, wet, animal touch, three strokes, and he repeated his admonition—"Don't touch it!"—moved over to do Ty.

"What does it mean?" I asked.

Larry, already painted, shrugged, bent his head over his chest, squinting down.

"It's witchy," he said.

"Witchy!" yelled Steph, stepping directly into the sun streaming from the sky window. The side of her bare torso glowed for an instant in the impossibly bright sun, like metal, and she twisted—the red symbol on her chest—suddenly, horrifyingly—the red turned the texture of *true skin* on a polished metal surface—like all of her was metal, artificial, hollow, and the red a stripe of true animal life! Then she stepped away and the vision and the thought vanished.

I blinked.

Tod, watching me, saw. Nodded slowly.

"Yeah," he said.

"Yeah what?"

He stepped closer to me.

"Witchy," he whispered. "Witchy."

"What does it mean?"

He looked at me, sunlight and shadow scalloped over his face like a mask, thin red paint design dripping in a line down his chest, veins in his neck pulsing—and I saw his eyes for the first time—really saw them. They were like stones. They would have no problem staring at anything for an hour, a year, a century—eyes like closed gates, like walls.

"Do you want to know the secret of how to get *Solid Mind*?" he asked me.

I didn't move. Staring at him staring at me with those cold stone eyes—I felt the panic start. I felt the thing in me that isn't a thing vibrate in the socket of my skull—felt the diving board extend from my face . . . from my eyelids . . . from my lips . . .

Ian and Sarah stood beside me now. The others still on the far side of the barn, laughing. I heard Steph's high voice, she was saying something, singing it. Ian and Sarah pressed closer.

"Do you want to?" Ian asked.

At that instant a deafening sound poured through the barn:

BRRRRRAHHHHH

An insanely loud drone . . . a sound like metal, no like animal, no like metal animal.

BBBBRRRRRAAAAHHHHHH

Louder and longer . . . the sound lasted for twenty frenzied heartbeats. I saw Ian's lips moving in the sound, moving without sound.

Sarah's smile detonated.

BBBBRRRRRAAAAAAHHHHH

I turned, saw Steph with a huge horn in her hands, her cheeks puffed out and her eyes bugged as she blew into it. And when she dropped the horn laughing, Sarah, Tod, and Ian looked at me expectantly.

I blinked.

No panic. It was gone. Totally gone. My body was my own, vacated by the unthing, by Pan. I felt delicious fluid movements gathering in my limbs, felt the *give* as my angles bled away into the air, saw the shadow cast by my head on my chest tinted red by the sign Ian had painted.

"Did you recognize that note?" Sarah asked.

And then Steph raised the horn and blew again, and the note sounded.

I recognized it.

"More Than a Feeling." It was the moment when the UFO's doors slid open. That was the sound. That was the note. Prized somehow out of the song, out of the song's sacred heart. I looked in wonder at Steph, holding the long, curved horn in her arms. Or did the horn come first? Was the horn older than the song? Older than the seventies? Did the song grow up around the note of the horn, hiding it? Spreading it?

"Belt Day," whispered Sarah as silence rushed back into the room, and the alien note receded.

*

Five minutes later we sat on the couches and passed around the labelless brown bottle. Tod was the first to drink.

"Two short swallows," Ian warned.

Tod took two gulps, passed it to Larry, sitting next to him.

Ian stood before us, with the sky window behind him.

"They say the old races celebrated Belt Day at night, with bonfires," he was saying. "But that's totally wrong. Last year—you remember—our first real Belt Day—I had the revelation. You remember, you remember, you remember when I had the revelation? The revelation! That we had to do Belt Day *in the fucking sun*."

"In the sun!" Larry said, wiping his mouth.

He passed the bottle to Steph. The sun lay in visible rays on the air or heaped in the shadows. The broken pillar, the tie-dyed wall hangings, bare torsos, stereo speakers, unlit candles, light hair and dark hair, moving hands, still legs, the soft dark couches—some things shone in the visible sun, some shone like dark suns.

"And today it was like supposed to be cloudy," Steph said. "It was supposed to be cloudy. It was supposed to be cloudy but Ian—"

"I said the sun would come for us," Ian finished.

"Why is everyone repeating their words?" I whispered to Sarah, sitting beside me, arms crossed over her breasts, smiling. She leaned close to me without changing her expression.

"Belt Day?" she whispered. "Belt Day? Belt Day?"

"I said the sun would come for us," Ian said. "Because you remember my revelation, my revelation, my revelation is that those bonfires that you see in those stupid fucking sixties movies—"

"They're there to trick people," Tod broke in. "Fake suns for fake people. What's in the bottle, Ian?"

"Ecstasy," said Ian. "Plus herbsbane. Plus something else."

"It doesn't taste the same as last year," Tod said.

By now Steph had passed the bottle to Ty, who'd taken his two swigs, and passed it to me. And despite how good I was feeling, I wasn't about to drink it. Not when I'd discovered the secret to keeping Pan under control, to keeping the door shut on him, not when I was feeling so good, not when I'd read that pot intensified panic, and that other drugs were worse. I didn't know what ecstasy was, or herbsbane, but there was no way I was taking a sip of that stuff.

So I raised the bottle, and plugging its mouth with my tongue, imitated taking two swigs, then passed it to Sarah.

"It doesn't taste the same as last year," Tod said again.

"It's better this year," Ian said. "This year, *you don't have to drink it for it to work.*"

I froze. Sarah froze with the bottle raised. Everyone froze. And everyone turned toward me.

And then everyone began to laugh.

Adrenaline spiked in my throat—Just like the first time, I thought in a thought that was like a door in the back of my mind swinging open. Just like the last time.

"You didn't swallow?" Ty said, turning toward me. "Fuck, are you telling me you faked drinking this shit, Nick? You faked it *again*?"

But it wasn't like last time—it was like the inverse of the last time—because immediately Ian raised his hands and said,

"I said you don't have to drink it for it to work."

Even Tod was nodding.

"It's cool, you don't have to drink it for it to work," he said.

"He doesn't have to drink it!" Steph shouted.

"I said you don't have to drink it for it to work," Ian said, turning to Ty. "Now I said it three times. And you should know, Ty, that everything said three times on Belt Day is real and it's the law on Belt Day and it's against the law to even *think* something different."

There was a moment of silence. Ty nodded.

And actually it wasn't silence, I realized. The techno music, the insistent rhythm, the liquid movement I felt in potential in my calves, in the muscles of my stomach—it was coming from the speakers. Music had been playing the whole time we'd been sitting on the couch.

Or had it?

It was only the second time in my life when I wasn't sure whether something was happening inside me or outside me.

"This is awesome," I whispered. "This is the best."

*

Everyone sat on the couch for a while listening to music, maybe tapping their feet a little in time to it, but not talking much. There was a sense of anticipation. Like everyone was feeling around in their heads or bodies for the first sign that whatever it was they'd drunk was starting to work.

I observed false starts—Ty let loose a big smile, mumbled something, lay back with his head up, staring at the high slanted roof, where the dust motes shone in sunbeams. After a minute or so he sat up again, looking a little sheepish. Larry cracked his knuckles repeatedly. Steph seemed to be practicing some kind of deep breathing. *You don't have to drink it for it to work.* But I didn't feel especially different. Happy and loose—unusually relaxed, as I'd been the whole morning. But nothing strange, really.

And then, slowly, something started to happen.

Ty smiled again—but this time the smile was tuned to a different frequency. Before, it was like he'd been smiling for us—trying to convince himself he'd felt something by convincing others. But now—his smile wasn't for anyone else. And his eyes—pupils dilated—I could see it even from the side, but when he turned to face me I felt a stab of panic. The whites of his eyes seemed swallowed up by swelling color. His eyes looked like . . . like doors, I thought, the panic rising a little more now. Like stones. Like *real* stones. And I realized Tod's eyes hadn't truly looked like stones at all but now Ty's eyes . . . they looked like black stones.

"Holy," said Ty. "Holy."

Everyone was watching him now. He was perched on the edge of the couch, facing me, his impossibly dilated eyes staring sightless into the sunblind air.

"Holy shit," he finished.

And I turned to say something to Sarah—*what's going on*—and stopped. The words stalled dead in my throat. Because her eyes had *dilated*—like her eyes were their own sunglasses—of the impossible coolness of stone. She smiled down into herself, a smile like a stone thrown backward down into the pool of her, falling, getting farther away with every breath.

And now everyone began to move. Nodding and smiling, eyes dilated. They got off the couch with their bare torsos flashing in the barn's alternating sun and shadow. Tod crept over to the stereo, turned it up, the high sound like pixel gemstones tumbled over the low sound like a river, like a god's deep breathing.

They started to dance.

Without speaking, as if they'd planned it, as if they knew what to do without speaking, Larry and Ty pushed the couches back to the walls, clearing the vast central space of the loft. Ian picked up the broken fluted column, picked it up easily, as if he was much stronger than his thin, birdlike frame suggested, and dropped it against the wall.

Everyone arranged themselves into a circle. I'd jumped off the couch when Ty started to push it—pushing with the inward-facing smile on his lips, with his eyes like pools of shadow. I stood there clenching my hands. They formed into a circle.

And I was part of it. Larry held my left hand—Sarah held my right—then on her right Tod—on his right Steph—on her right Ty—on his right Ian—on his right Larry—and we were moving, dancing, spinning slowly in a circle as the music sped up.

A weird dance—sidestepping—every few steps they would all *dip* in unison—and then go up again—and then *dip* in unison—and then go up again. And I tried to follow. I tried to bend down when they did, but a half second too late, I'd be going down when they were going up again. I tried to predict when they went down but I couldn't predict it—it seemed impossible to predict—it wasn't every third or fourth or second step, but sometimes on the third, sometimes on the ninth, sometimes three in a row. As if they all were hearing some signal, some sound, some cue I couldn't.

My heart was pounding and every time we went round—we were going faster now, I was panting, they all had their inward smiles and gatelike eyes, they moved like water—every time we went round—every time we made a circuit—every time I passed the broken fluted column on the wall—the panic in me waxed.

We spun until sun and shadow blent. Sun and shadow became one uniform substance, one color that wasn't a color. We spun until the walls became a band shining, a ring around us, we spun and the music changed. I started to hear it—I started to hear a very low sound—a pressure not a sound—an *indentation* on the air. When it came they dipped. And every time it came the panic in my head got stronger. My eyes were wide open—there was nothing to focus on—no need to move my eyes around—no danger of staring too long—the world moved quicker than I could look. Panic was loose—it was loose—Pan was loose in the room.

And then we were stopping and Tod or someone had turned the music lower and everyone was out of breath and now they were smiling for each other again, laughing. No one spoke but the laughter came in chords and groups and beats like words, like music. I was standing there with the panic totally loose in the room and Ian walked over to me and said, "That woke Pan up, right? Right? Right? The dance woke up Pan, and it's ok, it's Belt Day, it's ok Sarah told me, it's Belt Day, how do you think I got cured? Are you ready?"

I couldn't talk. I couldn't remember what to say. The panic vibrated every molecule of the thing of my body, beat each material cell of me like a drum. My throat felt sore as if I'd been shouting, but I hadn't made a sound.

"Follow Sarah," said Ian.

The room annihilated by sunlight. My heart throbbing, thrumming, going so fast now there was no space between the beats. Sarah took my hand. I couldn't speak. If I opened my mouth it would be Pan—it would come out of my mouth—he would come out of my mouth—that was all I could think. I was biting down so hard my jaw hurt. Sarah took my hand. She took my hand. My hand.

We passed through the door of the loft into darkness where two sunbeams yawned and spread like the transparent wings of a bat.

"It's down in the crawl space," she said. "We all go. You're first because you need it."

She led me down the stairs, speaking in her lovely, low Svetlana voice, burred with the fur of shadow.

"We all go, it's cool, it's just a Belt Day thing, it's the Belt Day thing, you don't have to say any words or anything, it's not like the sixties movies, you just go in and you come out and it's natural."

She was whisper-talking the whole way down the stairs. My breath was totally out of control—I didn't even try to control it. I could actually hear it rasping in my throat.

And then, at the bottom, on the ground floor, she led me over to a corner of the nearly pitch-black barn. No not pitch-black—coils of sunlight—black coils of sunlight heaped. The air in the barn must have been eighty degrees by now—black heat—she led me into it, and opened a short door, and she bent over and I bent over and then we were in a place without light.

And I felt her bare chest pressed against my bare chest and panic turned red. My heart shuddered. My panicked breath for an instant became the eager impossible hunger of an animal, a dog, a possum, a goat—lapping up the air—feeling her bare chest on mine, and between it—we were so close—between her breasts I felt the fur-like burr of the dried red paint.

Then she reached out and I heard a click and we stood under the illumination of a single bare lightbulb.

I backed away blinking and it was just panic again, regular unred panic. She smiled. The light wavered infinitesimally as the string that turned it on swung across the bulb.

"Right down the stairs," she said. "And just crawl into the little tunnel."

She smiled at me. I had stopped trying to control my expression. I don't know what I looked like. I felt as if Pan visible might extend from my eyes—His horns out of my eyes.

"Are you serious?" I managed to say.

She laughed.

"It's just an old Belt Day thing, we do this every year, you go into the tunnel and you're supposed to see something that's important to you, or will help you, or something. Ian and Steph and Tod and me set it up yesterday. It's harmless but Ian and me, I mean it could actually help you, this shit is really old, Belt Day comes from Pan's time, like."

I looked down the short flight of stairs. The bulb cast a flat white light on the dirt floor below.

*

It was the crawl space. Sarah's shadow poured across the dirt floor. She stood at the top of the short flight of stairs waiting.

"It's at the back," she called down.

I could hear my heart beating. I felt panic alive in my head like a swarm of flies. And I told myself, Nothing has happened, a contact high, they're all on ecstasy, nothing impossible has actually happened. And each word as I thought it turned into a fly, joined the swarm in my head. It's like a game, like a game they play, Belt Day, it's not even real it's a game.

Inching slowly forward all the while, crouched down. The crawl space must've been five feet high at the most. The ground was littered with empty jars, ancient lengths of unidentifiable cloth or tarp, short piles of unpainted slats.

Then I saw it. It looked as if a tent had been stuffed into the narrow end of the crawl space, where the low wooden ceiling slanted down to meet the floor. I could see the green flaps. A tent, wadded into the corner, with a small, open space barely big enough for a person to wriggle into.

"Just crawl into it!"

Sarah's high laughing voice echoed behind me.

I got down on my hands and knees. The dirt released an old smell. And I realized there was no way I could go back. Once I'd gotten on my hands and knees in the dirt the panic in my head was so strong that I understood, I understood, I understood that I couldn't get up and turn around and go back like this.

I had no idea what was happening to my face.

I had no idea what expression Pan was excruciating my features into—it could be a tube. It could be a tube! I thought in horror. The front of my face could actually be a tube right now, I thought in thoughts like swarms of flies. Crawling on my hands and knees made it worse, like the front of my face—I couldn't see it! I couldn't feel it!—as if it had become a snoutlike *tube* from which Pan extruded!

I killed the thought, digging my nails into the hard dirt, and pushed into the narrow tunnel. Fabric brushed my hair, the sides of my naked torso, cold tent fabric raked my arms. I pushed into the tunnel.

A light ahead, a dull reddish light. Faint, though the end of the tunnel couldn't be more than a couple feet more. I pushed in farther. My head came loose from the fabric into a small, open space. There seemed to be a moving red light somewhere. I couldn't tell where the source was. The red shadows of my shoulders crawled on the dirt floor. On the dirt wall I saw the shadow of my chin—just a human chin, no snout! The red light moved. Total silence except for my fast breathing, and—

Something else. Something was here. The walls were made of packed brown dirt, red in the dim light. As my eyes adjusted I saw signs and symbols painted on the walls—signs and symbols in red paint, growing redder when the moving red light passed. I couldn't stand up. I couldn't sit up. The low ceiling of wooden boards slanted down to meet the floor a foot ahead of me. The space was maybe three feet square. The symbols on the walls seemed to rotate as the red light swung and moved. They looked like claws, like broken letters. The light seemed to be coming from just behind me, but I couldn't crane my neck around to see. The dirt walls, the dirt floor, the wooden boards seemed alive with weird, crawling symbols.

But that wasn't it. There was something else here. Something truly alive.

It darted across my vision.

The panic grew stronger than I'd ever felt it before. Then, much more slowly, the thing crept back into view.

And it turned.

It looked at me.

And when the thing's tiny, black, dilated eyes turned toward me I felt the unthing inside me vibrating, vibrating, on the diving board . . .

Gone! The thing—the tiny animal—whatever it was—gone. The red light swung slowly across the intricate symbols. When I put my fingers to my face they came away wet with tears.

*

I wiped my face dry as best I could on the rough fabric of the tent, then backed slowly out of it. Crouch-walked back to the stairs, then up, to Sarah's expectant face.

"Well?"

I shook my head.

"What? What is it?"

"I feel . . ."

"Yes?"

"I feel," I said. And I was feeling around inside me, feeling into the vacancy what had left me had left in me.

"I feel fucking awesome."

And it was true. The panic was absolutely gone. Not even a trace of it. My thoughts lay smooth and quiet in my head—they moved like . . . like nothing. They felt like nothing. They sounded like nothing.

But my body . . . I felt the liquid pools of movement, force, strength, desire, curled easily in my limbs and in the muscles of my stomach.

Sarah's smile detonated. She hugged me and we turned around like that. The ceiling was so low my head kept brushing the lightbulb. The bulb moving, the light swirling slowly, like a white version of the hidden red light in the tunnel below—her breasts—her arms around my neck . . .

Then we were on the ground. There was a thin rug spread over the floorboards. We struggled out of our jeans—the slowly rotating light exposing animal fur and tensed muscles beneath our smooth bellies. She was on her hands and knees before me—I couldn't see her face—I couldn't see her face but her whole body thrummed and tensed and coiled and uncoiled and tensed and thrummed with the Svetlana energy—that *savage smile*—opening inside us—inside me as I pushed into her—she tensing and squirming against me until the *savage smile* tore through us both—

Like we were balloons, like we were one single balloon—tore through us as easily as if we were a balloon. And we collapsed in liquid, calming, joyous waves holding the string.

Afterward she traced the painted symbol on my chest with her forefinger.

"You know it's a mouse," she said.

"What?"

Her body shook with laughter.

"It's just a mouse! Down there, in the tunnel. Tod feeds them to his boa. You have to drug them before you feed them to the boa, so that's why it didn't bite you or scratch you or anything."

"A mouse?" I repeated.

"Yeah," she said. "For real Belt Day it's supposed to be a goat, or maybe even like a wolf or something crazy. And we were talking and Tod was like, let's just use a fucking mouse!"

And she started to laugh out loud and I started to laugh too, and we laughed until someone started banging on the door and it was Steph saying ok lovebirds, that's enough, it's my turn for the tunnel now, you've had enough . . .

*

Everyone discovered something in the tunnel. Ty said he saw his father's middle name—which there was no way any one of us could know—written in red paint on the boards of the ceiling.

Larry said the mouse told him a number, which he was pretty sure was a lottery number, and he was going to get his older brother to buy him a lotto ticket with it, that night, that very night, the instant his brother got home from work, and if he won he was going to buy a white Rolls-Royce lined with the skin of white tigers.

Tod said the tunnel was a *buzz concentrator*. He claimed he'd experienced the most pure and intense buzz ever inside it.

Steph didn't tell us what she found.

And Ian said he didn't need to go into the tunnel. He'd done it two years ago and it made him a new person and he never needed to again.

Sarah and I mostly sat holding hands on the couch the rest of the afternoon. We sat in the sun and shadow while the others smoked pot, played music, told jokes, danced, argued, laughed. We sat together on the couch until the sun shrank into a red design on the floor, and the evening breeze drifting in through the sky window finally dried the sweat from my chest.

I realized she'd fallen asleep, nestled against me.

PART II

SUMMER

9.

Drip Drip

It's June, a little more than a year after the events of Belt Day. I'm sixteen. On July 4, I'll turn seventeen. I spend the nights either at the barn or with Sarah. During the day I work at Ace Hardware.

The store manager, Keith, would probably view the description of my activity at Ace as "work" with skepticism. In fact, my energies were almost entirely devoted to avoiding work. But this in itself was a job at least as demanding as any of the spirit-killing mundane tasks Keith assigned me—assembling TV stands, putting prices on cleaning supplies, scrubbing the bathroom mirrors.

I was in constant motion. When you're trying to avoid work, the worst thing you can do is to stay in the same place. It's impossible to conceal the three stigmata of idleness while stationary—the hanging hands, the half-open mouth, the unfocused eyes. I moved rapidly in circuits through the store with a quick, purposeful stride calculated to render me invisible.

"Everybody Plays the Fool" by the Neville Brothers came through the speakers. The store had a loop of five songs. Corporate had figured out the maximum average time customers spent in the store and bought the rights to exactly that many seconds' worth of songs.

"Everybody Plays the Fool" was unquestionably the worst. The chorus features a whimsical flutelike eight-note synthesizer hook. This was perhaps the fourteenth time I'd heard "Everybody Plays the Fool" that day. When I started working at Ace after school in the spring, I'd only heard it about twelve times per day, three days per week. But since classes had let out, I'd heard it approximately thirty-two times per day, five days per week.

Walking onto the main floor that day, I thought, It's killing me. This thought disturbed me, not because of its content, but because of its form. It contained something that I hadn't experienced since the opening of the Church of Pan. It had that quality, the quality of water that isn't water. One of the real, old thoughts.

Drip.

It's killing me—I felt a shiver of recognition when the thought trickled through my mind—*it's killing me*—just a shiver, like a single cold drop hitting your scalp out of a clear blue sky. Hitting the underside of your scalp . . . But I forgot about it almost immediately.

Because, as I turned into the paint aisle, I saw Keith standing there at the other end with his head and neck swiveling toward me.

His main-floor smile froze.

I couldn't reasonably pretend not to have seen him. Yet I was steeling myself to do just that when . . .

My eyes locked onto his.

And it was as if my gaze was a bright bridge of water—and my body—his body—the walls—the white laminated floor tiles—rocks, boulders, and stones—falling.

A look of bewilderment creased Keith's face—my gaze broke off. When I looked up again he was gone.

I went to the employee bathroom and locked the door and read the book I'd brought with me that day. *Melmoth the Wanderer*, written by a relative of Oscar Wilde's mother. Some impulse—the memory of the ancient *Ivanhoe* technique of suspending uncanny states in another's words—kept me on the closed toilet seat, turning page after page . . . sunk in the atmosphere of a corrupt monastery . . . Melmoth creeping into the disgraced monk's stone cell, with his demonic offer.

Once the shadow of a severed head slanted across the print. I gulped and turned the page at once, picking up midway through a new paragraph, hurling myself headlong into the sentences.

"When he spoke, not a puff of sulphur came out of his mouth . . . The night was intensely hot, and the moon glowed like a sun over the ruins of Saguntum . . ."

I read until the light below the crack in the door vanished and I knew the store was closed. Then I let myself out the rear entrance and ran to catch my bus.

I examined my hands in the wavering light of the overcast summer afternoon, streaming in through the warped glass of the bus window. They looked . . . fine. Like hands. Like part of me.

The next day—moving through the store on my circuit, twenty seconds behind Keith—I allowed my mind to return to that moment in the paint aisle.

What did Keith think had happened? That look that crossed his face—a quarter second of *bewilderment*, of *lostness*. I was sure he didn't have a vocabulary for making sense of it. He lacked a lattice of words for catching what had or hadn't happened between us. I'd learned that adults swiftly forget beings and events they don't have words for.

Reflecting on this fact, I felt relieved. But then I thought—what *had* happened? And the thought itself seemed a little . . . unstable to me. Not exactly water-like, but . . . unsolid. It had a buzz to it, like an old refrigerator.

I ran through the catechism. I checked my hands. They weren't tingling. Normal breathing? Check. Normal heart rate? Yes.

Odd, I thought. This isn't a panic attack. But my thoughts felt strange. They felt weird in my head. Which was a symptom of panic.

A loose symptom.

It's escaped a panic attack, I thought. Seeped out.

The thought felt loose and sort of buzzing in my head.

What was happening?

The catechism of the First Church of Pan taught me how to keep Pan's gate closed by not wondering about the symptoms. It taught me to identify the symptoms of panic, diagnose the attack, then breathe into the paper bag until the symptoms were gone.

In fact, though I rarely allowed myself to think about *why*, even the symptoms of panic had grown rare since Belt Day. Sometimes, when I wasn't paying attention, the memory of the sensation of something *leaving* my head, *pouring* into the open black tunnel eyes of the . . . thing, the animal, the *mouse*—that memory would course through my body, a sensation I knew I hadn't made up or hallucinated. Just as you know, when you remember the taste of cinnamon, that you've really tasted cinnamon. You haven't made it up. No one could make *that* up.

Whenever I thought about this, and as a way not to think more about it, I would remember when Father Snow in religion class had described the difference between us and the Protestants. The Protestants relied solely on *grace* for salvation, he explained, whereas we also relied on *works*. And that was better, because the visitations of grace were unpredictable and mysterious, whereas works were solid, everyday, dependable.

Relying solely on grace, Father Snow had said, would be like quitting your job because you'd bought a lotto ticket. But we Catholics, he explained, bought lotto tickets and *kept* our jobs—that was the difference between us and the Protestants.

And then Ty had asked if that meant we bought the lotto tickets with the money from our jobs, and if *that* meant that grace actually came from works, that grace was, perhaps, a use or misuse of the earnings of work, and Father Snow threw a book at Ty's head, but I remembered the distinction between grace and work, and when the sensation of something *leaving me* went through my body like the taste of cinnamon, when the sensation of an *absence* arose in my mind like the memory of the odor of cinnamon—then I thought,

The symptoms, the paper bag, the closed door are the *work*. The thing in the tunnel, if it was anything, was *grace*.

And the work was the important part. The real, solid, dependable part. I had the work. Should I experience again the symptoms of a panic attack, I knew what to do.

But if a symptom somehow got loose from an attack, breathing into a paper bag wouldn't help. The bag only helped full-blown panic attacks. And now, walking through Ace Hardware avoiding work, I wasn't having a panic attack. Just strange-feeling thoughts. And every second that went by, the thoughts became harder to tell from normal thoughts. Without the tingling hands, without the speeding heart, without the crucial markers, panic thoughts don't feel like panic for very long.

They just feel like thoughts. After a few drips, you can't tell the difference. Once you become fully soaked, you don't notice the rain anymore. Thought is just thought. Insight. And the insight falls like rain, wherever you are.

I stopped walking. I was standing in Ace Hardware. In the garden-tools aisle. Under colorless fluorescence. And upon the tines of the rakes, the tongues of the hand spades, the teeth of the rotary tillers, the beaks of ground breakers, the glossy sides of the hoses—insight fell like rain.

These are animals. These are animals too. These things are not different from animals.

They are animals. These are the husks, the waiting bodies, the body traps of animals.

Stare at them.

Enter them.

10.

Sissyfuss

I decided Ace was to blame. I'd discovered the *seeping* in its aisles, after all. And the seeping had spread.

It's killing me.

The things I'd been reading, the music I'd been listening to, Ty or Tod, computer games, even the company of Sarah began to seem like extensions of the hardware store. Other rooms, neglected display shelves. Their words, their colors, even their smells seemed not sufficiently unlike Ace to pull me from its orbit.

I fantasized a sound or a color brash and big and bold enough to punch a hole in Ace's substance. But it didn't take me long to realize that brash and big and bold *was* Ace's substance. Big reds and wild yellows, bright fluorescence, catchy tunes—the bars of my prison.

I saw that a true alternative to Ace culture wouldn't be, couldn't be *deeper* than Ace. It wouldn't be *sharper* than Ace, a color or sound strong enough to *rip* or *tear*. Make a tear in the Ace substance—as the intense and loud music they sometimes played in the barn did—and you simply revealed new, deeper levels of Aceness.

It's killing me.

The brightest color imaginable, the most shocking sounds—all that was *in the direction* of Ace. At the time, I intuited this. Much later, when I read Ian Kershaw's biography of Hitler, I grasped it intellectually. Kershaw wrote that Hitler himself could never keep track of everything happening in a nation as large and dynamic as the Germany of the nineteen thirties. He didn't have time to come into your office or kitchen or barracks or concentration camp and tell you what to do. Instead of dictating exactly how everyone should act, Hitler became a Sign pointing in a Direction. Everyone could look at their own situation and ask themselves—which direction is Hitlerward? And anyone could know *this* is the direction of Hitler—a slightly bigger flag in the yard, boots a little shinier, a bit less tolerance here, a harder attitude there . . .

So each person moved themselves, little by little, in the direction of the Leader. And the whole German world sailed Hitlerward at a speed that no level of totalitarian top-down control could produce. Kershaw called this the "working towards the Führer" theory.

In the same way, Ace was a *direction*. More vibrancy, more color, more boldness, more intensity—this was the direction the store—with its bouncy music, its garish colors, its tools like animal bodies, like *body traps*, its inescapable, shadowless lighting—pointed. The deathly spiritual threat I longed to escape through sensory intensities was in fact inexorably carried forward on a tide of louder sounds, sharper colors, more intense sensations. Even sex, I thought in horror standing one day in the aisle at Musicland, even sex with Sarah was in the direction of Ace!

The true escape, I realized, stopping suddenly in the colorless desert of the classical music section, was not a tear or a rip in the Ace substance, but a small, unobtrusive *fold*.

So I picked out the least-interesting-looking CD I could find, a CD that had no image at all on its plain red cover. Just words:

J.S. Bach. Orchestral Suites. Academy of St Martin in the Fields. Neville Marriner.

*

That afternoon I sat on my narrow bed at Dad's with the lights off. My cheap headphones over my ears, I slid the disk into the player. The summer sun filled the thin white curtains, spilled rich golden light on the carpet. I lay in shadow and pressed play.

When the music started, it was like an architecture inside a color. The color was red—the cover had given me that hint—but within it were lines and circles—the bones of the color.

This is extremely high-level music, I thought. I didn't understand any of it. But it didn't matter. I had the feeling that my listening was like the sketch of a god's eye—that I was picking up the bits and pieces of a sensation that required a greater body and mind than my own to cohere.

I listened very, very closely.

I felt I possessed, in the unfolding complexities of the music, the materials of a Higher Intelligence's perspective on the world—on afternoon light, for example.

I felt intensely grateful that I owned the CD. I could listen to it as often as necessary—undoubtably it would take many hundreds of listenings, many hours of study—but it contained everything I needed.

(In retrospect I detect a strong vibration in these thoughts.)

When the first track ended I considered starting it over. I should get this one down before moving on, I thought. But the next track had already started, and the rods and cones of the god's eye swam in the key's thick liquid. C major, as I would learn.

The first suite went on like that. It wasn't an experience, but the raw materials of a greater experience than I was currently capable of. Even at that distance, at that level of incomprehension, it opened an entirely different dimension from Ace. The second suite too hovered just out of focus—a blur of movement, like I was an ant, crawling over a speaking human's lips. I didn't understand. But I was learning. The first movement of the third suite—the sounds possessed the same hieroglyphic quality; the sensation of unknown meaning vibrated in the notes.

But with the first slow tone of the second movement of the third suite, I *felt* it.

And a scene appeared behind my eyes—not like a dream image, more like a daydream—unfurling without any effort, pure responsiveness to the music.

A Roman scene—*Salome* atmosphere. A large hall, marble columns lining each side. Figures, resplendent in richly colored togas—purple and red and gold—lay on cushions spread on the mosaic floor—lay in the same posture as I, stretched in reality upon my narrow bed. At the far end the hall opened on a sunset scene: the sea lapping gently at the foot of a flight of marble stairs—sensation of vastness—the red distance of sunset slowly filling the vast chamber.

*

The next time we were at the barn—an afternoon after work—I pointed at the broken three-foot-high marble column on the floor. Some weeks back, at the low point of the Doors fanaticism that had gripped the barn—Steph had covered it with a tie-dyed throw.

"Take that fucking thing off," I said now.

Ian, Sarah, Ty, Steph, and Larry all looked at me, surprised.

"What?" Sarah asked.

"Yes!" said Ian.

He got up fast on his long, thin limbs and snatched the cloth away.

"That hippie rag's a desecration."

"Actually," said Steph calmly, "Greek and Roman statues *were* brightly colored. The paint just flaked off over the centuries or whatever, which is why everyone thinks they were plain white. But really they were brightly colored, so the tie-dye is, you know, historically accurate."

Ian snorted derisively.

"I'm interested in ancient Rome," I said.

Sarah smiled, the edges of her mouth indefinite in the dim barn light, a Bachian distance in her expression.

With the column unveiled, and the wood walls like a red glow in the dimness, the barn itself took on a Roman atmosphere—the sky window like a sketch of the seascape from my Bach vision. Even the smell of the weed was not out of place. I pretended it was incense, rising from the ritual of a Roman cult. Like church incense, I thought, smelling the air. But with something witchy added.

Tod nodded sagely.

"Philosophy comes from ancient Greece and Rome," he said.

"'The Myth of Sisyphus,'" said Ty.

We looked at him, surprised. He shrugged.

"My mom gave it to me to read. By Camus."

"Cay-moo," Ian corrected.

"What's it about?" I asked.

"It's a very good philosophy," he said. "Totally anti-Christian."

Tod and Steph looked interested.

"Sisyphus," said Steph. "The guy who was punished by standing in water and getting very thirsty and when he tried to drink the water went down."

"That's Tantalus," Ian corrected.

Ty took a giant bong hit.

"Sisyphus," he said in a high voice as he held the smoke, "was this guy who'd been cursed by the gods to have to roll a giant boulder up a big hill. And it was almost impossible, but he kept pushing and pushing and pushing and finally he got it all the way to the top."

"Fucking exhale," said Sarah. "Jesus."

Ty let loose a snaky stream of witchy-smelling smoke.

"And then," he said deeply, "the rock rolled right back down to the bottom again."

"And he had to push it back up," Steph guessed.

Ty nodded.

"What did he do to get cursed like that?" asked Larry.

"I don't know," said Ty. "But Camus said life is like that."

"Like what?"

"Like having to push a giant boulder up a hill and then having it roll back down."

There was a second of splendid silence—and then all of us except Tod and Ty doubled over with laughter.

"That's the stupidest fucking thing I've ever heard," I said.

Ty shrugged, offended.

"It's philosophy."

Tod was nodding.

"It means life doesn't have any meaning. Life doesn't have a shape or an end. You could die at any time. There's no reason to get up, to go to work."

"No reason for you," I said. "You're rich."

Tod shook his head.

"You're missing the point."

"*I* have a job," Ty said. He worked as a caddie, hauling around rich guys' golf bags for money. "And I think it's a good philosophy."

"How is it a good philosophy?" I asked. "How is it different than like, an insult. Like an insult to life."

"You didn't let Ty finish," said Tod.

Ty nodded, his big eyes bloodshot in his dark face.

"Because you can make your *own* meaning," he said. "Pushing the rock up the hill, Sisyphus feels like he's overcoming obstacles and shit and it's meaningful to *him*."

I stared.

"That," said Ian solemnly, "is what meaning looks like to most people. That's what mystery looks like. Like pushing a rock up a hill."

"Solid Mind?" asked Sarah.

Ian nodded.

"It's like they're pushing the rock of their own heads up the hill. That's meaningfulness to them."

"Well what else is there?" Ty said.

I looked carefully into Ty's eyes. He seemed sincere. Stoned, but sincere.

I'm not like him, I thought. I'm not like him at all.

*

That night, when listening to the second movement of the third orchestral suite, I discovered something else in the tone, or in its slowness. Something like sorrow, I thought. And then I thought how wonderful it was that I was feeling the music, and studying it, discovering in it new feelings, and then feeling *them*.

Bach is like math class for feelings, I thought.

I played it again. I listened. A sorrow . . . No, a longing. That's different, I thought. The Roman figures lying in the columned hall, watching the sea—they longed for something. For what? I listened through the music, down into myself, an inward eye opening, focusing—

At the top of the steps that led down to the sea, a gate had developed. A gate of silvery bars—you could see the sea through it.

No handle. Not an opening/closing gate. The sign of a presence that neither entered nor left, but appeared, as if from nowhere.

The *longing* sluiced through the bars.

*

The next day was Friday. After work, as usual, Ty picked me up and we drove over to the barn. There was supposed to be a party that night. Larry and Steph and Sarah and Ian and Tod were already there.

"We party every night," Steph said. "How's tonight going to be any different?"

"Every night," Ty said. "Like the Myth of Sisyphus."

And then Larry said something unexpected.

"Ty told it wrong. About the Myth of Sissyfuss."

"Sisyphus," corrected Ian.

"Whatever," said Larry. "Ty said it all wrong. First he pushes the rock up and it falls back down. Ok. It does that a few times. Three, four, five, six. A bunch of times. Twenty, twenty-two. But in the end, he gets the rock up the hill, *and it stays put.*"

He sat there looking around at us with a self-satisfied grin on his face. Ty asked him how he knew so much about the Myth of Sisyphus since he'd obviously never read the book and couldn't even pronounce the name right. Larry replied by telling him how much smarter he was than everyone else. Test me, he said. Ask me a question, go on, ask me anything.

Larry was always insecure about his intelligence. He probably had the lowest intelligence of anyone who ever came to the barn. Eight years later he would sneak through the open second-story window of his ex-girlfriend and stab her new boyfriend while he lay sleeping beside her. I heard he got him in the arms. The guy survived no problem. A sitting duck like that and Larry couldn't even hit the torso.

He stabbed the guy in the arms—twice in each arm. That's extremely difficult—almost impossible. The guy would wake almost immediately upon being stabbed, and the very first thing he'd move would be his arms. Yet there were two stab wounds on each of the guy's arms according to Steph.

Larry isn't the smartest guy in the world, Tod used to say, but he might be the fastest.

Now Larry was poking me in the arm, demanding I agree with him.

"About what?"

"About the Myth of Sissyfuss!"

I didn't say anything. Larry got agitated.

"You *know* I'm right. I saw your face the other day when Ty was talking about it. You didn't believe him either."

But suddenly I couldn't look at him. It wasn't the on-the-diving-board feeling. It wasn't that. It was just that Larry's face suddenly looked . . . flat. Like a mask. His face looked like a flat mask with two holes poked where the eyes should be.

And I could see . . . I could see . . . I could see quite clearly that the smoke of nothingness, the smoke of nothing at all, his eyes, the dark smoke, not black, black is *something*, black is the concentration of color, no not blackness but dark-gray or brown smoke, curled in the tunnels where his eyes should be.

I saw all this in an instant, without any feeling at all, without panic, calmly and even so to speak coldly. I saw it and I looked down.

"What are you thinking?" Larry demanded.

Steph laughed—a high, piercing laugh. Tod moved toward me.

"Yeah," he said. "Yeah, Nick, what are you thinking?"

"Right then!" Ian said sharply. "Right there!"

"You should say," whispered Sarah.

I was looking down. The coffee table was piled with empty pop cans, empty pizza boxes, empty boxes of cigarettes. The naked bulb of the light fixture shone directly down on all that trash. Conventional people would call the light yellow, but the color the lightbulb threw down was actually brown.

"What are you *thinking*?" Tod sneered.

"I'm thinking I've got to get out of this brown light," I said truthfully, at last.

The tension went out of the room. Ian snorted and retreated to a corner.

"Who ever heard of brown light?" Ty said.

I looked cautiously up. Normal faces. Normal kids. Staring at the color of the air.

"Look at it," said Ty.

*

Me and Tod went to get the liquor for the party. We were underage, of course, but we had a plan. It was very hot out—still in the eighties. The metal of Tod's car purred in the way material objects purr in heat. Inside it was hot and reeked of stale cigarettes. The smell of the summer body. Hot black metal bones, no lungs, speed.

Strapped in, going sixty down Route 176, passing the old Chiltern place—miasmatic paranoid thoughts spread out from my head like the car was a censer.

I wondered what Tod was thinking. I wondered if his thoughts changed the mood of landscapes. I knew Tod divided people into those who had Solid Mind, like him, and those who didn't, like me. "I could wake up on Jupiter," Tod said once, "and all my habits and thinkings would function the same." I looked at him now, when we stopped at a red light. His mouth hung open. The red stoplight was taking forever to turn. The longer it lasted, the browner its red light looked.

Brown light, brown light—the thoughts, agitated by the *seeping*, loped out of the miasma in my head like rabbits out of a dust storm. Like that famous photograph of the Dust Bowl—the thin farmer and his two thin sons heading toward a terrible house, horizon obliterated by an ocean of dust. We'd seen it in junior year history.

Riding in Tod's car to get the liquor, it occurred to me A) That the barn was not fundamentally unlike the house in the Dust Bowl photo (old, made of wood); B) The Brown Dust of the Dust Bowl had been transmogrified into the Brown Light of the barn; C) The Brown was outside the house in the Dust Bowl photo; D) It was inside the house in the barn.

Seepage.

Tod started talking. He observed that he'd been waking after sunset every day of the summer. So what, I said. I had to get up at 5:30 a.m. for Ace. Tod said that it made you feel weird, never seeing daylight until near the end, when it was almost dead. I said that all daylight showed was what everyone saw—teachers, parents, people on TV, people with jobs, people without jobs. The yellow residue of all their looking: daylight. Stale views and glances of random everyone congealed over every object, every landscape, even the places you'd never been to, the ones you'd never be able to get to if you traveled your whole life, covered with the sticky yellow scum of people's looking and staring—for all intents and purposes that *was* daylight, it was the fucking definition of daylight.

"Maybe daylight is the rock," Tod said obscurely. "Sissyfuss's rock."

He pronounced it that way deliberately, Larry-style. *Sissyfuss.* Turning Larry's stupid mistake into Tod's obscure intention. I felt there was a key in that to Tod's personality, his subtle malevolence, but I couldn't quite grasp it—it floated just out of reach. Like the first two suites of Bach, I thought.

We arrived at the liquor store. Tod went around to the trunk and got the wheelchair out and unfolded it and wheeled it around and opened my door and helped me into it. This was the worst part. It would have been so much simpler if I'd been able to just get out of the car by myself and then get into the chair, but Tod pointed out that they would have security cameras. Plus someone could be watching through the glass, he said. You never know, better safe than sorry.

So I scrambled into the wheelchair directly from the car seat without using my legs, which is not easy. I must've looked pissed because Tod whispered into my ear,

"Act sad."

I nodded and wheeled myself up the short ramp onto the narrow band of sidewalk that surrounded the liquor store. Then I sat there sweating in the wheelchair, knocking at the glass door, until the clerk finally got off his ass and opened it for me.

"Thought your friend woulda helped you," he said as I wheeled myself through.

My friend. I'd always considered this to be the weakest part of the plan. "What do you think they're going to think?" I'd told Tod. "They see the car pull up, they know I'm not driving. They see you help me into the chair—and then you just watch as I wheel myself up and bang on the door for like five minutes until someone opens it? You're just standing there watching?"

"They can't see my face if I don't come into the store," Tod said. "If they see my face they'll know I'm in high school. It'd cancel the whole effect of the chair." "Well how old do you think I look?" I said. "Yeah but you're in the chair," he said. "Who's going to deny booze to someone in a wheelchair?"

We'd been through it a dozen times. But somehow I never knew what to say when the clerk asked me why my friend didn't help me. It seemed so wrong.

"He's drunk," I said now. "He thinks you can't come into liquor stores if you're already drunk."

The clerk stared at me.

"He's superstitious," I said.

I wheeled away before he could ask me any more questions. I wheeled myself to the vodka aisle. The only bottles I could reach were the gallon jugs of Aristocrat, which was lucky, as they were by far the cheapest. They put the cheap stuff low to the ground for the disabled and kids. People grab from the shelf they can reach. I grabbed three bottles, and headed toward the checkout.

It sounds easy, but it wasn't. This is how I did it. I held the three gallon jugs of Aristocrat against my chest with my right arm while I wheeled myself with just my left arm, which sent me veering wildly into the right side of the aisle. Then I switched arms, holding the booze with my left while I wheeled with my right. I veered into the left side of the aisle, stopping myself at the last second from colliding with a shelf of glass bottles by grabbing hold of the wheel with my bare hand. It burned. Then I switched again. In this way I zigzagged slowly toward the front of the store.

My hands were raw from braking the wheels. The clerk was back behind the desk. He had a clear view of me all the way down the aisle—thirty feet easily. I considered putting two of the bottles on the ground, holding one bottle between my legs, wheeling down the aisle normally, and then coming back for the others. But I knew I'd never have the guts to make that trip twice, let alone three times.

So I zigged and zagged, the wheels making a horrible screeching sound on the tiles every time I braked, the hot rubber cutting into my raw palms. I bit the inside of my cheek to keep from crying out, trying all the time to keep a sad look on my face.

It turns out it's almost impossible to look sad when you are in pain. If you see a sad expression on a person's face it's practically a guarantee they are not in pain. The sad face is ice-cold, I thought, as pain and anger burned my cheeks. The sad expression is a form of social control practiced by individuals more or less completely free of pain.

I finally arrived panting at the checkout counter. The clerk's mouth was open.

"Just these," I said, heaving one of the bottles up to the counter.

"ID," said the clerk fast.

I theatrically checked my pockets, emphasizing how hard it is to check your pockets while sitting in a wheelchair.

"Shoot," I said. "I left my wallet in the car."

He stared at me.

"I've got the money," I fished out the wrinkled ten and the three wrinkled ones.

"I'm going to need to see your ID."

"You're going to make me go back out there?" I said. "Like this?" I nodded down at my legs.

"It's the law," he said impassively.

"I'm forty years old," I said.

I'd initially been skeptical about this number. Tod said it was perfect. It was way higher than anyone would expect a sixteen-year-old to claim. Beyond overkill. Forty was a sledgehammer brought down on the skull of reason and resistance, Tod said.

The number had its effect. The clerk's eyes widened.

"I don't have my license with me," I said quickly, hoping to force him to a decision. "It's not in the car."

His eyes narrowed.

"I can't sell you this without an ID."

"I cannot fucking believe," I said, "that you're going to deny a crippled forty-year-old man alcohol so close to July Fourth."

"Get out of this store," he said.

"I need it," I said.

"Get out of here."

"I hope you end up in a chair like this one day," I told him.

"I'm going to call the cops."

"You need their help?" I taunted. "To deal with a crippled old man?"

Then he actually picked up the phone so I left. I considered just picking up the chair and walking out I was so disgusted. But I didn't want to give him the satisfaction. Obviously I wasn't forty. But he couldn't know I was lying about being crippled. He might suspect, but he couldn't know for sure.

So let him watch, I thought. Let him see the desperate, sad, crippled individual wheeling out of his store into the hot night after he threatened to call the cops. Let him see. Happy Fourth of July.

The security camera recorded Tod helping me from the wheelchair into the car. Two thin boys, a wheelchair, and the terrible metal shape of the car—static obliterated the horizon.

*

"We'll try Connor's next," said Tod.

"No way," I said. "I'm done. This has never worked. Not once."

"Come on," he said. "It's your rock. Your meaning."

Houses and trees sped by. Not that you could see them. But there were places where the dark kind of collapsed into itself. My thoughts were vibrating again. Then Tod said something but I didn't listen. I was thinking about the life I might be having behind the clerk's brown eyes.

*

When we got back, everyone was disappointed that we'd struck out at the liquor store. But then Steph pointed out that no one really liked to drink anyway, that there was a ton of weed, and that the whole idea of having a party had been *Sisyphean* in the first place.

"What do you mean by that term, Steph?" asked Ian, with an inscrutable expression.

"I mean it's like pushing a rock up a hill when it's just going to fall down again."

"The rock stays up," said Larry.

Everyone ignored him. My head hurt. They started smoking pot again.

Ian had a little black notebook he'd taken to carrying around and was drawing in it, with a red pencil. Occasionally I felt like asking him what he was writing, or maybe even pretending to get something, walk behind his back, and then peer over his shoulder.

But no one else seemed to think it was at all unusual that he should sit there in the same position on the couch, not smoking, not talking, sit there for hour after hour with the red pencil scratching on the rough paper—and so eventually I forgot about him.

Sarah sat next to me with her legs pulled up and a dreamy smile on her face. Her barn look, I'd taken to calling it.

Ty and Tod and Steph and Larry passed the bong and occasionally spoke. They spoke in the low, loud, long syllables that had recently become a barn tic. It'd started as some kind of joke, but now they did it without laughing.

I thought of it as the late-nite barn voice.

"What rhymes with *hooouuuuussseeee*?" Tod asked in the voice, exhaling.

Larry hit the bong. Held the smoke. Exhaled.

"*Loouuuusssseee,*" he said in the voice.

They all nodded.

This is a new game, I thought. My headache was worse. I'd been getting headaches a couple times a week lately. *Ache* was the wrong word. It wasn't a consistent ache. It was a tiny, muted sensation in a very specific part of my head—on the right side—and deep.

Ping.

The sensation itself wasn't painful exactly . . . It wasn't pleasant either, but it wasn't exactly pain. It was the impossible rhythm of its occurrence that was maddening. *Ping. Ping.* There might be four together, on four successive heartbeats—and then nothing for forty minutes.

Then,

Ping.

Like a code . . . like a kind of Morse code, I thought. *Ping. Ping.*

I sat on the couch waiting for the next one, staring dully at the circle of smokers. Now Steph was exhaling the gray-brown smoke. Now she was about to speak in the voice. And now she was speaking the voice:

"What rhymes with *house* is . . . *houuuussssseeee*," she said.

And it was eerie how deep she went. How deep her voice seemed to go. It actually kind of shocked me.

I sat up straighter.

Ping.

Ty passed. He looked tired. Stoned and tired. So Tod took up the bong again.

"What rhymes with *house* is . . . *grooouuussseeee*."

And now I was sitting up straighter because now I knew what game they were playing.

"What rhymes with *house* is . . . *ploooowwwsssseeee*," said Larry.

None of them laughed. *Plowse* wasn't even a word. I looked from face to face to face. Like stone. No hint of a smile.

Ping.

They are very clearly, very deliberately, I thought. They are clearly and consciously and deliberately avoid the word *mouse.*

"What rhymes with *house* is . . . *sooouuussseee*," said Steph.

Ping.

Ping.

Ping. Ping.

11.

The Fear of Sleep

Ty dropped me off in his mom's minivan. There was a book in the back seat with the words *The Myth of Sisyphus* on the cover. When I got inside, I stood for a moment in the hall. Remembering Larry's masklike face. Steph's low voice. *Hhoouuussse.* I shook my head, took a deep breath. I needed to stop thinking. I needed TV.

I turned it on, surfed around until I found an old episode of *Gilligan's Island* on the outer reaches of basic cable. I felt better. The color of television shows from that era is maximally soothing. Not too bright like Ace, not too deep like Bach. Certainly no brown light in it. Soothing. The color bleeds out through the shapes just enough to ensure there are no real edges anywhere.

And the color . . . No one knows how color really looks to anyone else. It's the definition of a private experience. All we share are the names.

The sole exception to the rule of the total privacy of color experience can be found in the television of the *Gilligan's Island* era. Due to an accidental feature of this primitive technology, the color of television made in the middle nineteen sixties is essentially public, rather than private. The sky in *Gilligan's Island* isn't the color of the sky outside, and it's not the color of the sky in eighties television. No, we know everyone sees *Gilligan's Island*–era color identically from the *inside*. We can tell this isn't our own private feeling from the way it feels. It doesn't feel like my feeling. It feels like everyone's.

Try this experiment. Turn on a modern TV show and freeze the screen on a shot showing the sky. Now walk around the room and view it from different angles. Get a water glass and reflect a little of the color on the glass. Turn the lights on and off. You'll notice that the color changes in tone very slightly, just like real color.

Now perform the same experiment with the sky in *Gilligan's Island*. What you'll discover is that, whether the lights are on or off, whether the color is reflected on a water glass, stared at directly on the screen, or peeked at from a prone position underneath a translucent coffee table—the color remains exactly the same.

The engineers designed that color so it would show up uniformly on shoddy sixties televisions, but they inadvertently created the first and last collective color sensation in the history of human civilization. Watching *Gilligan's Island* is the closest I've ever gotten to seeing the world as someone else does.

After twenty or twenty-five minutes of *Gilligan's Island* on mute I felt sufficiently relaxed for sleep. I undressed, turned off the light, and got in bed. It was late, past midnight, and I had to be up by five thirty for Ace.

As I lay there with eyes closed, I anticipated the slow cessation of thought—the gradual lengthening, first of the spaces between thoughts, and then of the spaces within thoughts—followed by unconsciousness of which I had no direct knowledge, but inferred.

My thoughts grew spacious . . .

. . . and suddenly collapsed.

Because I saw it, painted on the darkness as vivid as life. The thing in the tunnel. Its eyes like tiny black stones . . . like holes. Like *open mouths*.

Unconsciousness? I thought.

The usual slow dissipation of my being across time in the moments before sleep, the curious distribution of fading consciousness over six or seven minutes at once, lapping over the invisible barrier of sleep, reversed. I poured back into the present at 12:17 on my red digital alarm clock.

My eyes shot wide open. Exactly what, I thought, is *UNCONSCIOUSNESS*? And *HOW* could I just *LET IT HAPPEN*?

*

Unconsciousness seemed at that moment unspeakably horrible. Intolerable. I glanced around fearfully at the shadowy shapes of the *things* in my bedroom. The rumpled pile of my jeans, my shirt. Bulk of the dresser. The knob of the door, like an animal bone.

These things, I thought, are *asleep*. They are asleep *right now*. That could be me, I thought. That's what I was about to be. I was seconds away from it.

And that's as close as I ever want to be again, I thought.

Not me, said the thought in my head.

No more sleep. We'll have to figure out a solution to this death thing too. But in the meantime, don't close an eye. Try not to blink, even.

*

I felt like you do when you narrowly avoid a car accident. The living tissue of the brain—glimpsing the void—floods the body with adrenaline.

My entire body rigid with a thousand volts of pure energy. My thoughts, flicking out their forked tongues at the heavy liquid of sleep, tasting deadly poison, uncoiling, pushing their erect spines down through my arteries, stabbing my heart.

Relax, I told myself. Think about something pleasant.

I thought about the color of the sky in *Gilligan's Island.*

The brown light of the Barn flashed under my lids.

I thought about Sarah.

"The rock stays put," hissed Larry, pointing down below the floorboards, where sleep pooled and streamed.

I thought about Ty.

"I have something to show you," said Carl. His face in sixties color, nonrelative, inescapable.

My eyes shot open. The clock read 2:21 in red digits.

Closed my eyes. Remembered my Ace insight. Saw the plump shining handle of a rake; its fine animal teeth . . . look at it . . . *stare* at it . . .

WAKE UP! YOU ARE ALMOST ASLEEP!

My eyes open, adrenaline spiking in my legs.

3:02.

Every time I closed my eyes, I grew weaker, more exhausted, less capable of resistance to the occult symbols of Pan: brown light, mouse, Sisyphus, Carl, Ace . . .

This sequence played through my mind in a thousand variations.

What does it mean? I thought. Where do thoughts come from?

When the alarm went off, I realized I'd fallen asleep, and horror racked my whole body.

Never again! The thought screamed.

Then I saw it. The summer daylight, peeking between the slats of my shades. The color of the sun shone through the phantom thoughts.

I stifled a sob.

The color was like a bright rope, tossed down into a dungeon where I lay, without hands to grasp it, without arms.

Thoughts swarmed around it like flies.

*

One more night of that was enough for me to break through an unspoken agreement with my father and directly raise the possibility that I was mentally ill.

"I think I need to see a psychiatrist," I said.

It was Saturday. We were eating breakfast together, Raisin Bran and English muffins. The dining room's single window showed the deserted asphalt of the Chariot Courts parking lot.

He looked at me.

"All right," he said. "Right now?"

"It can wait till Monday," I said.

On Monday Dad called our family doctor and got a referral. Thursday I showed up at the psychiatrist's office. Dr. Host.

"It's pronounced like 'horse,'" said the receptionist. She whinnied like a horse. Dad laughed.

"Oh that's good," said Dad, wiping his eyes.

I tried to smile. I'd slept maybe eight hours in total since Friday.

A button on the receptionist's phone lit up. She raised the receiver, put it to her ear, listened.

"Dr. Host will see you now," she said.

She caught Dad's eye, made a little whinny.

"That's a good one," Dad said.

I walked through the door into the doctor's office.

*

He was maybe Dad's age. Small, thin, ashen-haired, desiccated, serious. He sat behind a large wooden desk with a shining polished surface. Two dolls and a manila file folder lay atop the desk. The dolls were wearing underpants.

He saw me looking at them.

"Diagnostic tools," he said. "I work with patients as young as three."

I gulped, nodded.

He studied me.

"I don't think we'll need the dolls today," he said.

The corners of his mouth inclined into the world's most subtle smile.

"At least I hope not."

"Uh," I said.

"A joke," he said, waving his hand. "We're here for, let's see"—he opened the file, scanned its contents—"panic attacks? Hospital admission in, ah, February of last year?"

I nodded.

He looked up at me expectantly.

"Still experiencing panic attacks?" he asked, when I failed to speak.

"Um," I said. "No."

"Excellent."

"I used to have them," I said. "But they stopped. Basically."

He raised an eyebrow.

"Basically?"

"Lately they . . . they, um. I mean, I have these thoughts, like in a panic attack, but it's not a panic attack."

"What kind of thoughts?"

"Oh," I said. "Well, first I was worried about . . . things."

"Worried."

"Yeah, and now I, uh. I'm kind of. Afraid to fall asleep."

His face lost the remaining vestiges of a smile.

"Afraid," he said.

"Yeah, um. Of falling asleep. It's weird."

He closed the file without moving his eyes from my face.

"First you had panic attacks," he said. "Hands tingling, fast breathing, racing thoughts, correct?"

I nodded.

"And now the panic *attacks* have subsided, but you experience *thoughts*—persistent worries or fears, dwelling on subjects in ways that appear excessive. And these thoughts eventually produce in your body *physical panic symptoms* that, while lacking the intensity of an actual panic attack, might linger for extended periods of time. Whole nights, for example."

I was amazed. He got it. I breathed a sigh of relief. I wasn't going to have to tell him about the Ace tools or Carl or any of it.

Dr. Host leaned back in his chair.

"Your condition," he intoned, "is known as Generalized Anxiety Disorder. GAD frequently exhibits the development you describe. A period of panic attacks, followed by persistent anxious thoughts on a wide array of subjects, often accompanied by insomnia, difficulty concentrating, and mild depression."

So it had a name, I thought. It was known. And the name didn't seem all that bad. Dr. Host hadn't said the words *insane* or *psychotic.*

"Panic attack disorder," the doctor continued, "is today easily treatable with benzodiazepines such as Valium or Xanax. Today we enjoy great success with medication-based treatments for panic attack disorder."

I'd heard of Valium. Tod said it was good to smoke pot and take Valium.

"I have to take Valium?"

"No," he said. "You appear to be having trouble concentrating. I said Valium is for panic attack disorder. You have Generalized Anxiety Disorder."

"Oh," I said. "What do you use to treat Generalized Anxiety Disorder then?"

He steepled his hands before him on the desk.

"Nothing," he said.

My stomach churned.

"Nothing?"

"Nothing," he repeated. "BZDs are very effective over the short term. They're ideal for the intense bursts of fight-or-flight response triggered by panic attacks. But Generalized Anxiety Disorder, as its name implies, is located not in three-to-five-minute blocks of time, but spread out over the entire length of a patient's existence."

"The entire length of existence?"

"Yes," he said. "The panic is slightly diluted, as it were, and poured into thoughts, which efficiently transmit the panic across the entire twenty-four-hour spectrum."

"Oh," I said.

"BZDs, which are effective in the short term, lose their efficacy over the long term. The antianxiolytic effect diminishes rapidly. In addition, they become habit-forming. BZDs shouldn't be taken for extended periods. They are strongly contraindicated for GAD, which typically lasts years."

"Years?"

The corners of his mouth inclined.

"I'm speaking euphemistically," he said. "Simply trying to indicate that the disorder's time horizon is far in excess of anything responsibly treated with BZDs. By years I just mean that GAD is without a cure, and never goes away."

"Oh," I said.

I looked at the dolls with underpants. Their primitive expressions looked frozen at the instant of being thrown from a speeding car.

Or the instant of falling asleep.

"If you had come to me when you had panic attacks," said

Dr. Host. "I could have treated you with a high likelihood of success. Now there's nothing I can do."

"Nothing?" I asked dully.

"Well almost nothing," he said, opening a drawer and taking out a pad of paper. "There's therapy."

He wrote the therapist's name on the pad. Dr. Crawford.

*

Dr. Crawford could see me the very next day. Dad got home from work early and drove me to the office. It was in a strip mall out in Vernon Hills, one town over. Dr. Crawford proved to be a youngish, attractive woman, maybe in her early thirties. She shook Dad's hand and then my hand. Dad sat on the single couch in the tiny waiting room and she led me back to her office.

"You've probably heard horror stories about psychotherapy," she said. "But there's no reason to be alarmed. I don't work with Freudian gobbledygook. I'm a cognitive behavioral therapist. Everything we do here is evidence-based and scientific."

I nodded. I tried to think if I'd ever heard any horror stories about psychotherapy. Maybe *A Nightmare on Elm Street*? Freddy Krueger, gloves with knives sewed onto the ends . . . But that kind of thing couldn't be legal, surely?

I'd gotten maybe three hours of sleep the night before.

Dr. Crawford motioned for me to sit. Her office was small, but cozy. There was no desk, just two large, comfortable, sofa-like armchairs, a bookshelf, a filing cabinet, and a table piled with electronic equipment.

"Behavioral cognitive therapy," she said, "or BCT, is solution-based. We're not interested in spending a lot of time trying to figure out what caused your problem, whether you were abused as a child or whatever."

I started.

"I was never abused," I said.

"And if you *were,*" she said. "You'd say exactly the same thing."

She looked at me. There was a long pause.

"I was not abused," I said again.

"We could go round in circles," she said, "trying to figure out whether you were abused or not. We could spend years. But we're not interested in causes. We're interested in solutions."

I nodded cautiously.

"The first solution we're going to try," she continued, "is something we call biofeedback therapy. Have you heard of biofeedback therapy before?"

I shook my head.

"Well it's *very* effective. Basically, I'm going to teach you some breathing exercises. And I'm going to put this little biofeedback device on your finger to track our progress."

She reached over to a table loaded with electronic equipment and grabbed a small white cup—about the size to fit over a fingertip—connected by a wire to a small white box with a digital display.

"The concept is very simple," she said. "When you become anxious, the temperature in your extremities drops. This is due to what we call the fight-or-flight response. Your body reacts to fear by pushing your blood to your heart and brain, releasing adrenaline, preparing you to take immediate action against a threat."

She smiled.

"If a tiger jumped out of a bush while you were on the savanna, say," she said, "this reaction would help a lot. That's why mother nature gave it to us. But in cases like yours, the response goes haywire. It gets triggered when there is no threat. But the good news is you can train yourself to diminish the response."

Dr. Crawford slipped the tiny cup over her index finger. She pressed a button on the box. The display read ninety-one.

"Ninety-one degrees," she said. "That means I'm relaxed. Now let's try yours."

I held out my hand and she placed the cup over the index finger of my right hand. The box read seventy-eight.

"Hmmm," she said. "Pretty low. Not so good. Do you feel tense?"

I nodded.

"Anxious?"

I nodded.

"Ok, now I'm going to teach you some relaxation techniques. You will be able to see your finger temperature go up as you relax. You will be able to see how you are pushing your temperature up, all by yourself. This is what we call reinforcement. Your subconscious mind will gain confidence in your capacity to eliminate anxiety through these techniques. And soon you won't even need to use them. As soon as the anxious thoughts start, your body will begin to reduce the fight-or-flight response. And without the fuel of the physical response, the anxious thoughts themselves will wither and die. Make sense so far?"

I nodded uncertainly.

"It'll make more sense once you see it start to work. Ok, now close your eyes."

I closed my eyes.

"I want you to take a deep breath through your nose. That's right, good. Pretty good. But next time *hold* it and count to three seconds. Ok, hold it! Now exhale *slowly.*"

I felt very uncomfortable sitting there with her while my eyes were closed. Closing your eyes in the presence of a stranger, I thought, seems like a bad idea when you're trying to relax. How would that work on the savanna? Some dude you've never seen before, some guy from a strange tribe, with a huge stone axe, weird tattoos, bones in his hair, he comes up to you and you *close your eyes*?

"Keep breathing, Nicholas!" Dr. Crawford said. "Your finger temperature is still going down. Breathing *slowly* is very important. Now inhale. Ok . . . One . . . Two . . . Three. Now *exhale. Slowly*, more *slowly.* There. That's good. Pretty good. You can do better."

I tried to put the weirdness of closing my eyes in front of a total stranger out of my mind. I concentrated on breathing. In: One, Two, Three. Out.

Concentrating on breathing, I thought, is basically the worst thing you can do if you're trying to relax. Breathing only works right if you *don't* think about it. Like walking. If you *concentrate* on walking, I thought, you're more likely to fall over. Much more likely. And breathing is worse, I thought. If you pay too much attention to it, you realize how strange it is.

Plus, I thought, Dr. Crawford was perversely privileging exhalation. But inhaling makes more rational sense than exhaling, when you think about it. You need air. Your brain needs air. The more you think about breathing, the more you'll inhale, and the less you'll exhale.

"Slower!" Dr. Crawford shouted. "Exhale slower. Come on. Exhale for three full counts. One. Two. Three."

It was really hard. Basically all the breath would come out at One. I tried to keep pushing the air out, but by Two I was bone-dry. I'd have to inhale a little by Three. I tried to inhale while making it look like an exhale. Not easy.

"Ok," said Dr. Crawford. "Your temperature is still going down. That's ok. Just forget about your breathing. Don't worry about your breathing. Just breathe naturally. A little slower if you can. If you can't, don't worry about it."

"Can I open my eyes?" I asked.

"Not yet," she said. "I don't want you to see the reading on the biofeedback monitor yet. It would be negative reinforcement."

"I won't look at the monitor," I promised.

"Just keep your eyes closed," said Dr. Crawford. "We're going to try some guided meditation. This is very powerful. This will definitely get that number up. Just wait one sec."

I heard her open the file cabinet and shuffle things around a bit. And then I heard the sound of a tape being placed in a deck, and the sharp snap of a pressed play button. Music filled the air. Soft, tinny, cheap-sounding, airport-type music, coming from what sounded like very, very inexpensive speakers.

This music, I thought sitting there with my eyes closed, is not relaxing. It's the opposite of relaxing. With eyes open it would be bad, but with eyes closed it's terrible. With eyes closed, I thought, there's no way to keep the music in its place. With your eyes open, you can say, it's over there, the music is over there, coming from that shitty boom box, and I'm over here.

But with eyes closed, I thought, when you ask yourself, *Where is this music?* the only answer is *Here*. Inside me. The music is here inside me. With eyes closed, I thought, the music is literally inescapable.

To make matters worse, the music seemed to be getting softer. Dr. Crawford was turning the volume lower. The music was now at exactly the volume level where it becomes impossible to tell with eyes closed if it's still playing in the external world or if it's been turned completely off and what you're hearing is your own mind, mindlessly repeating the tune . . .

They say, I thought, that people who die in a car accident imagine they're still driving for up to three minutes before the fact of their death catches up to them . . . It was that kind of music, that kind of volume . . . It was in my head in a way that implied it might *only* be in my head.

A gentle, insistent, tinkling tune. Very insistent. Familiar, as soon as it starts, already familiar. Very familiar . . .

Too familiar.

"Is this," I asked, "'Everybody Plays the Fool'? Is the music you are or were playing an instrumental version of 'Everybody Plays the Fool' by the Neville Brothers?"

"Don't worry about the music, Nicholas. Just try to breathe. I'm going to start the guided meditation now."

"Wait, can I just ask if this is an instrumental version of 'Everybody Plays the Fool' by the Neville Brothers?"

"I don't know what it is. It's just a tape made for this kind of session."

"Can you check?"

She was silent for several seconds. I don't even need to ask, I thought. It couldn't be anything else. The six-note line from the chorus. Played on what sounded like a glockenspiel. I'd recognize it anywhere, at any tempo, on any instrument. I'd recognize that tune even if I'd been dead for a week.

"Yes," she said finally.

"Can you turn it off?" I asked.

I opened my eyes. Dr. Crawford's hand held a tape cassette with the title *Ultimate Relaxation*. But she wasn't looking at the tape. She was staring at the biofeedback monitor. I followed her gaze. The monitor read sixty-five degrees.

"I've never seen it go that low before," she said.

12.

The Second Church of Pan

Dr. Crawford gave me a biofeedback monitor to take home with me. She told me to continue practicing with it. She said this out in the waiting room, where Dad was sitting on the little couch.

"Keep practicing and you'll continue to see improvement," she said.

I thought her choice of the word *continue* odd. But she didn't say anything about a follow-up appointment, so I didn't argue. I was glad to get out of there. Leaving, I already felt more relaxed. I put the cup on my fingertip in the car and the temperature went up to seventy.

"Did that help?" Dad asked.

"Yes," I lied.

And with that word, I closed the door on medical help. Or medicine closed the door on me. Either way, it was over. The psychiatrist had nothing for me. The therapist actually made it worse.

We drove home through the suburban twilight, not talking. We passed the stunted trees, the thin poles of power lines, the thin poles of traffic lights, the low retail buildings, the little houses, the thin poles of signs. Darkness coming out in the spaces, darkness like a gathering of thin poles, first in the low sky, then on the roadside, then in the car.

My wakefulness cleared a tiny space in the darkness. Like an arctic explorer, under his tent with an alcohol lamp, as the blizzard rages. A tiny pocket of light, my wakefulness, fitful flame under the translucent tent of my skin, keeping the darkness from collapsing onto itself, blotting out the world.

*

As the days passed, my consciousness developed a queer economy. The intense wakefulness of night was compensated by a very low level of awareness during the day, a quasi consciousness that resembled light sleep, and sometimes even crossed over into sleep.

This is Pan's body, I whispered to myself, moving through the aisles at Ace. The hardware store no longer bothered me. During the day, hours could pass like seconds. The world under the fluorescent lights shone in *Gilligan's Island* color. No edges to things.

I placed my seventy-degree index fingertip on the sharp corner of a metal shelf and pressed. When I took it away there was an indentation like the blade of a bread knife, a faint echo of mild pain. So the world still has edges, I thought. I just couldn't see them. If it was up to my eyes alone, I could pass through walls.

My eyes alone, I thought.

I remembered that distant spring night in the barn, when I'd felt my looking standing on the diving board of my face, ready to leap out.

Now, I thought, panic has made its home in my body. Instead of threatening to leap out, as in the days of the attacks, it has turned around. That panic vision has burned down my eyes like wax candles, and now it's burning through my interior, dissolving it.

My body like a pool of water, I thought, in which Pan's vision floats. In which His thought moves in electric charges.

I streamed through Ace in liquid form. But at night I paid for every minute that passed so easily during the day. I could read all of *Ivanhoe*, I thought that night, staring at the red digits of the alarm clock, in the time it takes 3:02 to turn into 3:03.

3:02. I closed my eyes, remembering everything I could about *Ivanhoe*. The preparations for the tournament. The tournament. What happened after? Oh yeah. And don't forget about the one guy's dog. The one the Saxon lord tried to kill.

The Saxon lord had Carl's face, but that was ok. Rebecca had Sarah's face. That was ok. You couldn't stop characters in books from growing real faces when you closed your eyes. When I got to the end of everything I remembered about *Ivanhoe* I was about to open my eyes, but then I remembered the whole subplot about Robin Hood, and so I went through all that. Finally, I opened my eyes.

It was still 3:02.

*

I had become a semisacred personage in the Barn.

"How many hours of sleep did you get last night?" Tod asked.

"Zero," I said.

Tod, Sarah, Steph, Ty, and Ian sat back, deeply impressed.

"I told you," Tod said. "I told you, Ian. The first time I brought him back here I told you, didn't I?"

"Told him what?" I asked.

"Yes," said Ian.

"How can you be . . . afraid to sleep?" asked Steph, wide-eyed.

"Because sleep is the cousin of death," I said.

She laughed. I didn't say anything for a while. I felt a kind of rage bubbling up in me.

"Steph," I said. "Do you want to die?"

Everyone laughed. I didn't. After a while Steph said, "Um, no."

"Anyone who says they don't want to die," I said, "and yet allows themselves to fall asleep each night is worse than a fool. They are traitors to consciousness."

"Say more," said Tod.

"Their heads and faces are the puppets of shadow," I continued, the adrenaline of insomnia flowing through my veins. "They are the marionettes of the enormous continents of matter, the endless spaces between the stars, the rock and gas of planets. The toys, the fools, the underlings, the cultists, the cultic fanatics of the endless unconsciousness of matter—that's what these people are who buckle up their seat belts, who tie their shoes, who say prayers when the airplane hits turbulence, who won't allow guns in their homes, who take only the recommended dosage, who swallow multivitamins, who don't smoke, who don't steal, who drive the speed limit, who push their rock up the hill, who vote, and who fall into the abyss of unconsciousness every night, who place their necks on the altar of night, who let the knife of the unspeakable transition to emptiness, to ending, to nothing, come down on their necks while they're thinking about Florida, about waffles, about breasts, about money!"

Sarah clapped her hands, delighted. Ty was grinning.

"Their lives," I said. "*Your lives*, perforated by death. One third of your so-called life *is* death. If things looked as they truly are, you'd see these people dragging around one third of their body weight in pure matter, pure dirt or rock or mud, a fifty-pound sack of mud tied to their leg, they'd drag it through the hallways of their jobs, they'd strap a seat belt to it.

"'This is the dead third of me,' they'd say, introducing themselves at parties. 'Say hello, dead third.' Dead third says nothing. Everyone laughs. Outer space laughs. The wooden floorboards laugh. The iron gate laughs. And soon the living two thirds of these people say nothing too. If one of them irritates you, just relax. Wait. They are never more than sixteen hours away from the condition of dirt, the condition of the discarded carapaces of beetles, of furniture."

Ian opened his mouth, started to say something, but I waved him silent, went on.

"These death-fearing people," I said. Spit was flying out of my mouth. I was spitting the words. "These fucking people who will talk your ears off about the dangers of tobacco, speak the language of nothingness all night long, their mouths stuffed with nothingness every night, they lap it up, greedy as pigs for the stuff of their own death! 'Ooh, I'm tired,' they say, and with monstrous perversity settle into their beds and eagerly lap up the tasteless taste of no sensation at all. Soon they'll lap it all day long too! Lap nothing with their tongues till their tongues fall off. Till worms eat them. Till they turn to dust."

And it seemed to me, in the dim, smoky light of the barn, that I could actually see dust inside the wavering boundaries of the grinning bodies around me.

"And in between," I said, I was sitting ramrod straight on the couch. "And in between, and in between," I said for the third time, "in between the hideous unconsciousness that precedes their birth, about which not one of them has the decency and self-respect to feel even a twinge of unease, between their unbirth and their death, which they profess to fear above all other things, between these two nothings they dance, the merry marionettes of matter and endless space. Listen! You can hear them piping their little tuneless ditties to the universe of unfeeling, unconscious, undead, endless matter all day long, you can feel them pushing the rock up the hill, it falls down, they push it up, it falls down, and you can see them lying dead on the soft altars of nothingness all night, and if dead shapes of endless nothing could talk, they'd sound exactly like them."

I sat back, suddenly exhausted. Everyone was smiling and laughing.

"Good," said Ian. "You're learning to speak from out of it."

Ty shook his head and lit the bong.

*

It was early August. We'd soon be back in school. I was only working at Ace two evenings a week now. Ian would've already been back east but he'd been suspended from college for the semester. Something about causing terror to his girlfriend.

Sarah wore a tie-dyed T-shirt. So did Tod and Steph. So did Ian. So did Ty. They were all on acid except for me and Ian.

"What were you saying about your body being like a pool of water?" Sarah asked me in a slow, LSD drawl. Her pupils huge in her eyes, her mouth Svetlana ecstatic.

"Wait," said Steph. "I want him to tell us again about how there's no edges to things."

She giggled.

"I can see ants in your hair," she said. "Not really."

"No," said Tod. "Really."

"Do you," asked Ty, "really believe all that shit you were talking about sleep?"

"*I* don't," I explained patiently. "My generalized anxiety does."

"You should go to a doctor," said Ty.

"I did," I said patiently. "I told you. They couldn't help me."

Ian stood up. He got off the couch and stood in the center of the floor. The sky window was now more or less dark. The candles on the tables and the floor threw fantastic shadows—the room spangled with six or seven elongated black insect-like Ian shapes.

"What did you just say?"

I looked up at him. It was night, so the panic had begun to boil in the liquids beneath my skin. Thought had begun to jump and move in me like electricity in water.

"I said I did go to the doctor. They couldn't help me."

"No," said Ian, jerking his shadows with a jab of his arm. "Before that."

"I said I have an irrational fear of falling asleep."

Ian stood there silently.

"That's wrong, and it explains the other thing you said."

"Wow," said Sarah.

"What the fuck are you talking about?" I said.

"The doctors couldn't help you," said Ian. "Because your fear of falling asleep *is rational*."

"Whoa," said Sarah.

"The doctor's premise," said Ian, "is that the fear of sleep is irrational. And they can help some people, people whose weak minds have only a weak hold on rationality. But people like you, Nick, have a strong hold on rationality, and people like you can't be helped by the doctors. People like *us*."

"Don't listen to Ian," Steph said. "He drove his girlfriend crazy. Literally crazy. She's in the mental hospital. That's why he's suspended."

"That's not true," Sarah said.

Everyone looked at the shrouded Ian thing at the center of the long insecticine shadows.

"No one can turn anyone into someone they aren't," said Ian. "I just help people become who they are."

"What do you mean the fear of sleep is rational?" I asked.

"I mean there's something in you. Something you think you want to go away. But deep down you know. And so you grip your head down on it, you don't let it go, you don't relax, not for a second, you won't let it out. You won't let *him* out!"

I stared at him.

"Come walk with me," he said. "They diagnosed me with GAD too."

I didn't move.

“You should go with him,” said Sarah.

She put her hand on my arm. Her fingertips were easily ninety degrees.

“First you tried to ignore the thoughts,” Ian said. “Then you tried to make them go away. Now it’s time to face them.”

I stood up. He walked over to the stairs and descended; his shadows sucked down after him into the dark stairwell. I followed.

*

Their property had a path that wound through the woods between the barn and the big house, and then snaked along the edge of a wide lawn, before hitting another stretch of woods, and ending at the pond they called the Dead Sea.

Ian strode forward with long strides, looking ahead, smoking cigarette after cigarette, his long hair hanging over his back, his thin arms moving as he spoke, the smoke of his cigarette intermittently visible in the light of the moon through the trees.

“You see the moon,” Ian said. “There are two ways to think about that. One is to say that the night and the moon are different. The night is dark and the moon is bright.

“But the other way is to say that the moon absorbs the night. When you look at the moon, you are seeing the night. The night has become visible in the moon. If it was day, you wouldn’t see the moon. The moon is what the night makes visible. It is the visible part of the night.

“How much night do you need to make the moon visible? All of it. So the moon and the night are not two things. They are one thing.

"It is the same with panic," Ian said. "Panic and life are not two things. They are one thing. When you are aware of the panic, you are seeing the truth of ordinary life. The darkness of ordinary life makes the brightness of panic visible.

"The goal of the therapists is to turn you away from the thoughts of panic, away from the truth of panic, back to ordinary life. But this is impossible," Ian said, striding through the moonlight. "Because panic is not an interruption of ordinary life, the way asthma or diabetes is an interruption of ordinary life. When ordinary life is at its fullest, when it is most truly itself—just then, does panic arise. Just as the moon rises at night.

"That is why panic most often erupts at age fifteen. This is when the human being bursts into the fullness of life. Origen says the number five in the sacred texts refers to the five senses. He says the number three refers to the Mysteries. Fifteen. Five by three. The senses bound by the Mysteries.

"Cardinal Newman says in his *Apology* that he first felt his calling at age fifteen. Augustine says he understood the nature of the flesh at age fifteen. The thirteenth-century Zen philosopher Dōgen attained insight into the transience of life at age fifteen.

"You told me you first experienced panic last year, when you were fifteen. It was the same with me," Ian said, stopping now, staring into the trees at the edge of the path.

"Those people back at the barn? Ty, for example. He is not alive. Not really. Solid Mind. A mind of habit, a mind of flesh. No space for panic to arise. No night for a moon to become visible. Speaking to him of these matters is like a shovel going into loose dirt.

"Panic is absolute clarity," said Ian, beginning now to stand on one leg, raising his arms at his sides. "It sees that only ceaseless vigilance will help us. It sees that with every cycle of sleep, the rhythms of nature wear us away, like a river falling on the face of a stone pharaoh, first our eyes go, then our mouth, and then what does it matter if we live or die?"

He put his leg down. He made an imperious gesture.

"Pan says—Wake up! Don't go to sleep!

"Ask yourself: Does panic feel like a fog? Like a distortion of reality? Or does it feel like *truth*. As if someone whispered into your ear—*Wake up! These thoughts are sacred—this presence in you—sacred—don't let him go—you feel his power—don't let him go—not until you've put on his knowledge along with his power!*

"Can you wonder now? Can't you see that the fear of sleep is *rational*?" Ian started walking again, moving faster now. I scrambled through the brush encroaching on the narrow path to keep up.

"Instead of trying to flee from the clarity of panic thoughts," said Ian without turning his head, "dwell with them. With your eyes half-open, sit with them. Inquire into the movement of the thoughts in your mind. Sit in the half-lotus posture and watch your thoughts very, very carefully.

"The unity of moon and night cannot be taught. It is already known. The god within you knows it. Listen—he will tell you. At the very heart of panic, at the pinnacle of unbearable clarity—"

*

We had arrived at the clearing of the Dead Sea. The moon spilled an inverted pyramid of light across the pond.

"What?"

Ian sucked on his cigarette, stared at the pond.

"At the pinnacle of clarity, what?" I repeated.

"Nothing," he said.

I couldn't see his expression. He could be smiling, I thought.

"What do you mean, nothing?"

"Just nothing," he said.

He wouldn't say anything else, all the way back to the barn. When we climbed up the stairs he sat on the couch and looked down at the floor. His long face looked like a horse's skull. Sarah laughed. She sidled up to me and whispered,

"Doesn't Ian's face look like a horse?"

I nodded.

"Do you know the old saying that you can lead a horse to water but you can't make it drink?"

I nodded. She laughed.

"Ian told me one time about another version of the saying. Do you want to hear it?"

I nodded for the third time. Her whispering tickled my ear.

"You can put the skull of a horse next to the water but you can't make it drink."

I stared at Ian's long face in the light.

"Ian said," said Sarah, "the skull version of the saying is older than the other version. Way older."

Before I left that night Ian gave me a book about meditation. I asked if it would help with the panic. He said that was the wrong way to look at it. I should be asking if the meditation would help the panic. He said the answer was yes.

Sarah listened while we talked and she smiled.

*

The meditation book said I should sit in a lotus or half-lotus position on a cushion on the floor and count my breaths. It was sort of like the therapist's exercise, with the important difference that the meditation book didn't say anything about how paying attention to my breathing would be relaxing. Which was a relief, because I knew it wouldn't.

I didn't know what a lotus position or a half-lotus position looked like, so I sat cross-legged on my bedroom floor. The book said to count breaths by counting every exhalation, starting with the number ten and then counting down to zero. When I got to zero I was supposed to start over. The book said I probably wouldn't get to zero, not for a long time. It also warned me not to shut my eyes. I should keep them half-open. This last piece of advice made a great deal of sense to me, after my experience at the therapist's office.

I sat down cross-legged on the floor and started to breathe.

Inhale . . . exhale: Ten.

Inhale . . . exhale: Nine.

Inhale . . . exhale: Eight.

After eight I lost track. Because I was thinking about Ian and Sarah. I wondered just when and where they had been having their little conversations. Sarah and her *Ian said*, *Ian said*, *Ian said*.

Sarah was with *me*. She'd never, the whole time we'd been together, said anything about hanging out with Ian alone. And yet here she was, this walking encyclopedia of Ian's sayings. Like that bizarre saying about leading a horse's skull to water.

True, she seemed to make fun of Ian a lot. Comparing his face to a horse's, for instance. But I knew enough about girls now to know that when they liked someone they made fun of them. She didn't make fun of me as much as she made fun of Ian.

Even with my eyes half-closed, I could see their faces clearly. In the carpet, in the whorls and curls of the carpet, I saw both their faces.

I opened my eyes all the way. There were no faces in the carpet.

I got up from my cross-legged position. Enough meditation for today, I thought.

*

After a couple days of meditation I thought it might be a good idea to keep a meditation journal. For recording the things I learned when I was meditating. Insights. I wasn't sure if this was exactly what Ian was talking about when he said to learn from Panic, to listen to Panic. The meditation book didn't say anything about a journal. But I thought that maybe I would have important insights when I was meditating, insights that could help me to sleep again maybe, and I didn't want to forget them.

Actually that's not true. The truth is that I started to write down the thoughts that came during meditation so I could *stop* thinking about them. Because very soon I discovered that if I didn't write them down, I couldn't stop.

Ian and Sarah, for example. The next time Sarah and I had sex, I couldn't get it out of my mind—*Where and when has she been seeing Ian?* We were in my bedroom, my dad was out of town, and we were in the middle of it, and I was closing my eyes a little, thinking, and suddenly Sarah says, "Keep your eyes open."

I almost had a heart attack. *Keep your eyes open.* Hadn't Ian said that, in the forest, by the pond? *Keep your eyes open!* Those were his very words.

"Why are you stopping?" Sarah gasped.

"What did you say?"

"I said why are you stopping."

"No before."

"What?"

I said never mind and kept going but when she left I wrote it down in my notebook. I wrote down, "Ian and Sarah." And then I turned off the light and went and lay down on my bed with the smell of Sarah and closed my eyes and tried to calm down.

With the failure of the First Church of Pan, and then the failure of psychiatry and therapy, I had few tools to deal with the old and new panic symptoms. The *work* no longer worked. On insomniac nights, I returned, helplessly, like a Protestant, to the original scriptures: *Salome*, Sarah's speculations, the mystic vocabulary of the *presence of the god.* Now, lying there sleepless, my mind began to interpret my symptoms, my experiences, my relationships in terms of dark patterns.

I got up and turned on the light and wrote one down in my notebook.

"'Beauty is a shape open to feeling'—Sarah."

Then I turned off the light and got back into bed. The next time I got up I wrote,

"'Keep your eyes open'—Ian. And Sarah."

The next time I got up I wrote,

"Salome: Panic sometimes feels like you can go out of your head. Ian: 'Keep your eyes open.' Sarah: 'It can go out of you.' Ian:

'Your head clamps down on it.' Sarah: 'It can go into other things too.' Ian: 'You don't want it to go.' Sarah: 'Beauty is a shape open to feeling.' Salome: She takes his head, she owns it."

I put the pen down.

I got back into bed. This is just a pattern, I thought. There are patterns in life. That's what panic is showing me. There's this pattern here about me, panic, Ian, Sarah, keeping my eyes open, Salome, the mouse, the possibility of leaving my own head and going into . . . a mouse's, or Sarah's. Or Pan—Pan leaving my head and going into Sarah's.

I had the feeling that if I wrote this pattern down, I wouldn't believe in it.

That's not exactly true. I had the feeling that if I didn't write the pattern down right away, I *would* believe in it.

I lay in bed, thinking about the words I'd just written, until an ancient memory fell through my thoughts. It was before the divorce, in the apartment in Mundelein. My little brother, Alex, was napping in his crib; I must have been eight. Mom had kept me home from school that day—she'd keep me home at least a couple days every week, when there were no appointments for her housecleaning business.

Those afternoons the time seemed to pass quickly; I was never bored. We'd look through the real estate section of the newspaper together. I'd pick the ones with the highest prices, and we'd marvel over their gardens, the ballrooms, the enormous windows. Mom's choices were more realistic. Two-bedroom town houses. And look! A three-bedroom house, cheaper because it's near the highway.

She'd tell me stories of Russia. She'd tell me about her father, who died when she was young. He had three fingers, a war injury.

She told me about this game he'd play with her. He'd ask her how old she was, and she'd say I'm five, or I'm six, I'm seven now, Papa—and he'd say no you're *one*—counting slowly on his fingers—*two, three*. And then he ran out of fingers and gave her *this look*, and she'd laugh until she couldn't breathe.

One afternoon—and this was the memory that slid through my mind as I lay in my bedroom at Chariot Courts, trailing the atmosphere of those winter days—one afternoon, she took out her thick black book. It was the book where she kept her work schedules, each page a carefully lined weeklong block, with the code, V. for her, and E. for Elsa, her first employee. And each day divided into two-hour cleaning blocks—for apartments—and four-hour blocks—for houses. Weeks full of absence, page after page of empty grids, some with two appointments, maybe three.

She'd take out the book, write out weekly schedules far into the future. Six months out, eight months. "By then I'll have three employees," she'd say. "What should we call the new one? How about W., such a funny letter."

But today, the day I remembered that night, lying sleepless on my bed in Chariot Courts, she opened to a blank page, near the end of the book. I sat next to her, curious.

"We are going to write down our bad thoughts," she said. "This is how we get rid of them."

I looked at her, bemused.

"I will go first," she said.

Then she took the book, started writing. I tried to watch her, without appearing to, but she caught me.

"Oh no, Nicholas," she said laughing. "That's not how it works."

Her face turned serious.

"If another person sees the thought you write, it won't go away."

She looked at me until I nodded. She always looked at me until I understood, until I had taken her words *vnutri*, inside. This time she had only to look at me for a few seconds.

"If another person sees," she said, with her quiet smile now appearing on her lips, "then it will last forever. Do you understand?"

I nodded. She lowered her head and continued to write. I didn't try to look.

"Now you," she said, pushing the book to me.

She watched me as I wrote my bad thought. And now, lying in bed in Chariot Courts, I found I couldn't remember the thought I'd written. It must've worked, I thought, the practice must have worked, the thoughts vanished.

As I lay in bed in Chariot Courts, remembering that winter afternoon when I was eight, and thinking of the thoughts about Sarah and Ian I'd just written, I thought, This is an ancient practice.

The rituals of the Second Church of Pan are like any other religious practice. It's not like therapy, where you do something for a single specific reason. I wrote down the fears that came to me in meditation not for one reason, but for two. To see them—to face them—and then to forget them. And the ritual of the Second Church of Pan didn't do nothing, like therapy. It did at least two things.

I got maybe four hours of sleep that night. Not great. But a start, I hoped.

13.

Hollows

A few days later I was at work, standing in the spray-paint aisle with my hand on the push broom, listening to "Everybody Plays the Fool." The second Keith showed up, I'd start pushing the broom down the aisle. But I felt the chances of that were minimal. First of all, the spray-paint aisle was the least-frequented section of the store. It had so few customers I'd often wondered why they didn't put some other kind of product there. But then my coworker Tom pointed out that while the number of customers was few, when they came, they bought in bulk.

You'd think bulk customers wouldn't have bothered with retail, but the typical spray-paint customer had a special characteristic that made wholesale impractical for them, and that brings me to the second great advantage of the spray-paint aisle. Approximately ninety percent of the spray-paint customers were teenagers, bent on graffiti and vandalism. Not the kind of customer, in other words, I had to worry about if they caught me standing in the aisle holding a broom, not sweeping, singing tunelessly to "Everybody Plays the Fool."

And I did sing. It was a deliberate choice. In retrospect, I can see that choosing to sing along to "Everybody Plays the Fool"—choosing, in other words, to totally surrender to "Everybody Plays the Fool"—marked the entrance to the final phase of my condition. In memory my singing stands like a kind of insane, gold-spray-painted gate to Pandemonium. But at the time it felt like a smart decision.

Here's how it happened. I was standing in the spray-paint aisle, holding the push broom, when the first notes of the familiar—horrible—synthesizer hook rang out of the speakers. I closed my eyes; my stomach lurched. And then I thought, No. I'm not hiding anymore, I can't hide from it anyway—earplugs forbidden, no way to close your ears—I'm done pretending to hide. I'm going to face it, like Ian said.

In fact, I thought, I'm going to *make fun* of "Everybody Plays the Fool." I actually giggled. I'm going to make a fool of it, I thought. I said to myself, Yes, when the words start I'm going to *make fun* of this awful song, I'm going to *pay it back*, I'm going to *give it a little taste*, I'm going to *punish it*, I'm going to *sing along*.

And when the lyrics started, I opened my mouth and sang along in a deliberately tuneless, ironic way:

"Everybody plays the fool . . ."

But as soon as the words left my lips, the irony, the punishment I'd intended to put into my singing, the humiliation I'd visit upon the song with my singing—all this vanished without a trace. Suddenly, all that mattered was that I was *singing*, I was finally *singing along* with "Everybody Plays the Fool," I felt enormous relief—it felt natural, it felt right. I was inside now, at last I was *inside the song*. It couldn't hurt me anymore.

"Why are you singing?" asked Carl.

I opened my eyes. He was standing directly in front of me.

"Is this your favorite song?" he asked.

At that moment a large redheaded woman in a gray pantsuit stepped into the aisle.

"Oh no, Carl," she said, scanning the contents of the shelves. "If you think I'm buying you more spray paint, you've got another think coming, young man."

Carl stood looking at me. He had bright-blue shoes on, a blue shirt, light-blue pants, and a blue sweatband around his head. A more extreme outfit than I'd ever seen on him. It was Saturday.

"How'd you find me here?" I whispered.

I felt foolish as soon as I'd said it. Say not one more word to this damned brat, I thought.

"Who's your friend?" said Mrs. Carl, moving closer and giving me a suspicious look.

I started to push the broom.

"Hey," said Carl.

I didn't look at him.

He came up and pushed something at my arm. If his mother hadn't been right there I would have put him on the floor. But as it was I had no choice. I snatched up the thing he was pushing at me.

It was a Polaroid picture of Ian, looking above and to the right of the camera, a majestic expression on his face.

Carl always had a hook.

"Where did you get this?" I asked.

"He gave it to me," said Carl. "He's my friend. He's my best friend."

"Well," said Mrs. Carl. "Your *other* friend looks like he's busy right now."

Grabbing her son firmly by the arm, she marched him out of the aisle. As they walked away I could hear her berating him, asking him why he couldn't play with friends his own age, why he had to hang out with a creepy hardware store janitor.

*

"Ian has some weird friends," I remarked.

Sarah was driving me to the barn in the new Jeep Grand Cherokee her father had gotten her for her sixteenth birthday.

"You're the weirdest," she replied.

She turned and flashed a smile at me.

"I mean that in a good way."

The wind blowing through the half-open window, patterned by passing cars, trees, and telephone poles, resolved into the rhythm of "Everybody Plays the Fool." The late-afternoon Sunday sky turned a private shade of blue. As Sarah pulled up at the last stop sign before the Barn, I noticed an empty spray-paint can lying half buried in the grass.

I'd slept four hours the night before. I could see every detail of the ancient can's dented surface.

The golden eye of its nozzle winked at me.

When we got to the barn, Tod and Steph and Ian and Ty were already there. Everyone except Ian appeared to be tripping. Ty and Steph and Tod were arguing about why the stereo didn't work. Ian remained silent, smiling in a quiet, superior way. Following his gaze, I saw that the stereo's black power cord had been detached from the long orange extension cord that wound across the floor before drooping down through a hole into the barn's cavernous first floor.

I decided not to interfere. But I paid a price. The absence of music magnified the unsettling senselessness of the barn's ambient sounds. Ty's nervously tapping shoe, the creak of the old couch as Steph shifted on it, a birdsong outside, Tod's mumbling.

I had to bite my lip to keep from humming.

Sarah wanted to talk. We sat on the other couch and she smoked the bong when Steph passed it and opened her eyes wide and pushed the hair from her shining face and asked me questions—about the symptoms, about Pan's antipathy to sleep, about meditation—was it helping?—about whether I'd felt like I could *come out of my face* lately. I was too tired to resist. It seemed easier to talk than not. She listened greedily. Sometime after it got dark, she rubbed my arm. Her eyes shone in the glow of Steph's lighter, sparking across the room.

"Let's go," she whispered.

"Where?" I whispered back.

Her parents were home. My dad wasn't traveling.

"I know a place," she whispered.

Tod, Steph, and Ty were arguing heatedly about whether something you thought had happened, but that no one else saw, had really happened, if only in your mind, or if it hadn't happened anywhere. Ty defended against the others a complex theory that such an event not only hadn't happened, but was even more unreal than events that both hadn't happened and that no one thought had happened.

Only Ian watched us leave.

Outside, the late-summer sounds—crickets, weird summer static, rustling vegetation—like a radio dial set between stations.

I tried to yawn but it didn't work. A little shard of panic got caught in the yawn and I had to breathe through it—six or seven fast breaths shot through before I could close my mouth again. Each breath sped my heart a fraction.

"You ok?" Sarah called back.

"Where are we going?"

"Into the house."

Tod and Ian's house. I'd never been inside before. We'd always hung out at the barn, never at their house. I asked if it was all right. We were whispering.

"No one's home," she said, gesturing at the house-shaped depression in the darkness of the summer night.

I followed her.

*

The front door was unlocked. Inside, she moved like she didn't need the lights, like she knew the place. I stuck close to her, watching her body move and twitch in the dark, like heat lightning.

"Here," she said, stopping and opening a door.

She wasn't whispering anymore. Her voice seemed too loud. Inside the room she turned on a light, a light on a dimmer switch, she slid it up slowly, stopping just after the dresser, chair, and queen-sized bed began to glow, as if lit from within. I knew what was going to happen. She put her arms around my shoulders.

"What you were saying back there," she said, her mouth close to my ear.

"About being afraid of sleep?" I asked.

"It's like there's this other reality," she said. She looked into my face, her eyes wide with LSD. She brushed my cheek with her fingers. "There's this whole other reality ok and . . . I can see the outside of it."

She leaned closer. She pressed her hand to my face, to my chest, the words coming in a rush.

"I can see it, ok, I can see this whole other reality, I can see its *skin*." (Fingers trailing down my neck.) "Its *breathing*." (Hand pressed into my heaving chest). "I can see its face." (My cheek.) "And it's your face, it's—"

We were kissing. Her breasts pushed against my chest, my hand moving lower down her back, her fingers on my thigh.

"Am *I* beautiful?" she whispered, withdrawing her lips a quarter inch from mine. "Am I beautiful, Nick?"

Something . . . I couldn't remember it. Breathing fast now. She drew her T-shirt over her head, revealing her small white breasts, the marvelous areolae.

"Do I have a beautiful shape?" she asked, arching her back, her breasts closer now, I covered them with kisses.

"Yes," I said, closing my mouth over a nipple.

"Do I have a shape," she said, unbuttoning her jeans. "A shape . . ."

"What?" My eyes on the immaculate white of her smooth belly

as her jeans slid off, pink underwear purple in the dim light, dark curl over the top.

"Am I beautiful, Nick?" She put her arms around my neck. "Do I have a shape open to feeling?"

I blinked. I stood back, breathing hard. Stared at her.

"What are you talking about?"

"I want you inside me," she said.

*

"Inside how?"

"What do you mean how?" She placed her hand on the front of my jeans.

I throbbed under her fingers; my hands tingled madly.

She led me to the bed, pulling off my shirt. And then she was unbuttoning my jeans, and I was on top of her. I kept trying to catch my breath but kept catching hers instead, hot through her open lips.

"Look at me," she said, pushing my chest back.

I arched up, looked down at her, bewildered.

"What?"

"*Please* look at me." Eyes wide with *hunger*, her legs crossed behind my back. "Don't stop looking at me!"

I let go and looked—staring down into her open eyes with my heart bare, I could feel my face losing expression. Her face lay in the shadow of my thoughts—*like in the mirror,* I thought—*in the sky window, in the mirror, the mirror, in the sky window, that first time at the barn*. Her open mouth, open eyes, open face—like an astronaut's visor snapped back.

I pressed my eyes shut—like when you're a kid, when you're about to throw up and you clamp your mouth shut. My spine a dark, transformer humming, turning panic to lust and back—the phantom of Sarah's flushed face sliding under my eyelids—remembering when I was a kid, my mother used to say, "*Don't stare at people, never stare at people, don't you ever stare at people . . .*"

But my eyes were open again and I was moving over her and Sarah's face began to *lose its shape*. It got *longer* as I stared in the dim light, almost no light, lengthening—*flattening*—her cheeks pushing out into shadow—her nose sinking into the pool of her spreading face. I stared helplessly.

Her face spread and flattened and grew *much more beautiful*. Oh God. Helplessly wanting her face to grow *even wider*. Even flatter! Her face pulled itself out into an unspeakably beautiful inhuman shape, lying there on the pillow, a flat pattern of flesh in the dark—her mouth swirled and twisted in it.

My thoughts wild with panic and lust now, no difference—electric pain in my head as thoughts swelled, pushing forward, my head *too small* for them. The thoughts—they'd split my head open if I didn't force my eyes *wider*.

And now *her* eyes—opening! Her eyes like heaven—not her pretty green eyes, no, the other eyes, the beautiful secret eyes, wide with the no color of absence—under the magnifying shadow of my head, my thoughts, my breath—opening!—her face had become a lattice of widening pores—my head would split!

I wrenched my head away from her open face, buried it in the bed beside her as shudders racked my body.

Darkness.

Stillness. A cooling vacancy. And then—after a long time—light, feathery thoughts—brushing the raw center of my head.

I opened my eyes gingerly—the dim shapes of the room, her bare arms—the shapes full and round and normal again. I couldn't look at her face. I felt her hand on me, patting my back slowly.

"Wow," she said

I rolled away, pulling the sheets over me. Stared up at the shadowy ceiling.

"Was it ok?"

She raised herself on her arm. I turned to look—she was gazing down at me. Her face had its familiar 3D shape, dark curls tumbling, smile spreading invisibly through the gloom. I smiled too, in love and relief.

"I like you," she whispered.

"Did it happen?" Ian asked.

I shot upright in the bed. He was sitting in the armchair.

"What the fuck!" I gasped.

"No," Sarah said. I stared at her. She'd pulled the sheets up around her chest.

"I think it *almost* happened," she said. "His face started to go empty, but . . ." She shrugged.

Ian nodded.

"Almost," he said, looking at me thoughtfully. "That's something."

A shape open to feeling. I pushed myself to the wall, as far away from Sarah as I could get.

Some kind of trap. Some kind of sickness. Drug psychosis. They were *experimenting* on me.

"Pan is truth," Ian said.

"Get out of here," I yelled, embarrassed at how high my voice sounded. I took a breath, tried to keep my voice low and steady.

"Get the fuck out of here."

"We needed to see if you could do it with a Hollow," Ian continued, unfazed. "I needed to see if Pan could go into a Hollow person."

When I spoke, I ground my anger down into the syllables.

"You are fucking insane."

"And you're *holding back*!" Sarah screamed suddenly, standing up on the bed, stabbing a finger down at me, in Svetlana ecstasy of rage. "You're doing it on purpose! It's not fair."

"You are both behaving like children," Ian said. "Look, just get dressed and I'll explain."

He turned and walked out, shutting the door behind him. Sarah sank back down on the bed.

"You're holding back for a reason," she whispered.

And inched over to the side of the bed, dropped her feet to the ground, her back to me. I felt like hitting her. I felt like kicking Ian's ass. I should have followed my gut. I should have gotten the hell out as soon as she started up with those questions again, as soon as she started looking at me like that, tripping balls, with that *hunger*. Like I wrote in my journal—the pattern. I wasn't crazy, I was right all along, the very worst thoughts are the true thoughts, *insight*, prophecy!

If she tries to touch me again I'll kill her.

"And how does it even hurt anything?" she was saying. "I mean, ok, it was Ian's idea to try. With eyes open like that. But I mean why not? It's not like it *hurts* anything. I mean come on. And you *felt* it. It was about to happen. Come on, don't lie, you *felt* it."

I pulled on my pants and fumbled with my shoes, finally got out of the room. Didn't look back, didn't look at her. I stumbled around the house, turning on every light I could find, until I got to the front door.

*

I stalked back to the barn—intending to have Ty drive me home immediately. My mind kept going over the pattern—Sarah, her poem, Pan, Salome, Ian, Pan, going in, going out, Salome, Sarah's poem, Ian, Sarah . . .

And with every circuit it seemed more unreal. What had just happened grew more shocking, more horrible, more a betrayal—by Sarah, yes, but also by everything—the panic, *Ivanhoe*, Mom, me, the therapist, what or whoever it was thinking *this* . . .

When I opened the barn door Ian's voice boomed out from above. I ground my teeth. I thought about just walking back to the house, finding a phone, calling Dad, telling him to come get me . . .

But what would I tell him? It was late—I didn't even know how late. What would I say? Plus I didn't want to run into Sarah. Not in the house—not in the dark.

So I climbed up the stairs. They were all sitting on the couch—Ty, Tod, and Steph—watching Ian pace back and forth.

"Listen to this shit," Ty said, turning to me, grinning. His eyes were bloodshot. "This is some next-level shit."

"You're just a Hollow," Ian said.

"He's been pacing there for ten minutes calling us Hollows. This is better than that video game, you know, the one where . . ."

"Ghosts and goblins," said Tod.

"I told you he drove his girlfriend insane," Steph said, grinning. "That's a proven fact."

"Or did you just think it?" said Ty.

"Shut up," said Tod. "We're not going into that again."

"Ian's on the next level," said Steph. "He's really on the next level this time."

She pointed. Ian paced back and forth against the wall. The sky window shone blackly. Ian's shadows lengthened and contracted as his pacing brought him closer and farther from the single candle on the floor. Lengthening and contracting—like breathing, like the Barn was breathing.

"These three are *Hollows*, Nick," he said.

"You mean we have Solid Mind," said Tod. "And your mind is as loose as what's-her-name's booty."

"You mean Karla," said Steph.

"I mean you are *Hollow*," said Ian. "Listen."

*

I believe Pan goes out of me in dreams. *Pan.* Sarah discovered the word—but *I* possess the truth to which that word points. And the truth sometimes leaves me. And it goes into *them*. People like *you*, Steph, and *you,* Tod. I can't control it. Going into Hollows, I mean. I can't do it when I'm awake. Not yet. But it goes out of me in dreams. I used to be like you, Nick. I used to fear sleep, I didn't want to lose it. Him. But now I know I can't lose him. He comes back, he comes back stronger, and when he comes back I put on a little more knowledge with his power!

I wake up knowing things I can't know. Things about other people. Pan must sometimes go into them at night and come back before I wake.

I think the Hollows remember. When it goes out of me and into them at night while I'm dreaming. I think maybe their brains retain a Panic trace.

What would it seem like to them, I wonder, waking and remembering? Like a dream, Pan slipping into their heads, then slipping out again. They dream, and for the first time their existence lights up with real thinking. The movement of true thinking occupies their Hollow heads for the first time. How would they remember it?

Maybe as a blank among the phantom words and numbers of their memories. Or maybe as a twisted word, a heavy word, a sign. A word twisted and bent by the pressure of real thinking. The way you sometimes find a car door after a tornado. Tod and I found one once. You remember, Tod? It looked like a six. The wind had twisted it into a six. Maybe the Hollows Pan visits wake one morning with a six in their minds.

And maybe some of them know what it means.

Ever since I was little, I think some of them have known. Not many. A few. The ones who wake up with a twisted word in their minds and think, What is it? Something was here. Now it's gone. Who is it?

Shut up, Steph. Listen. Learn something. Once, when Tod and I were little, we had a neighbor, Mrs. Crawford. An old woman, she'd had white hair as long as I could remember. She lived with her old husband in a house at the bottom of the hill. When Tod and I would pass her house, riding our bicycles, she'd come out and give us cookies. Then one day she didn't give me one. She gave a cookie to Tod, but she wouldn't give me a cookie. Remember that? Tod? Say if I'm lying. Am I lying? No. The old lady didn't say anything, just turned away. "She hates you," Tod said. Do you remember that, Tod? And the next time, the same thing. Gave Tod a cookie, wouldn't give me one. Wouldn't even look at me. And then the next time . . .

I'm going to tell you something no one else knows. No one but me and Tod. The next time Mrs. Crawford saw us riding by on our bikes, she gave me a cookie. She gave Tod one, and then she said, "I've got one for you this time, Ian." She went back into her kitchen and when she came out, she had a cookie with dark-red sprinkles on it. It was bigger than Tod's, and Tod reached for it. "Not for you," she said. "For Ian. Yes, it's bigger because he didn't get one last time. This one is for Ian."

A round cookie with red sprinkles. I put it in my pocket and when we got to the stream in the woods, Tod said, "Let's give it to a squirrel, to see." So we put it on a rock, and then drew back and waited. And a squirrel with a long white tail crept down and started nibbling at it. The next day when we came back, the cookie was gone, and there was a squirrel with a white tail lying dead in the sun next to the rock.

Maybe it was coincidence. We were afraid to tell our parents, we didn't think they'd believe us. There was no proof. Just a dead squirrel. Maybe it really was a coincidence. It doesn't matter.

What matters is that on that day I began to awaken. "People

can tell you're different," Tod said. "Some people can tell you're different and they hate you for it." Tod spoke those words when we saw that white-tailed squirrel lying dead. That is a glorious memory for me. When I turned eighteen I got this tattoo of a white-tailed squirrel. Here, on my back, I'll lift up my shirt. There. You see?

That squirrel was a sacrifice. His death awakened in me the great question. Who am I? From then on, I asked myself that question every day. Not an hour passed when I didn't ask myself in some way, Who am I? The question wove itself into everything I did. Whatever I saw or said or wished or dreamed was threaded with that question.

It is easy for us, Nick, to look at others and to believe they think like us, feel like us. You grow up among people who look like you, who talk like you. Isn't it natural to assume they *feel* like you? Of course, they don't often talk about what it feels like to think. But you grow up assuming that's just not something people talk about.

And then one day you realize the truth. That no one talks about it because no one feels it. That a terrible absence of thought hides behind their words. "I think this," they say. "I think that." The sound of words from a Hollow mouth conceals an abyss.

14.

Only One

Ian stopped pacing. At some point Sarah had crept in. She stood in the doorway watching. Ian turned to me.

"It is very important," he said, "that we discover how to transfer Pan to a new Host. A true, a lasting transfer. A sacred transfer, a movement! In case he be trapped in a dead body. Because you or I, Nick, could die at any time."

"I think I like being Hollow," observed Steph.

"I don't," Sarah whispered. "And I won't."

She smiled at me. Without warning, the memory of her naked body flew through my mind. Her melted face on the pillow. That horrid closeness of *panic* to *lust*! I forced a deep breath into my lungs.

"You're insane," I told Ian. "And you're an asshole."

Everyone stared at me. The candles—there were three of them now—flickered, pulling shadows out of mouths, noses. The sky window open—totally black—source of a warm, slow, sporadic breeze you could see in the candle flame whole seconds before you felt it.

"Whoa," said Ty. "We're just partying here, man."

"You need," said Steph, "to chill out."

"Everyone knows Ian's insane," Tod said. "But he's not an asshole. He's my brother."

The three of them sat together on the couch, speaking one after the other, like in a play.

"Plato said all prophets are insane," said Sarah from the doorway.

I looked at the three on the couch. The shadows of their noses crossed their faces at the same time in the candles' moving light.

"What are you talking about?" I asked.

"We're talking about drugs," said Tod.

"We're just partying with some drugs up here," said Ty.

"Up here in the sky," said Steph.

"*He's* not on drugs," I said. I pointed at Ian.

Steph and Tod exploded in laughter.

"Not on drugs," Tod wheezed. "Ian's not on drugs."

"Ian . . ." Steph gasped between gales of laughter. "Took so many drugs . . . the dude *is* drugs."

"Be quiet," Ian said.

And in the silence—in the shadowy room where the difference between eyes open and closed attenuated—where faces smeared on the air like you'd closed your eyes—I became aware of the feeling of my thoughts. Of the *buzz* in the thoughts—the panic edge.

What is happening, I thought. And the thought stood still in my mind, vibrating. It's not mine, I thought. I'm not me.

"Nick's afraid," said Sarah. "Look at him. He's totally afraid."

Tod and Steph stopped laughing. Ty, who'd been looking at them with a bemused expression, now squinted at me through the shadows swarming his face.

"Why are you . . . afraid?" he asked slowly.

Ian's face turned bright red. He strode across the floor to where I sat on the couch and leaned down into my face. I could feel the hot breath pouring from his nostrils.

"WHAT THE FUCK HAVE YOU GOT TO BE AFRAID OF?" he screamed.

I leaned back as far as I could in the couch, thoughts unsheathing from their words, becoming bright, loose arcs of panic.

Sarah moved to Ian, her hand on his back, patting him slowly.

"Calm down."

Ian stood staring at me wide-eyed, actually panting with fury. After several seconds he blinked and swallowed. Began furiously scraping his fingers through his scalp.

"Just tell me," he asked, speaking quietly while his eyes blazed with rage. "What's the worst thing that could happen to you?"

I crossed my arms protectively and edged toward the far end of the couch.

"Let's imagine the worst," Ian continued, stepping closer. "Let's say, just for the sake of argument, that Nick is scared because the very worst thing that could ever happen is about to happen to him. Right here in the Barn. Ok, now what is it? What's the worst thing that could happen to Nick here in the Barn?"

"He could die," Steph said, and laughed.

Ian looked at her with astonishment. Looked back at me.

"You're afraid of dying?"

Everyone looked at me.

"Sarah," Ian whispered.

"Calm down, Ian," she said. She was standing right behind him.

"Get the mice."

"Are you sure? You—"

He turned around.

"Get the mice! Get the mice! *You.*"

He stabbed a finger at me.

"Get up and follow."

I turned to Ty.

"Ok," I said. "Let's go."

Ty sat on the couch, looking from Ian to me.

"And after all it's true," said Steph. "It's all true, after all."

Tod nodded slowly.

"Ian knows," said Steph. "He knows. He said it. He has the knowledge and the power."

Ty wouldn't listen to me. He wanted to see. I didn't want to be alone up there, and so we all followed Ian and Sarah down the stairs, and then down the hatch and into the crawl space. I'd gone past having any feelings at all. My only thought was I didn't want to be alone in the dark. Stick close to Ty. Whatever happens, stick to Ty and we'll be out of here as soon as this shit is over. And I'm never coming back.

*

We followed them down the stairs, down the other stairs, and into the narrow hallway of the crawl space. The tent was gone. The red symbols had been scrubbed off the far wall. And there was something new. A floor lamp, with a harsh, Ace-bright fluorescent bulb. Steph and Tod whispered and then Steph giggled as we moved in a jagged group into the center of the low corridor.

"What rhymes with *houusseeee*," Steph whispered.

She giggled again.

I stood blinking in the harsh light.

"Who cleaned off the runes?" Ty asked.

"They were just decorations," Tod said. "You don't really need them."

Ian was pacing. I gazed apprehensively at his spastic movements, his formal ill-fitting clothes, his skull like a clenched fist atop his skinny, twitching neck. His soft, pale, long blond hippie's hair fell down his shoulders, clashing with his formal clothes, with his clenched expression, with everything.

"*Afraid to die*," he muttered derisively. "*Afraid* to *die?* We'll see about that."

I actually wondered if he was going to try to kill me right there. I took a cautious step backward, toward the stairs—then the door at the top swung open and Sarah came through. She carried a large Tupperware container with a wire mesh top. It was full of things—things that moved.

"You take the nasty shits," she said, grimacing, and shoved the container into Ian's arms. He fumbled with it, then set it down.

"Gloves?" he asked.

"Right there," she said, pointing at a shelf built into the side of the hall.

"*Mouse!*" Steph squealed.

Ty's eyes widened. Tod shook his head, smiling. Ian pulled on the long green gardener's gloves, and then gingerly peeled back the mesh top. He slowly pulled out a plump gray mouse and set it down on the concrete floor. Its black eyes didn't move. Its tail scraped the pavement sluggishly.

"He drugs their food," Sarah explained.

Ian drew out another mouse, and placed it next to the first one. Then another. He rolled the top back over the Tupperware container and stood up, glaring at me.

"You watch," he said.

And then he got down on his haunches, crouched down right above the first squirming rodent, and began to stare at it.

"Shovel," he hissed without moving his eyes.

"Ok," said Tod.

He picked up an old metal yard shovel with a wooden handle that was leaning against the wall. He threw it over his shoulder like a rifle. Ian stared at the mouse. His eyes got wider. He wobbled a little on his crouching legs, straightened himself with a hand to the floor, and stared.

The mouse moved very slowly. It was still within a few inches of where Ian had deposited it. Its fur glowed under the bright lights. Ian's eyes grew wider. I imagined the mouse stretching in his vision, losing its third dimension, spilling out. Holes opening in its fur . . . I imagined Ian's thinking, standing on his face like on a diving board . . .

His mouth flopped open. His jaw unclenched, his eyes lost focus. I held my breath, wondering what it was like. The harsh fluorescent light, refracted through the mouse's coal-black eyes. The interior, a dark flux of organs, its tiny heart pulsing—its head—full of the sound of its squeaking voice, the sound hissing out as *Pan* entered!

Stop it, I thought, you're giving in.

Tod had the shovel in his hands now. He raised it in the air over his head and brought it down on the squirming mouse with a resounding *clang*. I jumped. He'd splattered the thing's guts for nearly a foot in all directions.

"Not me," he said, catching my revolted gaze. "Watch *him*."

"Holy fuck," said Ty.

Ian had fallen back, and lay sprawled on the concrete. I stepped over, looked down at his face.

His eyes . . . screwed up tightly. His face red, mouth open . . . He was *laughing*. Convulsed in silent laughter.

His lips contorted and squirmed—horribly, as if in sadistic parody of the mouse—then he opened his mouth and brayed.

"*Afraid to die*," he laughed. "*Afraid to die*. Oh God! I want to do it again! Tod!"

Tod gave him his arm and Ian pulled himself into a crouching position. He shot me a wild, gleeful look, and then focused on the next mouse. This one had managed to crawl maybe a foot away—Ian shuffled forward on his haunches, catching up with it—staring.

Tod followed with the shovel, watching Ian's face as it lost expression. This time when he brought the shovel down, I was watching Ian's face too. As soon as the deafening *clang* rang out, the expression poured back into his slack features as if sprayed through a fire hose. He wobbled on his thin haunches, mouth opening and closing silently—and a thin *squeak* trickled out of his lips.

"Hear that?" he said, looking sightlessly into air. "Mouse's last words!"

He pursed his lips and the awful, distorted *squeak* came bubbling out—the rodent syllable descending whole octaves in the man's voice. He fell backward laughing.

"Is this illegal?" asked Ty.

"Ok, no more," Sarah said as Tod pulled Ian up.

"I *like* it," Ian said, already staring greedily at the final mouse. "The first two were to convince Nick. On Belt Day, Pan went into the mouse. But you think he stays there, Nick? You think he's gone? You think you can get rid of him like that? With an open head like yours? A *missing* head? The first two were to convince you. The first two were to convince *you*. Are you convinced? But this one's for me. I *like* the feeling of dying! It relieves the pressure."

When the shovel came down this time, a bit of red matter splashed his glasses. He fell back with his choking laughter echoing through the room.

I stood over him as he lay on the concrete. He was breathing deeply now, a sleepy, contented look on his face. Sarah dropped a rag on his chest.

"Glasses," she said.

"Dying is *nothing*," Ian mumbled, his eyes closing under his filthy glasses, the rag lying untouched below his neck like a bib. "When your host dies it's just like exiting always is. But faster. And there's . . . I don't know how to explain it. You come back with a splinter of the thing in you. A splinter that gets pulled out fast, you can feel it getting pulled. It's a gas."

He opened his eyes, met my gaze, smiled lazily.

"I'd blow my own brains out to show you dying is nothing," he said. "But I believe it's a blessing for Pan to have access to words. So until we find out how to transfer it to another actual human, I guess I'll be." He tapped his head. "Duty, you know?"

He closed his eyes again.

"I think I'll take a little nap now."

He yawned.

*

The motor purred. Streetlights slid up the windscreen.

"They keep those mice to feed Tod's boa constrictor," Ty said, his left arm hanging out the window as he drove. "He showed the boa to us one time when you were at work. Big as fuck. He brought it up to the barn."

"So you're saying what just went down back there is ok?" I asked.

The night was hot—nearly eighty, probably. But I felt cold. I rubbed my arms, hunched forward in the passenger seat.

"I'm just saying," said Ty, "those mice were bred to be *eaten*. You know the boa has to eat them alive, right? Boas eat mice alive. That's the way it is. So from the mice's point of view, what Ian did wasn't any worse than their other option."

"Are you still tripping?" I asked. "Should you be driving?"

"I'm fine," he said. "I'm just saying that we should look at it from the victim's perspective, ok? You have to look at things from the victim's perspective. And from that point of view it isn't really that bad."

"Ian's a maniac."

Ty shot me a glance.

"He's got some obsession about you, that's for sure."

He shook his head.

"The only two dudes in the place who *don't* do drugs," he said. "You guys should be like in a *commercial* for drugs."

"Don't lump me in with Ian," I said.

"When someone obsesses on you that hard," Ty said, "you're lumped in. That's all there is to it."

"I'm not going back there."

He laughed.

"If you're afraid of Ian," he said, "you're just a . . . a mouse."

He laughed again. I watched the trees go by in the dark, thinking that I probably would go back. That's the problem with symptoms like mine. When you keep them closed, you know what your condition is. Generalized Anxiety Disorder, like the doctor said.

But when you open the door of the symptoms, it could be anything. It's your thoughts, it's your mind, there's no one else in there, there's no one else who can say what's real and what's not. Anything can feel like anything. And that thought itself is a symptom.

So when Ian claimed he knew, that he had *knowledge* of what my symptoms meant, when I'd already toyed with his ideas, when I was dealing with the fear of sleep, weakened by sleeplessness, becoming prophetic, becoming retroprophetic, looking back over the past year and seeing *patterns*, seeing the patterns and listening to the words, overwhelmed by Ian's total conviction, and Sarah's . . . it wasn't so easy to just walk away.

"Tod's right," said Ty, interrupting my thoughts. "You take things too serious."

"You would too if you had this fucking mental illness or whatever it is that no one seems to know how to fix," I said angrily.

He didn't say anything for the rest of the drive to my house. But the silence had a different quality to it. The sound of my anger stayed in it. And it added a strangeness to the atmosphere between us. Ty and I rarely spoke seriously to each other. Or rather, both of us were never serious at the same time. One was always laughing, one was always gone, high, disappeared. It was only when someone else was there that we could communicate seriously to each other—obliquely.

But when Ty slid into my driveway and put the minivan into park, he didn't lean over to give me five. He didn't make a joke. He didn't say anything about future plans. He just sat there. He turned off the engine. The car went dark. And I sat there too, waiting.

"Mental illness," he said finally, face lost in darkness. "It's retarded."

And part of me felt relief—this was just another stoned joke to him after all. Part of me felt disappointed. But before I could formulate some kind of joke to burn him back he started to talk again.

"It's retarded to think bad things happen for a reason."

"What do you mean?" I asked cautiously.

This was new terrain. Ty's voice sounded new and strange, unpeeled from its typical prelaughing condition.

"Two years ago," he said, "my mom wanted to go to the beach or whatever and he didn't want her to go."

He stopped. The Chariot Courts parking lot had a single tall light. It shone through the windscreen, on Ty's hands, still wrapped around the steering wheel. He started to speak again.

"Dad," said Ty. "My fucking dad." He was talking fast now. "Dad was always talking about how she was a slut, about the things she probably did when he wasn't around. I was sitting there in the living room playing Super Nintendo and I could hear them yelling in the kitchen. And then he says, 'Now look what I'll do.' And I hear the sound of one of the kitchen drawers jerked open. And now my mom, she's screaming in a different way, not the usual way. And I get up and look, and I see but I can't move. He's got her shirt off, and he's got this big sharp knife we have for cutting meat. And he grabs her arms with one hand, and he slices her across the back with the other hand. The one with the knife."

"Jesus," I said.

"Yeah. And then he says, 'You can go to the beach and show them motherfuckers your nice scar now if you want. And they can get it too.'"

Ty stopped talking. He hadn't moved his hands from the steering wheel. I hadn't taken my eyes off his hands the whole time he'd been speaking.

"They can get it too," he whispered.

I didn't know what to say. I felt he could hear my heart, pounding in my throat. Eventually he started to speak again.

"It's retarded to think bad things happen for a reason. Like Ian back there, I could understand the mentality. My mom got like that for a while after my dad cut her. She went to church like three times a week. She made me go sometimes. She said how everything happens for a reason. People will make a church out of any bad thing."

He turned his head and I could tell he was looking at me even though I couldn't see his eyes.

"You can make a church out of any bad thing. About not being able to sleep or whatever. About mental illness. But there isn't any reason why bad things happen. You laughed at the myth of Sisyphus book. Well, I didn't tell you the whole thing. It's not even in the book."

He took a deep breath.

"Every time the rock rolls back down the hill it crushes someone," he said. "Think about that. A huge boulder rolling back down the hill? That's the other side of the story. That's the other part of the myth. They talk about how he pushed it up, but what about the other part? Why push a rock up the hill in the first place? It's a huge fucking rock. You think Sisyphus is stupid?

"Yeah, life don't mean shit, ok, and that's tough luck for my mom. But check this out. That also means that nothing you do means anything either, and that rock, you could roll it right down the hill onto any motherfucker you want."

Ty stopped. Looked away again, staring out over the steering wheel.

"And that's tough luck for my dad."

I'd never heard hate like that. His voice vibrated with it. I said something like yeah, or fuck that guy, or something similarly inadequate and got out of the van and went inside.

And as it got later, lying awake hour after hour on my bed, my perception of the evening's craziness got weaker, until my sense of a baseline normalcy dropped all the way down to nothing. Soon the stigma of insanity, the protective wall of *this is all insane*, that was gone, only the words left in the dark now . . .

Beauty is a shape open to feeling . . .

He slices her across the back . . .

Hollows . . .

Salome, the symptoms, Sarah . . .

What rhymes with house*?*

Show them motherfuckers your nice scar now . . .

Salome, Ian, Hollows . . .

They can get it too . . .

Get the mice!

Pan.

And at three a.m., a memory from the evening seized me. Something I hadn't remarked at the time. I sat up in the bed. When Ian had screamed, in total and sincere incredulity, "Afraid to die?" I'd looked away, unable to hold that insane gaze—and when I looked away, I saw Ty's face. And he was grinning.

Ian standing there pointing and screaming, "Afraid to die? Afraid to die?" Ty grinning. There are many churches, I thought, spiraling now into the last circle of insomnia. There are many churches, there are many churches, I thought, lying there, the red digits of the clock huge in the darkness. Many churches. I couldn't tell which way was up and which way was down.

There are many churches, I thought, many, many, many churches, there are very many churches, I thought.

But there is only one God.

15.

The Family

The next day was hot. I rode my bike to get a Slurpee at the 7-Eleven, two miles down the road. The smell of cold sugar hit me as soon as the glass door slid back. The hot blue morning pushing against the store's windows, fluorescence like the underside of eyelids after staring at the sky. Blue raspberry Slurpee, the most magical of flavors. I watched the clerk as he counted out my change and played with the idea that thinking didn't feel like anything to him.

When I got back Ty was sitting on the little hill with the unopenable Chariot Courts gate, his mom's minivan parked in front of my town house. The whole morning I'd wondered, and as soon as I saw him, I knew. He had the old, solid, normal, usual, unserious Ty look on his face. "Bored," he said. "Woke up bored. Sunday. We should go to the barn." "What about all that crazy shit last night," I said, and Ty closed his eyes. "If you say you're scared of Ian again," he said, "I'm going to poison you. I'm going to put poison in your food."

And at that moment—listening to Ty's normal jokey voice balancing on the memory of his slow, serious words of the night before—I had a prophecy. Ty's going to kill his dad. And suddenly it was like a key slipped into a lock—Ty's bright laughter as Ian bellowed, "Afraid to die?"

"What?" said Ty.

I shook my head.

"Then let's go."

I didn't put up much of a fight. Ty's attitude left no opening I could find to prize the seriousness open again. And I didn't want to anyway. I wanted to see Sarah. The cool ease with which she could turn our relationship into a kind of board for Ian's weird role-playing game—if that's what it was—it made me . . . want to see her. "You're holding back." I didn't want to hold back. Thinking of the shape of her face, of the smell of her—no, I didn't want to hold back again.

I wanted to see her—to *tell* her . . . I wasn't sure exactly what I wanted to tell her. It was easier to put on Ty's attitude as camouflage—the Barn's never boring, no reason to think anything there is real or serious or lasting, the crucial thing is it's not boring—we rode out.

It was probably around one p.m. when we got there. Larry was asleep on one of the couches. Steph was already smoking pot. It smelled like summer—the heat coming off the grass of the fields outside, rising through the pores of the wood, blowing in through the open sky window, through the door every time it opened—heat infused with the smell of dry grass and the smell of the pot smoke Steph put into the air. Smell of the sugar from my Slurpee.

Larry woke up.

"Heard Ian got at them mice again last night," he said, stretching and grinning.

He didn't wear a shirt in summer.

"Where is everyone?"

No one answered him. I walked down the steps and stood outside, to get away from the pot smoke. I looked at the chimneys of the house in the distance. I wondered where Sarah was, whether she was with Ian.

My thoughts felt dull and inert in my head. I sat on the barn's front step, leaning against the wall, on the far side of the door. I bet I can fall asleep right now, I thought. If I lived in a culture where people slept during the day, I thought, I wouldn't have any problem.

It seemed impossible to fear sleep at that moment, with the heat, with the sky so bright it didn't really have a color, it looked like sleep, nothing had a color . . .

Larry woke me up, sitting heavily down next to me, nudging me with his deeply tanned arm.

"I thought you didn't sleep," he said.

"What time is it?"

I felt like I'd been unconscious for hours. I rubbed my eyes.

"You think I can't read?"

"What?"

He pushed a book at me. I took it. Looked at it without understanding, still waking up.

"You and that book *Ivanhoe*," Larry said. "Tod loves that story. About how you read it all night thinking you were having a panic attack when really your mind isn't solid and it just slides around everywhere and makes it so you can't sleep or have sex or whatever."

"What? I can have sex, how—"

He waved his hand.

"This book right here, it's just like *Ivanhoe* except it's true."

I looked at the worn paperback in my lap. Picked it up. A garish cover with a half-naked barbarian cutting a monster's head off with an unbelievably enormous sword. Read the title. *Nifft the Lean*.

"My favorite book," Larry said.

"This isn't anything like *Ivanhoe*," I said. I didn't know where to begin. "*Ivanhoe*'s like a classic and this . . ."

Larry snatched the book away from me. Began flipping through the pages.

"Ok," he said, looking up at me. "Ask it something."

"What?"

"Ask it something. You don't have to tell me. Just think of a question in your head, think of something that's bothering you, or something you want to know about, or a mystery or something."

I was about to get up, but I felt weak—a nap after weeks of insomnia leaves you drained. So I sat back, thought *whatever*, and then, cutting through the daylight's superficial glow—a shard of the previous night entered my mind. Ty's dad, I thought. I pictured him as I'd seen him countless times, nodding at us, while working on his car, or walking heavily through the living room on the way to the kitchen or the bathroom while we played video games. *Cutting* Ty's mom—did he really do that? Why?

"'Dismal, eternal, remorseless gluttony,'" Larry read slowly. "'We came to see the hideous vitality of that place as a single obscene shape, its multiform jaws forever rooting in its own bleeding entrails—guzzling and growing strong upon itself.'"

He looked up at me gleefully.

"I just picked that out of the book at random."

Prophecy, I thought. I sat up straighter, rubbing my eyes furiously, trying to get a handle on things. This was *Larry* . . . this cheap, ridiculous book.

"It worked, right?" He was grinning. "I could tell by your face. You asked and it worked. Ok, again."

I shook my head.

"Get out of my face, Larry."

He laughed.

"Don't you want to ask one more thing? Come on and ask one more thing and I promise if it doesn't work I'll never ask you again."

I settled back against the wall. The Bach image swam into my mind—the grotto, with the sleepers on the floor—the arch through which a sun set in a pink sky. And Larry must've seen the thought passing through my eyes, because he flipped through the book, stabbed a finger down, and read out a whole page.

"'The essential horror of its aspect you could not at first identify. The sounds of it had an awesome musicality, and the prospect a barbarously rich coloration, which conspired to exalt and bewilder your senses. The shingle footing the cliffs was jet-black . . . It was only belatedly you felt the horror of the enclosure of so huge a sea. For though the light that broke through the clouds might suggest earthly sunset colors, it was quickly recognizable as a demonic imitation . . . Such subearthly luminosity, in varying hues, had been our sky for weeks now—never a real sky, of course, never a transparent revelation of endless space, but always a kind of bright paint masking the universal ceiling of stone imprisoning this world. . . . This bottled sea, for all its terrible vastness, gave you not the awe of liberation, but its black opposite, the awe of drear imprisonment's infinitude.'"

Larry looked up, awe floating in the shallow blue of his eyes.

"You were thinking of an ocean," he whispered.

I nodded. Coincidence, I thought weakly.

"This book," he whispered, pressing his face close to mine, "this book BEATS THE SHIT OUT OF *IVANHOE*."

I jumped, startled. He laughed.

"Where did you get that book?" I asked.

He shook his head.

"You can't have it."

"Do you even know what infinitude means, Larry?"

"It means your book is my bitch," he said. "Listen."

The sound of a car engine cut through the heavy air, the high whine of cicadas.

"Here they come."

He nodded at the far end of the driveway, where it met the road. I could see the slow flash of white metal through the trees. I reacted to it, like it was her, like it was her walking. Sarah's car, I thought obscurely, is another of her bodies. A pattern, I thought. White astronaut's helmet, visor, her closed eyes, her white Jeep, "More Than a Feeling," spaceships, false skies . . . I was still waking up.

The Jeep unsheathed from the trees, slowing, then stopping.

Ian got out of the passenger side. I was prepared for it to be awkward, but the look on his face instantly erased all possibility of awkwardness. Direct, intense, unembarrassed, purposeful. Sarah got out next. I thought she maybe looked a little awkward, a little sheepish, and I thought, Ok, we'll get this shit straight, we'll get this shit together. Then she opened the back door of the Jeep and Carl got out.

*

He was wearing an uncharacteristically restrained outfit: jeans and a Cubs shirt, Cubs hat. He stood there clutching a Slurpee between Ian and Sarah, like a unicorn.

"What the fuck?"

It was Tod, coming down the driveway from the house. Wearing sunglasses. Karla, one of Steph's friends, walked slowly behind him, also wearing sunglasses, and a tight tie-dyed T-shirt. Smiling. Tod frowned.

"Get this kid out of here."

"Ian brought me," said Carl.

Tod stared.

"Ian is my collegiate big brother," Carl explained.

Ian nodded, put his white bony hand on the kid's head.

"I'm showing him how a person should be."

Then he smiled in a way that undid the effect of the daylight. A smile like a crack in the day—summer brightness turned insomniac white, the hue behind sleepless lids.

Tod looked for a second like he was going to argue. Then he shrugged. He was holding a beer can. I watched the can's aluminum skin. For a moment I couldn't tell whether the sky was bright or dark.

And then I felt Sarah, who'd been avoiding my eyes, looking at me, and I looked up and it was last night, in the bed, in the house, her head on the pillow, me looking down at her, and now, standing there outside the barn, my heart shuddered. She looked away, and the whole scene locked back into place, everyone moving, me and Larry bringing up the rear, trudging back up the barn stairs, blind in the sudden dark, with the thick smell of summer, the odor of pot, the taste of Slurpees.

*

Upstairs, people kind of milled around, looking at Carl out of the corners of eyes. He stood there beaming, holding some kind of folder. Only Larry seemed unbothered by his presence, sitting down before the bong and proceeding to light it. Carl's lips wrinkled in distaste. Steph shrugged, walked over, and turned on the stereo. Ian and Tod argued.

"Keep your voice down," Ian kept saying.

Carl walked up to me.

"What are you doing here?" I asked.

"I told you," he said. "Ian is my collegiate big brother."

"What the hell is that?"

"It's a school program. They like pair us with a college student and I got paired with Ian. Isn't that cool?"

He smiled wider.

"You know," he said, "you and me and Ian are a lot alike."

"No, we're not."

I was watching Sarah, who was sitting on the couch next to Larry. It looked like he was teaching her how to roll a cigarette. He'd recently started rolling his own. He'd read about it in a magazine, thought it was real high-class.

"Yes," said Carl. "You want to know how?"

I wanted to get away from him, but my options were limited. I could go over to where Ty and Steph and Karla were smoking—but then Steph and probably Karla and maybe even Ty would give me a hard time about not smoking. I didn't want to sit on the couch with Sarah and Larry. And I definitely didn't want to be over with Tod and Ian.

"Because," Carl continued, "we're all from broken families."

I looked at him.

"What?"

He nodded eagerly.

"My parents are getting divorced!"

"And you're happy about that?"

He shook his head.

"No. I mean, they only put me with Ian because his parents are divorced too. You know, I never really felt *comfortable* with the others, those lame kids on the bus. Ian calls them Hollows."

He giggled.

"What does your parents, being divorced have to do with the kids on the bus?"

Carl's eyes widened.

"Don't you know?"

Steph had turned the music louder. The Doors, one of their worst songs. I looked down at the sheaf of papers Carl was carrying.

"What's that?"

He beamed proudly.

"It's my book," he said.

He thrust the papers at me.

It was a handmade book, its covers made out of black construction paper, three punched holes on the side, the ten or so big white pages secured to the covers with string. "For ages 6–12," it said on the back in neat white crayon. I flipped it over to the front.

Where Do Thoughts Come From?
by Carl Friend

And underneath the title, a somewhat primitive-looking drawing of a boy lying on a bed, gazing up into space.

Then I couldn't think because Sarah was standing next to me.

"Let me see it," she said quietly.

I handed it to her without speaking. She contemplated it for a while, turning the pages.

"This is super cool," she said.

Carl's cheeks glowed.

"Thanks."

She looked down at him.

"I heard you say your parents are getting divorced."

He nodded.

"Mine are still together."

"I know," said Carl.

"You can tell?"

He nodded. Sarah seemed somehow deflated. She turned to me.

"We need to talk." She grabbed my hand and pulled me after

her, walking quickly to the stairs. She ushered me down, looking nervously over her shoulder.

When we got outside, she started walking, toward the house, and I didn't want to go to the house, but she said we needed to talk and I wanted to hear what she had to say, so I followed.

"*Please*," she said, pushing her hands out in an expression of exasperation. "Don't complain right now, ok? I can't take it."

She stopped. We were halfway to the house now. Out of earshot of the barn.

"Do you remember the first time you came to my house? Do you remember, ok, how we *bonded* over 'More Than a Feeling'?"

I nodded.

"And then you told me all this wild shit about how you could *come out of your face*? Remember that?"

I nodded again.

"I thought we were together," she said. "I thought 'More Than a Feeling,' ok, was like our *anthem*. Like, a song that's so normal to everyone, but to us, like we *know* it's a fucking UFO? Like a door actually goes up in the song, and there's this whole other place?"

She was getting angry, her face reddening under her summer tan.

"Yeah," I said in a low, calming voice. "But, I mean come on, that demented shit with the mice? And letting Ian *watch* us . . ."

"Just come on," she said.

We walked the rest of the way to the house. When we got inside, I followed her to the kitchen where we got Cokes out of the fridge. Then we went to the living room and stood in front of the big picture window, neither of us looking at the other. The window showed browning fields of grass, a sky of white heat.

*

Sarah said she'd always known something was wrong, that there was another way for a person to be, deep inside. So she was ready to believe me, when I came around talking about feeling like I had something inside me that could *come out of my face.* She said she told Ian one night, and he put it all together. He invented the Theory. Sarah said her first reaction was, that sounds like bullshit.

But then Ian said to her, "Why not believe if you want to? You can believe it—why not? Why not believe that not everyone's the same, that it could really be different inside a person?"

And Sarah said she wanted to. She admitted the acid helped. She said it didn't bother her if Ian's theory wasn't real. If it was a way to talk about things—things that were hard to talk about.

"But why," I said, interrupting at last, "is my *mental illness* so important to you?"

She looked at me for a while, tapping her foot irritatedly. Then looked out the window again. You couldn't see the edges of the clouds anymore. Just white, suffocated sky over dry fields.

"People compare things they know to things they don't," she said. "Like if you've never been stung by a bee before and someone asks you what it's like and you say it's like being poked with a needle."

She glanced at me and looked away. Back to the window. Like something was happening in the featureless color of the sky, the warp of the grass.

"When you compare," she said slowly, "something far away to something near, it brings the thing that's far away . . . closer."

I said nothing.

"But it also moves the thing that's close farther away. Sometimes you compare because you want the far thing to come closer. But there's always two sides."

I was trying to follow her.

"When we compare what your mind is like to mine," she went on, "*you're* trying to make the way it is for you more normal, to move it closer, so you can deal with it."

I nodded uncertainly.

"And *I'm* trying to move the way it is for me farther away."

I must have looked puzzled because she made an impatient sound.

"You know how when you got insomnia you compared sleep to death? Well, that made death—which most people think of as super far away and ultimately strange—it made it seem closer, more familiar. But it also made *sleep* seem super strange, much weirder than most people appreciate."

"So a theory of panic," I said slowly, "is a comparison . . ."

"That makes it possible to connect me to you," she finished.

She stood there in the light of the whitening afternoon, her profile flat against the vast picture window, and I saw that her lower lip was trembling.

*

Driving back home in Ty's mom's minivan, I said, tentatively, that I sometimes wondered whether my parents' being divorced had something to do with what I was going through, with not sleeping and everything. I felt Ty was probably going to just make a stupid joke, but he nodded, eyes serious in the staccato of passing streetlights.

"That's why Ian calls people like Sarah and me Hollows," he said unexpectedly.

"What do you mean?"

He shrugged.

"The family is pretty basic, right? I mean, it's biological. It attaches us, kind of, to the earth, to other species and shit. It's like when you're in a family, part of you, maybe most of you, isn't totally *in* you, isn't totally there at any given moment, but is sort of spread out through time—backward and forward—through the people in your family who are dead and the people in your family who aren't even alive yet."

"And so if your family breaks up?"

Ty was quiet for a little while, driving.

"I mean," he said finally. "It's kind of like *you* are, right? Like, you're not spread out at all. You're all right here."

He cast me a sidelong glance as he drove.

"And you're not very tied to the earth, let's face it. You're loosely attached to the earth, too loose. People can see that when you walk, even. It's why Jason and them make fun of you. They call it pussyness, but it's not. Looseness. Isn't that what you say your panic attacks make you feel like? Like you're about to come loose from your body, from all this stuff, from the earth?"

He gestured around at the world outside the minivan's spacious windscreen.

"I'm not saying it's all that great to have parents who *aren't* divorced," he added after a while. "I mean look at this shit with my mom and dad. It's just different though."

"Maybe you'll kill your dad," I said. "And then you'll be like me."

He shook his head.

"I won't ever be like you. If I kill my dad I'll be even more part of the family. Killing your dad is a very family thing to do."

He laughed. We didn't say anything for a while.

"I don't get that."

"I know," he said. "You probably never even think about killing your dad. That's because you don't have a family, not really, and so when you look at your dad you're kind of looking in at a family from the outside. But it's different when you're inside. I can't explain it."

He turned up the stereo.

*

That night, when I got home, I was strangely excited. I'd first begun to learn about panic through literature—about its contours, its features, the nature of the symptoms—things you couldn't discover on your own. You needed to read about someone else leaving their head, for example, before you could truly accept that you felt that way. What happened inside—deep inside, in the weird physics of consciousness—you couldn't translate into language by yourself. I understood that now. The first step was discovering the words that would let other people see it. But more importantly, the right words would let *me* see it. Without the right words, panic could feel like anything—like a heart attack.

Now I had a better grasp on the symptoms. I still didn't know what it was, in its essence. But I now had the insight that *what it was* depended on *where it came from*. And for the first time, I felt close to the origin. What the panic was—what it meant—depended, in some occult way, on *why* it started. Ian's crazy theory really had no way of answering that. But as soon as Carl had said "divorce"—I'd felt—*this is it*. What Ty said in the car only intensified my intuition that in the breaking of my family lay the secret of Pan's birth.

So I sat down with my legs crossed on the floor of my bedroom, in the meditation posture, and I closed my eyes, and I remembered.

I remembered the day my parents told me they were getting divorced. I had just turned twelve. It may even have been my birthday, though I couldn't be sure. All I really remember is that it was a hot, bright July day. The world, heated to the degree necessary to break a family.

In my memory there are no shadows in that day. No dark, cool spots. Everything relentlessly bright and hot. And windy. Wind blowing everywhere, I remember that especially, a wind without any cooling in it—a wind with no connection to the earth—blowing in space—loose—heated air whirling in bright blue distances.

And now, sitting cross-legged on the floor in Chariot Courts, I wondered if it was the wind I'd prophesied so many years before. It seemed like the kind of wind you could prophecy—like it was made out of the same stuff as prophecy—something the prophetic mind could touch. Not like a cool wind that blows low, that gets involved in grass and leaves, that almost has a color and a taste. In my memory my small white limbs are blown into hot white shapes on the lawn, where Dad had taken me to talk—hot white shadows like the ones left by the bomb at Hiroshima. We'd read John

Hersey's *Hiroshima* in school that year, in honors class. In reality the shadows couldn't have been white—we would have noticed—Dad would have stopped speaking and pointed to the shadows. But then again we were still a family, we were still spread out through time, like Ty said, and so maybe the shadows really were white outlines of us there on the dead grass, and maybe we didn't notice because when you're in a family you don't notice every little thing that happens in the passing present. There's so much more of you in the future and in the past.

But now, cut off from future and past, sitting whole and sleepless on my bedroom floor in Dad's inexpensive town house in Chariot Courts, I looked through my memory at the day my family broke and I saw no darkness. Even the shadows were white.

The day grew hotter and brighter. He must have told me, out there on the lawn, but I don't remember his words because it didn't feel like it was something he was saying, it felt like the day was saying it. The world.

And I remembered that I'd always dreaded the word *divorce*, that it had haunted my life unsaid for years, that every time my mother's mouth opened, every time my father's mouth opened, the word was there, a shadow cast by whatever words they did say, white shadows cast forward and back, since I was five.

And I understood now, sitting cross-legged on the floor at Chariot Courts with the first hour lit in low red digits on the darkness, I understood that the word *Divorce* was like a gate. Like an open gate, it had been there every day of my life, every word my parents spoke passed through the open gate, my name passed in and out of it, my grandparents passed in and out of it, their grandparents, and my grandchildren, we were all forever passing in and out of that gate, and the gate was always open, the word was never spoken, and then that bright day in the center of the year the word was spoken, and the gate closed.

The gate closed, I thought, sitting cross-legged in Chariot Courts, with the closed wrought iron gate in the drive beyond the thin walls of the inexpensive town house, the gate closed, not to keep me out, no, not to keep me out, I now understood, the gate closed because it no longer needed to open to let me through.

I was as free as air.

*

A few days later, Sunday, Dad and I were sitting on the couch in Chariot Courts watching an old black-and-white movie on TV. It was late afternoon, and the sunlit room enhanced the unreality of the television images. The natural light—glowing from the shapes of the carpet, the couch, our feet, the angles of the walls—somehow compressed the TV's illusory three dimensions, flattening them—so the screen looked like a book—a picture book.

I wasn't paying much attention to the plot of the movie. I was thinking about the Divorce theory, thinking how stupid behavioral cognitive therapy was, thinking that maybe if Dr. Crawford had been a real therapist she would've uncovered the Divorce theory herself and saved me all that craziness at the barn.

The TV showed a flat picture of men driving in a car, flat unreal black-and-white trees in the windscreen. The car stopped before the rectangle of a big wooden house.

Dad started to snore beside me. I wondered if Ian really believed the shit he said. I calculated how much my next Ace paycheck would be and wondered if I should get Sarah something. A necklace, maybe. How much would a necklace cost? Maybe a book would be better.

And then I stopped thinking because on the TV screen the men had gotten out of the car and they had opened the door of the house.

Without really following the plot, I had the sense that something was about to happen. Enough time had passed that I had the vague feeling that this would probably be the climax, and, like most black-and-white movies I'd seen, it would probably be lame. Some person lying on the floor in fifties clothes who was supposed to be dead. A close-up of a gun. That kind of thing.

And something like that did happen. The two men opened the door, and the screen showed a large hall, with a few pieces of old furniture. A chandelier in a bag hanging from the high ceiling. A close-up of cobwebs strung between a wooden chair and the wall. And there was actually a dead person, sitting in the center of the screen on another chair. A fat guy, slumped over, with a big envelope on his lap.

But I wasn't paying attention to the center of the screen.

Because in the corner, something was moving.

The director had probably put it there to add to the decrepit ambiance. The camera didn't focus on it or anything. A single mouse in the lower left corner of the shot, moving across the floor.

But I couldn't breathe. Because the way the mouse moved . . . it crept forward . . . stopped . . . nosed around a little, whiskers twitching . . . moved again . . . stopped . . . then a couple steps . . .

then it scurried off. Just the kind of movements mice make. Natural movements. Instinctual. Nothing shocking.

Except it shocked me. It nailed me to the back of the couch—it stapled my breath to my chest. Because I recognized it. That movement—the *rhythm* of its movement. I recognized it. Step. Stop. Step, step. Stop, stop. Step, step, step. Stop. Scurry. That rhythm. That rhythm.

The rhythm of the headaches I'd had earlier in the summer. The pings.

Ping.

(wait)

Ping. Ping.

(wait, wait)

Ping. Ping. Ping. Ping. Ping.

The same exact rhythm. Sometimes stretched out over hours. Sometimes compressed into minutes. But the same rhythm. And I knew, watching the mouse moving across the floor in the three seconds before the shot switched to the close-up of the dead guy's face—I knew it was also the rhythm, the rhythm, the rhythm *of the dance.* The Belt Day dance! When they danced in the circle and every so often they would *dip* in unison!

Dip.

(step)

Dip. Dip.

(step, step)

Dip. Dip. Dip. Dip. Dip.

It came back to me, the same rhythm, the same, and worse, much worse, much, much worse, sitting there on the couch with an inhalation stapled to the back of my chest and my heart so help me God totally stopped—much, much worse was that *I knew that rhythm from the inside.*

At the same time that I realized the identity of the mouse's instinctive movements with the pings—with the dance—at the same time I realized this—no—before I realized this—it was the *key* that enabled me to make the connection to the pings and the dance dips—a memory—I remembered—my mind flooded with the memory of *me* moving, stopping, waiting and watching, moving, scurrying . . .

What rhymes with house?

And it was like the taste of cinnamon . . . it was the kind of memory you couldn't possibly make up—like if you remember the taste of cinnamon, it doesn't make any sense at all to think, Maybe I made it up, maybe I dreamed it, maybe I imagined it—there's no way. Absolutely no way. It was that kind of memory.

I'd moved that way. On the floor. Inside walls.

Then the credits were rolling and Dad was waking up and there was no way to rewind it—it was just a TV movie—it was gone—totally gone.

Dad stirred on the couch next to me and stretched. The sun glowed on the pale carpet, on the black plastic sides of the television. And I got up and went up to my room and wrote in my journal. I wrote about the *Divorce.* I relived every moment of the day I learned of the *divorce.* I covered six pages in twenty minutes, all about the *Divorce.*

And when I was done, I felt better. I told myself that anything can happen when you're not sleeping well. Ian could make a church out of his mental illness if he wanted to. I knew the truth. It was the Divorce. Just the Divorce.

*

The moment on the couch was unnerving. But it was just a moment. A blip. Things were getting better, generally. And somehow, without ever saying anything more than what had passed between us before the picture window at Tod and Ian's, Sarah and I were ok again. Ok on the surface, at least. Under the surface, a tension remained. I made no mention of anything related to my condition, and she didn't ask. I think we were both waiting.

After several weeks had passed, after I felt sufficiently in command of what I thought of as the Divorce theory, sufficiently distant from Ian's theory, I tried to connect again—to connect my mind to hers, as she put it. I opened the connection obliquely, cautiously.

It was a Tuesday in mid-August. Sarah picked me up from work. When I exited the store, carrying my Ace vest under my arm, she was sitting in the first parking spot with the window down, smiling from her white Jeep Cherokee.

The early clouds had disappeared and the sun shone on the lawns and pavements. Getting out of work was always like a second start to the day, like waking after a nap in late afternoon. No harsh morning intensities of light and color; everything tuned down to a low glow.

The afternoon wore *Gilligan's Island* colors—green and blue and gold and brown—like sixties television, bleeding out a little over the edges of the shapes. Like dead people remembering earth, I thought. Remembering the trees, the pavements, the cars, the post office boxes: my hand, resting casually on Sarah's armrest.

The interior of Chariot Courts seemed especially flimsy on

such a day. The sunlight coming through the windows made the cheap dining set look like it had been cut out from a furniture catalog. We perched gingerly on the uncomfortable chairs, ate a snack of yellow bananas and dark cola, then went out back.

Out back there were two lawn chairs, and maybe eight square feet of pavement. A chain-link fence on two sides, endowing a perforated privacy from the neighbors' eyes, if they had eyes. I'd never seen them.

Our little patio was open in the back, showing a stretch of untended meadow, which petered out after a hundred yards or so into the parking lot of the liquor store facing the main street. In the past, Ty and I sometimes searched the dumpsters when we were bored. From here they looked like blue smudges.

"Here's the book I was telling you about," I said, handing it to Sarah. "This was one of Oscar Wilde's favorites."

She turned it over in her hands. This book wasn't from the library. I'd bought it at Borders with Ace money. The cover showed three white orchids against a black background.

"Charles Baudelaire," read Sarah. "Something, something, something."

"It's French," I said. "It means flowers of evil." I showed her the table of contents. "See? It has the English translation and the original French, in the same book."

She was wearing a shirt that looked like a vertical rainbow, stripes of color flowing down her slender figure. A spot of light glowed in each of her eyes. I wondered what Sarah would think of the book. It seemed like something truly new to me. It had the weird insight of *Salome*, a glimpse even of the familylessness insight, the divorce insight, but it was different too.

"Here," I said, taking it from her. "Let me read you one of the poems."

"Cool," she said, her smile widening.

We hadn't read anything aloud to each other since the library days. It made us nostalgic. The environment cooperated. Afternoon drew closer to dusk. The uncertain color of the liquor store guttered on the meadow's long green candle.

I felt somewhat self-conscious holding the book open.

"This is a good one for right now," I said.

I read slowly, trying to make it sound like it did in my head.

Twilight: Evening

It comes as an accomplice, stealthily,
the lovely hour that is the felon's friend;
the sky, like curtains round a bed, draws close,
and man prepares to become a beast of prey.

Longed for by those whose aching arms confess:
we earned our daily bread, at last it comes,
evening and the anodyne it brings
to workmen free to sleep and dream of sleep,
to stubborn scholars puzzling over texts,
to minds consumed by one tormenting pain . . .
Meantime, foul demons in the atmosphere
dutifully waken—they have work to do—
rattling shutters as they take the sky.
Under the gaslamps shaken by that wind
whoredom invades and everywhere at once

debouches on invisible thoroughfares,
as if the enemy had launched a raid;
It fidgets like a worm in the city's filth,
filching its portion of Man's daily bread.

Listen! Now you can hear the kitchens hiss,
the stages yelp, the music drown it all!
The dens that specialize in gambling fill
with trollops and their vague confederates,
and thieves untroubled by a second thought
will soon be hard at work (they also serve)
softly forcing doors and secret drawers
to dress their sluts and live a few days more.

This is the hour to compose yourself my soul;
ignore the noise they make; avert your eyes.
Now comes the time when invalids grow worse
and darkness takes them by the throat; they end
their fate in the usual way, and all their sighs
turn hospitals into a cave of the winds.
More than one will not come back for broth
warmed by the fireside by devoted hands.

Most of them, in fact, have never known
a hearth to come to, and have never lived.

Afterward we were silent. It was getting darker out, just like in the poem.

"The end is amazing," said Sarah at last.

I nodded.

"'Most of them have never lived,'" she repeated.

"Most of them," I said.

"Them," she said.

I nodded. The silence was intense and clear.

I didn't say a thing.

"Is that why . . ."

She hesitated, and I knew why. The idea of that part of the poem was hard to talk about without using Ian's language. The words we'd tacitly agreed to reject, that day before the window—these words flickered around the poem's words like heat lightning. *Hollows . . . Hosts . . .*

"Yes," I said.

She grew thoughtful. The colors on her shirt had begun to blend together. It was like she was moving farther and farther away. Actual darkness was coming now. I could understand why Baudelaire compared it to curtains. But I could also understand if someone compared it to distance. Like the air was filling with distance. Now our two chairs seemed as far apart as the patio and the liquor store.

Her eyes, like the dark smudges of the dumpsters.

"I thought," she said. "After . . . I mean I thought we'd never . . ."

She smiled. I couldn't really see the line of her mouth, it was too dim—but from the shape of her face I knew she was smiling. I was glad it was dark. My face felt hot. She must have felt it too because she started talking about the poem again.

"I wonder what it feels like to write something like that," she said.

I flipped through the book, and found it. The light was so dim I read the words more by memory than by vision.

"He says here: 'O Lord God, grant me the grace to produce a few good verses, which shall prove to myself that I am not the lowest of men, that I am not inferior to those whom I despise.'"

"'Not the lowest,'" said Sarah. "Not like the people who have never lived."

"If it's good," I said. "*Good* verses."

"What does that mean?"

"I've been thinking about that," I said as the darkness erased my lips.

*

I was *as free as air*. I'd known that since I'd unlocked the memory of the Divorce. But you have to work a realization like that into your life slowly. It's like you have a needle and thread, and the thread is the insight, and you have to thread it through every space in your life, no matter how small. So I revived the practice of the Second Church of Pan in the wake of my insight that I was *of the air*, and it deepened. It deepened further after I found Baudelaire.

Meditation captured the panic thoughts; writing them down neutralized them. But it wasn't long before a new panic thought occupied my mind. Baudelaire taught me to have new thoughts, to *transform* the panic thoughts—turn them into something else. That's what he meant by *good* verses, I believed. Strong writing. The fabrication of new shapes for my mind to move into.

Beauty is a shape open to feeling.

Not escapism. Not like video games. Good writing, I came to believe, was the careful, painstaking replacement of each part of this world with a part that looked the same, but was deeper, more mysterious, richer.

Not *better* necessarily. Not more comfortable, or kinder, or more expensive. That's what *flowers of evil* meant. You wrote about the boredom and horror and emptiness of this world—all the Chariot Courts' artificiality—but if you did it well enough, you'd have made it your own. A home for the familyless. And when you moved into it, panic wouldn't move with you. You'd have created a level of the world invulnerable to panic.

If the writing was strong enough, what remained after the purifying transcription would be Pan's beautiful carapace. The god itself absent.

And it was working. I'd started to sleep again.

After Sarah left that evening, I began my usual practice. I sat cross-legged on my bedroom floor, my notebook and pen beside me, half closed my eyes, and began to breathe. I saw the patio, just before dusk, Sarah and I sitting on the lawn chairs.

After eight breaths I had something. I opened my eyes, picked up the notebook and pen, and began to write.

"Afternoon drew closer to dusk. The uncertain color of the distant liquor store guttered on the meadow's long green candle . . ."

I didn't show anyone the writing I produced in my practice. It wasn't for other people. There was no plot, no characters, no dialogue. No beginning and no end. Just page after page of redescription.

By the end of August, I'd started to use a candle at night. The constant sun of the declining summer polished the days, and when I lit my candle in my darkened bedroom, the colors and shapes of the day poured down its gleaming sides into my room. The shadows of leaves, the angles of faces rotated on the walls my flickering candle set in motion.

I transcribed them, one by one. Gradually a frail, paper-thin replica of the day would unfold—tiny square by tiny square.

I went to sleep in the still nights of these artificial days.

Now, when I look back, I imagine Pan creeping out of my sleeping body, touching curiously the grotesque paper shapes of my idolatry, suppressing a laugh—the *panic laugh* that even animals fear—and climbing back inside me. Pretending to sleep.

16.

In the Air

The first insight came through *Salome*. The next was familylessness. The final insight came to me as a thing of the air. We were all together in the barn one last time. Endings had begun to cast their shadows out of the near future. The light in the barn thickened—it seemed browner than ever—a deep reddish brown. *Sepia* Ian called it. And you didn't need to have the gift of prophecy to feel something was about to happen. Larry said that twenty pages had fallen out of *Nifft the Lean* all at once. He showed the fallen leaves to us, holding them up so the late-summer light, streaming in through the sky window, yellowed them, made them seem even more ancient.

"They just fell out," he said. "Like hair falling out of my head."

"How is it like that, Larry?" Steph asked, smirking.

"Because it shouldn't fall out."

He had the wide eyes of total psychedelic incredulity.

The music now was strictly Ministry. Harsh aural mechanics always running in the background. Sometimes Ian turned it so low it was like the teeth of mice grinding. Tod said no one in history has ever listened to Ministry so low, but he made no move to turn it up. Ty said that when they were poor, when his dad was still in med school, his family had lived in a house where at night you could hear the teeth of mice grinding behind the walls. Steph said, "That's bullshit, mice don't grind their teeth." Ty said nothing. Steph said, "What did it sound like?" Ty said, "Like this."

The late-summer light spread in pools on the floorboards.

After I'd told Sarah the Divorce theory of Pan's origin, she'd told it to Ian, and then apologized to me for telling him. She hardly talked to him anymore, she said—and never about me. But she said he deserved to know—and here she used a phrase she'd heard her father use in similar situations—that I'd decided *to go in a different direction*. She'd said that after she'd told him, Ian had said I was wrong, totally wrong, but now he turned to me—we'd hardly spoken in weeks—and he said,

"Have you ever heard the Buddha's Fire Sermon?"

I shook my head. Everyone was suddenly quiet. Tod expelled a cloud of smoke and lowered the bong, listening. Ian's eyes had a cold, stonelike quality, like someone had scratched the color out of his sepia-toned face.

"The Buddha said your house is burning. What do you do? Do you first try to find out who set the fire?"

No one spoke. No one moved. The Ministry song ground itself down so low you could hear our breathing, like the song was inside our breath, like there were tiny machines inside our breathing.

"Or do you first put it out?"

Later Sarah would tell me that the moments after Ian had spoken the Fire Sermon were among the most intense she'd ever experienced. She said that he was abandoning the theory of Pan, turning away from the possibility of connection. She said that in the silence after Ian stopped speaking you could hear a person disappearing.

But in those tense, silent seconds, I'd been thinking about Carl. He was there, of course—he'd been there constantly throughout the barn's final days—his presence like a talisman of the end, like a prophecy. Like a *changeling,* Tod said.

And Tod said that in Celtic legends the fairies would sometimes take a real human infant and replace it with a fairy changeling, and you couldn't tell at first because all babies were so ugly, but when the other children grew, the changeling would remain stunted and deformed.

"It's like one of us has been replaced by a *changeling,*" said Tod, pointing at Carl. "Which one of us?" Ty asked. Tod said, "We can't know because the changeling has replaced him completely. Including his memory. That's how it works. The one he replaced was probably a great guy, a great friend, better than any of you," he darkly added. "And it'll keep happening. Soon there will be five or six of the things sitting here in the barn and we'll be gone."

"I hate everyone my age," Carl said. "I would never bring them here."

"I can no longer be your collegiate big brother," said Ian.

We looked at him. These were the first words he had spoken since the Fire Sermon.

"Why not?" asked Sarah.

"Because," he said. "I am dropping out of college. I am moving to Massachusetts and joining a Buddhist monastery. Everyone in the monastery has to get a job. I'm going to work in the Yankee Candle factory."

"The candles that smell like ice cream?" Steph asked.

Ian nodded solemnly. Carl looked distraught. People started talking again. Tod said that Ian had been expelled, so to claim he was dropping out was like telling someone who'd just dumped you that you'd decided the relationship was no longer working. Ty asked Ian when he was going. Steph began to laugh for no reason. Carl tugged my sleeve.

"What."

I'd been focusing on a fly. At first I'd thought it was the Ministry song, that Tod had finally managed to turn it up, but around the time that Ian started to tell everyone about his plans to drop out of college, I'd actually seen it. An unusually large black fly. Stumbling among the open rafters of the barn's slanted roof. The dark-brown light of late summer—brown like dehydrated urine, like molasses, like a Polaroid curling away from an open flame—shone down through a thousand cracks. The fly stumbled and buzzed through shafts of dark light.

"Maybe you could be my collegiate big brother," said Carl.

I looked at him. His little starved face. Ever since Tod had started calling him *changeling* I couldn't help but see him—not as a twelve-year-old—but as a reduced version of us. A version of one of us out of some other story, a dark fairy tale, a charcoal drawing of the real world. I didn't know enough then to understand that it was the future, that Carl was from the future, that in five or six years he'd *be* us. At the time I experienced his futurity as if he were drawn on the surface of the barn in a different medium. Pencil when the rest of us were in color. Or vice versa.

"I'm about to be a senior in high school," I said.

He looked at me, and then looked away. Then he looked back.

"Have you always done that?"

"What?" he asked.

"Moved your eyes around like that. Fast like that."

He blinked.

"I don't know."

The fly buzz—droning in longer and shorter bursts—merged with Carl's voice at *I* and *know*.

Sarah went and sat down on the couch next to Carl, so that he was between us.

"Carl," she said, "you could, like, be our kid. Mine and Nick's. We could be your high school parents."

She giggled. Carl started to talk again, but now the fly was so loud I was having trouble hearing. I watched them—Carl talking and Sarah smiling—and I wondered why neither of them mentioned the fly. I wondered how they could hear each other.

"Shut up," I said.

They looked at me. Carl, with his mouth open, talking—the fly buzz x-ing half his syllables.

"*Trou . . . here . . . treas . . . back.*"

I closed my eyes. The buzz got louder. I don't know why they call it a buzz, I thought. It's cut up, syllabic, like talking. ZZZZ—zz—Z—zzzz—ZZZZZZZ.

I opened my eyes again.

"I have to go," I said.

And my voice was very soft and quiet in my ear—it stood next to the fly buzz—under the fly buzz—like a person standing underneath a tree, I thought. A tree in the ear . . .

And suddenly I possessed the whole insight—the fly *buzzes* and *skitters* because I can *perceive* only a *tiny fraction of it*—a fraction of it at each moment—but it's a *tree*—it *is* a tree—a *huge black tree with jagged branches*—rising inside the barn—its branches brushing the high rafters—an absolutely still, silent black tree.

And that thought—that insight—*Pan*—the fullest insight I'd ever had—complete—a complete word of Pan's—a bit of his vision, like an opal, an eye—falling through my flesh like an open eye—prophetic, a complete prophecy—standing outside of time, seeing the black tree rising there in the barn—then vanishing—in less than a second, it was gone—my hands tingling—breath out of control.

ZZZZ—zz—Z—zzzz—ZZZZZZZ.

Carl talking, sitting on the couch next to me.

"I like it here. I don't like the kids my age. My mom is terrible now, ever since my dad left. It's terrible at home. I don't want to go home. I took the bus here. I can take the bus. No one needs to drive me. The stop is close. It's not far. I made it in like twenty minutes."

ZZZZ—zz—Z—zzzz—ZZZZZZZ.

And the last time I ever saw Ian he was putting his long index fingers into his ears. Carl had started addressing his pleas to him—*why, why do you have to go to Massachusetts, why do I have to go*—and Ian put his fingers in his ears, turning to me, smiling, as the fly buzz fell in black chunks through his face.

And it occurred to me, much later, at three a.m. it occurred to me that he'd been putting his fingers in his ears to stop the sound of the fly. Not Carl's whining voice, but the sound of the fly. That's what Ian had tried to stop by putting his fingers in his ears, and the sound of the fly hadn't stopped, and Ian knew that it wouldn't stop, and that's what his smile meant.

*

Three nights later, I was standing on the grass next to the Chariot Courts gate. It was hot, and our air conditioner was broken again. So I'd been walking around outside, enjoying the wind. It was a hot wind—it must've been over eighty still, even at night. But I liked it.

I closed my eyes and let it blow against my face. It must've been a little after midnight.

When I opened my eyes, the sky looked different. In the distance, north, the direction of Wauconda—the sky had a reddish glow.

When the wind started again, I heard the faint sound of sirens.

*

The news took a long time to reach us. At first, it was just that everyone failed to pick up their phone. We'd leave messages with Tod's dad or Steph's mom or Larry's grandmother and no one would call us back. Sarah had gone on an end-of-summer vacation with her family. Ty and I were on our own, again, for the first time in two years.

It was a Monday evening—I'd taken the bus over to Ty's after work. We walked around his neighborhood, talking. The days were getting shorter. You could mistake the coming dusk for a deepening of colors: a greater richness to the lawns, the painted fences, the absolute green of the leaves. The sky would grow a deeper and deeper blue right up to the point it disappeared.

We stopped at the park. Ty crossed his arms over the short chain-link fence, watching the late Little League game across the field. A cluster of parents clung to the fence. In the distance they looked like insects.

I leaned on the fence and said I didn't understand it. Something had happened. I told Ty about the red sky I'd seen, the sound of sirens. I said Wauconda was probably way too far away for sirens to reach me at Libertyville, that it was probably nothing to do with the barn. But then what had happened? I said that I could almost believe that Ian had finally snapped and killed everyone but then when we called the house why would their dad pick up the phone with the same tone of voice he always used?

Ty said he'd hit his dad once. His dad had been getting at his mom and Ty hit his dad and then called the cops. Ty said he called the cops because his dad had a gun somewhere in the house and Ty didn't know where. Said his dad kept moving the hiding place. Could've been on his person. "Plus I was sick of the whole situation," he said.

When the cops arrived his dad and mom both just stood there saying everything was fine, saying they had no idea why Ty called the cops, saying nothing happened. Maybe Ty was worried about the gun, they said. Maybe he'd seen something on TV, but look, here it is in the gun safe, with a permit and everything. It had never even been fired. It was for personal safety.

Ty said except for the one time with the knife, his dad got at his mom in a way that didn't leave visible marks. So Ty said he could understand that when Tod and Ian's dad picked up the phone when we called he might sound normal. Even when something was very clearly wrong.

"There's always two levels to a situation," Ty said then. "On one level my dad loves my mom. On the other level he's trying to kill her. And he wants to keep both levels going, like two snakes, over and under. Or like Streeling said, in physics, before you measure the electron, it's in two places at once. So my dad loves my mom and he's trying to kill my mom. And then I hit him, and the two levels collapse and now there's only one level."

I nodded. The sounds of the Little League game hung on the darkening air. I was thinking how I'd redescribe this moment, in my notebook that night. Thinking about comparing the kids' voices to the sounds of birds. Thinking about different ways of describing darkness.

"You hit him and the level where it made sense for you to hit him is the one that disappears."

Ty nodded solemnly.

"Or maybe," I said. "Maybe when you hit your dad you revealed the truth, you revealed the true level and then the false level, the illusion level, the level where he hates your mom, that level disappeared."

Ty shook his head.

"It's not about which level is true," he said. "It's about who is stronger."

I thought about that. The darkness had reached the point where the shapes of the baseball diamond were mostly memory. The sound of opening and closing car doors came from the street on the far side of the field. The high-pitched voices of kids, the dim, blurry bass of adults.

Tonight, I thought, I'll write about all this so it's mine. I'll remake these things out of the substance of thought. I'll make this a place I can fall asleep in.

I will fall asleep tonight, I vowed, in my redescription of this very moment.

The thought comforted me. I exhaled slowly. My fingers felt warm curled in my palm.

"Something happened at the barn," I said. "Maybe . . ."

"I don't care what happened."

His voice sounded hard, cynical. Different from the soft, stoned tone he'd slipped into since we started going to the barn. I hadn't heard that tone from him in a long time.

"Things have been getting sicker there," he said. "You were right. About Ian being insane. I thought it was just a game. But I was just keeping two levels open. I was helping to hide the level where shit was getting sicker."

The streetlamps were coming on now; Ty's dark jaw definite against the shadows of the field.

"What do they do now?" I asked.

"My parents?"

"Yeah."

He shrugged, pushed off from the fence, started walking back.

"They still got two levels going," he said. "They're still working two levels. But I'm out of the situation now. When I'm around, there's only one level."

"Then how do you know?" I asked, jogging a little to keep up.

"Because I can sometimes see bits of the other level. Loose bits.

Those books in the back of Mom's minivan. A certain look Dad gets. That kind of thing."

Maybe he's right, I thought. Maybe the level of the barn where we all laughed, where everyone made their weird jokes, where Ian developed his crazy Pan theory, maybe that level was a lie, but maybe he's wrong and it's better to have two levels instead of just one. Maybe it's better to pretend it could be Pan instead of Divorce, magic instead of mental illness.

And for some reason I thought about sitting next to Carl on the couch, watching his eyes moving. He has the panic for sure, I thought.

I wondered what I could say to him, whether I had anything to say that would help him, and I thought, Ian's Pan theory would be better than what I could say to him. Because there was nothing you could do with the Divorce theory. It had already happened, it was over, the gate was closed, rusted shut. And my redescription practice . . . My heart faltered when I thought about telling someone else about it. It felt too frail, too ephemeral. It was barely enough for me. If I talked about it, it would ruin it for sure. And what else had I really learned about my condition?

The fly insight . . . But there was nothing to say about that at all.

And I thought about what Sarah had said when Ian fell silent. *You could hear a person disappearing.*

I shivered.

*

By the time our senior year of high school started, the barn had begun its transformation into myth. We'd received conflicting reports about activity at the site, mostly from Larry, who had resurfaced but seemed more demented than ever. At one point he claimed Tod and Steph had gotten busted for selling acid. It had happened in the Kmart parking lot. They'd been meeting some sketchy guy Larry had warned them about when undercovers jumped out.

At another point he claimed that he had been molested in the barn when he was a kid by Tod and Ian's dad. He said he'd rode his dirt bike there a few nights ago and seen police sirens. He implied he was the one who'd called the cops, that he'd get money out of a lawsuit, it was pretty much a sure thing, then he asked us for twenty dollars.

He was sitting in the back of Ty's mom's minivan smoking weed Ty and I had scored from Jason, and he looked like a wild animal. He wasn't wearing a shirt. His tan skin glowed in the dusk.

"You're so full of shit, Larry," Ty said.

"It's 'cause those pages fell out," said Larry, exhaling smoke. "If those pages hadn't of fallen out I could ask the book."

"You don't know shit."

But he refused to admit that he didn't know what had happened to the barn or to Tod or Ian or Steph. He'd tell lie after lie. As soon as one became incoherent or Ty or I straight up called it bullshit, he'd start on another. Sometimes without taking a breath. His skin glowed like it was radioactive. He's a one-person level generator, I thought. He's trying to generate the extra level out of his own body and mind. And it's not enough, I thought sadly.

I was still redescribing my days in my journal, still sleeping. Every night, I would see ten thirty on my red digital clock, then ten forty, then ten forty-five. And suddenly my alarm would be going off, the bedroom flooded with late-summer light, and I'd be stretching, wondering how it happened. On one level, I'd cured my insomnia.

But on the other level, what happened when I slept was almost worse than insomnia. And it was strangely similar to insomnia. All night, I struggled in dreams with Ian. I sat in chairs in Ian's house while he stared into Carl's eyes, into Sarah's eyes. I stood at the back of college classrooms while Ian spoke. I saw him writing on a blackboard—drawing two heads in chalk. One head full of moving chalk lines, like snakes, like flies . . . the other head empty.

I watched Ian perform experiments. Sometimes Ian was my mom. And sometimes Ian would come up to me, and he would start to whisper, and I noticed his face was translucent—I could see the red digits of my alarm clock through his skin—and I knew it was me whispering.

These dreams had all the prostration, the impotence of insomnia. The things of the dream world took on a new conviction, like the surfaces of the real world during insomniac nights, when through the haze of thoughts—thoughts that had nearly begun to assume the density of a world—actual materiality would suddenly protrude. The nightstand. The wood of the bed frame. My cold hand. Red clock digits.

When school started, Ty and I discovered that the rumors around the barn had grown and multiplied, and a certain glamour now attached to everyone known to be affiliated with it. The barn's expanding myth had rubbed off on us. Jason told Ty that people were saying that we were gangsters, drug dealers, that the new Toyota Celica Ty's dad gave or loaned him—he left Ty in a state of dark ambivalence about this—was actually bought with the money we'd made from the operation we'd been running in the barn with the vanished Tod and Ian.

Just before the start of school Sarah reemerged. She'd called, saying she was back from vacation, but it hadn't really been a vacation, then said her dad didn't want her to talk on the phone, that she was in trouble but she couldn't say why. She refused to say anything about the barn or what had happened. She said she couldn't hang out after school either.

"Was it drugs?" I asked over the phone. "Did they get busted for drugs?"

She was quiet for a little while. I could hear the sound of her breathing. The in and out of her breath, an intimate sound—but it didn't sound intimate. I couldn't tell if she was about to cry. I couldn't tell if she was sad or indifferent or tired of answering my questions or sick of me or lying or nothing. The in and out of her breathing over the phone had the neutral, anonymous quality of a dial tone.

"I really can't talk about it," she said finally.

*

People at school looked at me and Ty differently now.

"The weird thing about being popular," Ty said at the end of the first week, "is you don't have to think about other people."

It was the truth. Before you get popular, you think popularity is having a bunch of new friends. But it's not like that. You don't make many or even any new friends. Popularity is mostly a change that happens to the people you don't know. When you get popular, those people start to look at you. There's a lot of them, way more than you could ever be friends with. Their looks light up your life.

You start to shine. Your gestures shine, your words shine. It's like the center flips, from being out there, out among them, to being in here, with you. You don't have to think or worry or wonder what other people think about you. They're the ones who have to think and worry and wonder what you think about them. And if you're not thinking about them, maybe they're not even there at all.

Part of me liked it, this new popularity. But part of me was uncomfortable. The change seemed too rapid. It felt uncomfortably switchable—the feeling we were the only real people in the school felt as if it could switch in an instant to the conviction that we were ghosts, and everyone else was real.

When Ty and I first realized that our reputations had changed, we thought maybe we should change lunch tables. We thought briefly about going to the table where Jason and the other popular jocks sat. Jason had invited us, the second day of school, the day the rumors about the barn had really gotten out of control.

But we decided that our new popularity would be more secure and durable and authentic and real if we didn't change tables. Our policy became don't change anything. Plus we didn't really like Jason and the rest of them.

The result was that we ate lunch at our own table, all by ourselves. High school seemed more spectral than ever. There seemed, somehow, to be fewer people in the school, far fewer, even though on the surface the classrooms and halls seemed just as full of still or moving bodies as ever.

Worst of all, it was impossible to redescribe. I'd sit at night with my notebook open and it was like as soon as I thought about school I'd go blank. I'd try to remember an incident from class, try to recall the color of the first changing leaves through the cafeteria windows, or a kid's face—and I couldn't do it. I'd start to breathe fast then. I'd end up writing about the walls of my bedroom—in the candlelight they looked rose, vaporous—I described them as clouds . . . I thought about the Bach visions . . . I imagined marble columns.

Sarah had a different lunch period than us, but I'd see her in the halls sometimes and she'd be warm, open. Nothing in her words or expressions seemed to have changed. She apologized for being grounded, said it would all be over in another month. Yeah, it had to do with her parents knowing what happened to Tod and Steph. No, she couldn't say anything about it, not even to me. She'd promised. She'd had to. They'd made her. No, not just her parents made her. She wouldn't do it just for them.

But between or beneath her words, behind or below her skin, a certain ghostliness had invaded even her. And when she breathed, when she stopped talking and it was my turn to talk, and she breathed, in and out, totally normal—sometimes I forgot what I was saying. I had to stop—hearing her breathe. It sounded louder than it should. I could hardly hear myself think. And the rhythm of her breath never varied. The same neutral tone, the same anonymity, the anonymity of another body, the anonymity of a *thing*, I thought, and then wondered where the thought had come from.

I tried to find out if she was seeing someone else, if she was going out after school after all, going out with other people. But there was no one I could ask.

"Now I know why Kurt Cobain is always killing himself," Ty joked.

"What do you mean *always*?" I said.

He just stared at me.

"I didn't say always."

I looked around but there was no one else who could confirm what Ty had said. Just the blur of kids at other tables, all of them turning away as my gaze swept the room.

*

For a long time only rumors rose from the crater the barn had made in our social existence. Then, at the beginning of October, a call. It was a school night. I'd been out with Ty, and when I got home Dad—who went to bed early—had left a note on the kitchen counter. "Your friend Tom called." Followed by a phone number.

I stood staring at it in amazement. Why would Tom—and the only Tom I knew was the one at Ace—call me? Then I saw that the numbers were Tod's.

I felt a need to talk to Ty—but he was probably still driving, and anyway it was almost ten p.m.—I couldn't call his house this late. The thought of calling Sarah crossed my mind—she had a private line—but I dismissed it.

I picked up the phone and dialed Tod's number. After a couple rings his father answered. He put the phone down. I could hear him calling Tod's name. My heartbeat pounded in my ears. Footsteps through the phone, getting louder.

"Hey."

"Hey! Tod, uh . . ."

"Why don't you come by sometime?"

And then, whispering:

"Bring me some weed."

I didn't know what to say.

"Nick, you still there?"

"Yeah, um. Why, I mean, what's going on? We haven't heard from you in like two months."

He was quiet for a little while.

"You haven't heard anything?"

I shook my head, then realized he couldn't see me.

"I can't really say," he said. "I mean, I can't leave my house. Not legally. I mean, for, for a little while still."

Couldn't leave his house? Not legally?

"Are you ok?"

"Yeah, yeah," he said quickly. And then he whispered again, a harsh hiss over the line.

"Bring me some weed."

"When?"

And he was holding the phone away, asking his father.

"Saturday," said Tod. "Can you get a ride?"

"I'll see," I said. "I think so."

"And don't forget about the other thing."

Then he hung up.

*

Ty wouldn't go—he said the place was bad luck. Plus, he said that what Tod said pointed pretty clearly to him being under house arrest. Probably he had gotten arrested for drugs—weren't him and Steph supposedly selling acid? Ty was pretty sure that's why there was so much acid all the time at the barn near the end. He said Tod was too hot. I said what did we have to fear, it wasn't like we were selling drugs.

I pointed out how we owed our new popularity to Tod, highlighted the hypocrisy involved in letting everyone assume we were great friends with Tod while failing to visit him even once during his house arrest, if that's what it was. Ty said fuck popularity, he'd never asked for it, all it seemed to mean is that he had less friends rather than more. Then he calmed down and said there was no hypocrisy. He *was* great friends with Tod. He was simply pretending that his great friend Tod was dead.

Then Ty went further and claimed that he was doing this for Tod's sake—that he, Ty, was pretending Tod was dead because Tod would be better off dead than going to prison, which is what it sounded like was going to happen if Tod was under house arrest and couldn't leave even to go to school. Ty said he performed this act of pretense as the last gift of one great friend to another. He said Tod would be dead in him at least; Ty would be the level on which Tod was no more. Ty made his own heart into Tod's grave.

There was nothing I could say when he got like that. He was like that more often now.

At least he copped an eighth of weed from Jason for me to take to Tod. He didn't even want any money for it. He probably felt guilty, I figured.

Sarah wouldn't go either. I asked her. We'd been talking, over the phone, maybe once a week. She was still grounded. I said well at least you can tell me now what happened, I'm going to see Tod. She asked me what Tod had told me, and I had to admit he hadn't told me anything, and she breathed into the phone.

So that Saturday it was Dad who drove me the twenty minutes up Route 176 to drop me off at Tod's for a couple hours. He had to go to the mall, and Tod's house was sort of on the way.

"Big place," Dad commented, as we rolled up the long drive.

"Thanks for taking me," I said. "I appreciate it."

"It's the least I can do."

He glanced over at me.

"I've been traveling too much lately."

"It's no problem," I said.

"It's not good for you," he replied.

The sky was overcast. The changing leaves, that looked so brilliant in the sun, turned brown under sunless skies. I didn't look forward to redescribing those leaves.

Brown light, I thought, as we rolled past the barn. So it hadn't burned down, I thought. Not literally. The structure looked ancient. Paint peeling on the boards—I'd never noticed it. Maybe that was something I could use . . . ancient light . . . peeling light . . . an unblinking eye . . . open until light itself starts to peel . . . Then we were stopping in front of the big house, and I got out and waved to Dad and walked up to the door and rang the doorbell.

Tod answered.

"Hey," he said.

He looked thin and tired. He turned and walked back into the house and I followed him, shutting the door behind me.

"My dad's out," he mumbled. "Where's the weed?"

I took the bag out of my pocket and gave it to him. My fingers were cold—I was half afraid that undercover cops would jump out of the shadows, that Tod was setting me up to try to reduce his sentence or something. Even though Ty had said there was basically nothing any cop could do with an eighth of weed—they wouldn't waste their time, he said.

Tod grabbed the bag, opened it.

"Dark green," he said. "Real dark green."

"Is that good?" I asked.

He shook his head. Then he stuffed the bag into his underwear. I didn't see it again.

He led the way through the cavernous living room, to a table before the big window overlooking the backyard, the window where Sarah's lip had trembled. The day was so dark he had the lights on.

The last time I'd been in that room I'd had other things on my mind, there'd been a lot I hadn't noticed. Now I examined the light fixture above the table. It had tinted glass that had probably been described as *old gold* or *antique bronze* or *ancient copper* in the expensive-furniture catalog his dad and stepmom bought it from. The light that came down from it was pure brown.

I sat across from Tod. He stared out the bay window. The window showed an expanse of dead lawn.

"Why can't you leave?" I asked.

"I can't say. I'm not supposed to. My lawyers said."

I pondered this.

"Where's Ian?"

"In Massachusetts. Like he told you."

"Oh."

We didn't say anything for a while.

“What about Steph?”

He just shook his head. I didn’t know what that meant. But I didn’t feel like I could ask him. We just sat like that for a while.

“Pretty boring, huh,” he said eventually.

He’d been looking at me from time to time in a furtive way. This wasn’t something he used to do. Now, after he said his piece, he kind of looked at me out of the corner of his eye again, and then went back to staring out the window.

“Super boring,” I agreed.

“These days,” said Tod, “Solid Mind comes in handy.”

He shot me another furtive glance.

“Yeah?” I said.

He was silent for another while.

“Ian,” he said at last, “or you. Probably go fucking crazy if you were in my shoes.”

“Your shoes?”

He shook his head.

“I told you I can’t say. Stop trying to get me to tell you.”

“I’m not.”

Then we were silent again.

“Anyway I got over all that,” I said.

He looked at me, longer this time. Looked back out the window.

“What’s it like?” I asked. “Not being able to go anywhere, I mean.”

“It’s like when steel warps,” he said, without looking away from the window. “I’m like steel.”

I didn’t say anything.

“My dad’s an engineer, you know.”

I actually didn't know that, but I didn't say anything and waited for Tod to go on.

"He works on bridges, shit like that. Steel, when you put a lot of pressure on it, it doesn't snap, not if it's good steel."

"Ok," I said.

"It warps," he said.

I was silent.

"That's where the idea of warp speed comes from," he said obscurely.

"I brought you a book," I said.

I still hadn't taken off my coat. Now I reached in my pocket and withdrew the copy of *Swann's Way* I'd purchased at Borders for him. I laid it on the table.

He looked at it. His eyes brightened and for the first time since I'd arrived something like feeling animated them.

"Thanks, man."

He opened it, flipped through the pages.

"This is great."

He was still looking at the book, but I could tell he wasn't seeing it.

"You're the only one," he said. "Who's even come to see me."

"What about Steph?"

He shook his head. The light in his eyes was gone now.

"Larry? Karla?"

He shook his head.

"Ian?"

"Ian left right after it happened," he said.

He put down the book. He was staring out the window again.

"You should really read it," I said. "It's basically the best book of all time."

"You know it's kind of funny," said Tod. "That it'd just be you and me, at the end."

Now, I thought, was the time to say the thing I'd come here to say.

"The barn," I said, "was the most legendary place I've ever seen. And you made it. You created it. Things got kind of weird at the end, so I wanted you to know."

He shook his head.

"You can't say what the barn was like," he said without looking at me.

"What?"

A kind of creeping went up my spine. It was cold in the house, I realized. Much colder than the early October day outside.

Tod stared out the window some more. Eventually he said,

"What do you mean you 'got over all that'?"

It took me a second to realize what he was referring to. Time seemed to be operating strangely in this conversation. Then I saw what he was asking and I told him the basics of my solution to panic. I told him about the Second Church of Pan, and the Divorce theory, in an abstract and selective way. I didn't tell him about my writing, about the redescriptions, about the fabrication of a complete different level of reality through writing. But I told him the basics. I said the proof I was getting better was my sleep. I was sleeping really well, I said.

He stared out the window. It felt a little unnerving to be saying that kind of personal stuff not knowing if he was even listening, and so my words got more and more abstract, until eventually I was saying "You know" and "You know what I mean" more often, and finally I heard myself say a sentence that was essentially composed entirely of "you know" and "you know what I mean."

I stopped talking.

"You," Tod said after a while, "are a fool."

A stab of anxiety hit my sternum. Senselessly, the tune for "Everybody Plays the Fool" went through my head.

"What?"

"You can't change the way you are," he said. "Not even Ian thought he could do that, and he's the biggest fool who ever lived."

He shot me a furtive glance. And I saw now that it wasn't he who was embarrassed to be seen. I'd thought his furtive glances meant he was embarrassed to let me see how low he'd fallen, sitting there unable to leave the house, under house arrest probably, waiting to go to prison, for all anyone knew. Seventeen-year-olds weren't confined to home without being able even to go to school unless something seriously bad had happened, something bad enough to basically change his whole future, to change it in such a way that school no longer mattered.

Tod was still there, sitting at the table in his own house, looking out the window. But his life was all wrapped up. What else could his situation mean? Naturally he'd be embarrassed to look me in the eye.

That's how I'd felt about it. The only clear idea I had about the shape of a human life centered on college. And the most basic key to going to college was finishing high school. Tod didn't have that now. His future had been amputated. I didn't know how or why. But I had a feeling that if I asked him, *What about school, aren't you worried you won't finish high school?* I had a feeling that he would say, *That's the least of my problems.* It was more than a feeling. Of course he'd be embarrassed to let me see how low he'd fallen.

But now, as he looked at me furtively after saying, "You can't change the way you are," a microexpression raced across his eyebrows, through the corners of his mouth, and I realized he wasn't embarrassed by me, he was embarrassed *for* me. He felt it was embarrassing to be a person like *I* was, like *I'd* become, and because we were alone, because it was just the two of us, the embarrassment had no outlet, and since I obviously didn't feel the embarrassment myself, *he* had to feel *embarrassed for me*, every time he saw my face, every time he met my eyes, he was overcome with embarrassment for me, and I could tell that it was almost unbearable for him, even with his solid mind, and I could see also that he believed that if I'd been in his place, and had to speak alone to someone like me, I'd feel so overwhelmed and panicked by embarrassment that I'd be unable to take it.

I understood all of this in much less time than it takes to write it. I looked down at the table. Now it was I who carefully kept my eyes away from him.

"You're a fool," Tod continued, speaking more quickly, more fluidly, as if my becoming properly embarrassed of myself had freed him, loosened his tongue. "You think you can change the way you are?"

I kept my eyes on the brown wood grain of the table. I was aware of how easy it would be to see faces in the wood grain. I didn't see any faces, I was just aware that it would be totally unsurprising if I were to see Sarah's face in the grain of the table, or Ian's, or even Carl's. My eyes were getting the on-the-diving-board panic fullness to them—my legs full of electricity. I closed my eyes and counted my breaths silently, and between the counting I said,

"You don't know what you're talking about. You're not a therapist."

And I knew he was watching me. I knew he was looking openly and without embarrassment at my face with my closed eyes, and eventually he said,

"Yes, I am."

I left and stood outside until Dad came to pick me up.

*

That evening when I opened my notebook to redescribe my trip to Tod's I heard a fly buzzing in my room. A late fly, an October fly, it bumped and buzzed against my window, where the last light of the day was dying. And as I looked at the fly I thought it was like the black tip of a brush, a paintbrush, and with its sound it was painting in bumps and buzzes and skitters.

And I thought, What it's painting is a tree.

I wrote that down in my notebook.

And then I wrote, "I can *perceive* only a *tiny fraction of it*—a fraction of it at each moment—a single stroke, a single buzz or skitter or bump, but it's a *tree*—it *is* a tree—a *huge black tree with jagged branches*—rising against the window—inside the room—an absolutely still, silent black tree. It looks like a *tree*," I wrote, "when you can see all the successive moments *at once*."

And then I sat back with my scalp tingling and I thought, What kind of redescription is this?

Usually I redescribed my various experiences in various mundane settings using metaphors and similes that essentially decorated reality. My redescriptions, I realized now, are basically and essentially decorations. They are like Christmas-tree ornaments hung on the ordinary tree of my life.

But this, I thought reading through what I'd written about the fly, is something totally different. *This* is about my ordinary reality seen from the perspective of a different kind of being. A being that sees time *all at once.*

I should have remembered. I should have known. But recall: It was incommunicable. When you can't communicate something, it's easy to forget it. And I'd never written it, never before even turned it into words, for the same reason I never wrote down things other people said. The whole point of the practice was that it was a translation from the substance of the world into the substance of thought, *my* thought. And this—*fly tree*—it didn't come from me. It wasn't something I could have thought of or imagined.

And then I finally remembered, and the panic sweat came out on my neck and hands. I remembered when I'd had the sense of a fly's movements as a black tree against a window before, and I remembered that it was *Pan's* thought, *Pan's* perspective, *Pan's* insight.

You can't change the way you are.

I put down my pen. I closed the notebook and pushed it away from me.

PART III

FALL

17.

Home

Almost immediately after my trip to Tod's, as if it had been in some obscure way connected with it, as if Tod's denunciation—*you can't change what you are*—was the preparation, or the spell, the words that would speak it into being—less than one full day after my visit to Tod—it happened. An epoch ended. Two years—my two years living at Dad's—were over. I was going home.

And when I saw the carpet and chairs and thin walls of Chariot Courts in the looming shadow of the return home, I thought, I'm not ready, there's something I should have learned, something I'm supposed to know, I haven't learned it yet. I need more time.

We were eating lunch together, me and Dad, the day after my visit with Tod, in our little dining room, which was actually part of the kitchen. There was no divider or anything. There was the kitchen, and then there was this table and four chairs we called "the dining room."

We only needed two chairs. Once, I suggested to Dad that we

move the other two chairs out to the patio—at least in the summer—the patio folding chairs were uncomfortable as hell. But he'd refused. He rarely put his foot down about anything, but he absolutely refused to even discuss moving any of the dining room chairs out to the patio. It was as if the removal of the chairs would undermine the dining room's tenuous existence. And then who knew what might happen?

Chariot Courts was a battleground between the idea of home and the armies of impermanence. Our dining room was a fortress. Once, after one of our school-night movie outings, Dad and I were walking back from the car when we saw one of our neighbors' windows with the shades up and the lights on. To see into the interior of another Chariot Courts residence—this had never happened. People kept their shades down in the windows facing the parking lot. It was like a law.

Yet here was this window, with the shades up and the lights on. We didn't actually stop, but we slowed our walking, we went into slow motion.

The open shade showed the space that corresponded to the little living room in our own town house. But the neighbor had no furniture in it at all, except for a single lawn chair. There were cans and a couple empty pizza boxes on the floor.

We didn't see the neighbor—I don't know if I'd ever seen them, I didn't know if it was a man or a woman, old or young. But we saw the open floor, and we saw the folding chair, and we saw that if you changed your perspective slightly, there were no rooms in the town houses at Chariot Courts. There were just open spaces where anything could happen.

This occurred early in September. A week or so later I asked

Dad if we could move two of the dining room chairs and he flipped out.

That was the first thing.

Then there was what he'd said in the car on the way to Tod's, about it being bad for me that he traveled so much.

That was the second thing.

And now it was Sunday, and we were having lunch, and he was looking at me funny. So when he finally said it, I wasn't even surprised.

He didn't say it right away.

"So how's your panic attacks these days?"

This in itself was relatively innocuous. He'd ask about the panic maybe once or twice a month, ever since the psychiatrist and therapist visits.

"Good," I said. "I mean, fine."

"They're not bothering you?"

"Nope."

"You're still doing the things the therapist taught you?"

"Yep," I lied.

Tod's words fell through my mind: *I am a therapist.*

Dad went back to eating his sandwich. But then he started talking again.

"Still," he said, "it's not good for you, Nicholas, to be here alone in the house all the time, with me traveling so much. It can't be good for you."

"It's not bad," I said. "I do my homework. My grades are good."

"That's not what I'm talking about. I'm talking about a home. This isn't any kind of home for a young person."

He gestured around.

"Well?" he asked. "Do you think this is a good home for a young person, to be here alone all the time?"

"It's not like I'm a little kid," I said.

Then he came right out with it.

"I talked with your mother the other day," he said. "Called her from the office. You should have a good home, at least for your last year of school. We agreed that you'll go back to live with her."

He'd said it, and now he returned to his lunch. He didn't look directly at me. It took a few seconds for me to be able to speak. Part of me was going up, part was going down.

"When?" I asked finally.

"There's no point in waiting," he said. "She'll pick you up Wednesday. I'll be traveling. You can just put the key in the mailbox."

*

Home? Mom's house was far more exposed to impermanence than Chariot Courts, even including the dire prophetic open spaces of the neighbor. The idea that in returning to Mom's house I could be returning home was a satire. It was a satire on the very idea of home. Mom's house was like a theater in which my essential homelessness would be broadcast through every level of my being. Chariot Courts may not have been a home. But it was at least a deferral of the question. Its shapes—the thin walls, the cheap furniture—an evasion of the revelation of homelessness.

But this danger to my condition wasn't something Dad could see. It wasn't on the surface. You had to live at Mom's house for at least a week to understand. And Dad had forgotten. The world of suburban adults didn't offer a vocabulary for understanding the uncanny desolation of Mom's house. And so he forgot. Now, years later, he couldn't see any reason why I wouldn't want to live there.

On the contrary, he could, if asked, point to many alluring features that made Mom's house appear far more homelike than Chariot Courts. First, her house, a stand-alone residence, was much bigger than Dad's. It had real wooden floors in the living room and hallways. It had a separate dining room, a living room with a stone fireplace, lots of windows. A vast yard—nearly two acres. And a brick pathway that led from the driveway to the front door. To the casual observer, the place emanated spaciousness, privacy, rest, elegance.

Dreamless sleep.

But appearances deceive. For instance, when you first drove up, you didn't realize that the yard was completely treeless. Rows of trees screened each of the neighbors' houses, another line of trees demarcated the back of the property. There seemed to be plenty of trees around. But in fact the house and yard sat atop a completely treeless hill.

The consequence was that there was nothing to stop the wind. Standing outside, it blew the words back into your mouth. It dried the tears on your face. Inside, it spoke all night and day in three syllables: the scream, the whine, and the thump.

Viewing the property from within a car with windows raised, Dad didn't experience the wind. Still less could he understand that the wind—bad as it was—actually served to conceal the very worst thing. The worst thing was always there, but you only came to know it when the wind stopped, something that happened maybe twice a day.

When the wind stopped you heard a highway.

At first, you'd think you were hallucinating, that your mind was manufacturing the sound of traffic out of the unfamiliar static of windless silence. No highway, after all, was visible. You could even go to the trees at the back of the property and peer through. All you'd see was the gentle rise of another hill.

But eventually, through intermittent spells of windlessness—accumulating over a period of weeks or even months—your ear would begin to pick out traffic sounds that you knew your mind couldn't have invented. The muted, distant, high-pitched grind of an accelerating motorcycle, for instance, rising through the dull roar of traffic, then dropping back.

There's nothing in my mind like that, you'd think. If I was imagining a highway, I wouldn't imagine that.

Soon you'd start to hear the highway *through* the wind.

So I'm hearing highway sounds, you'd think. So what? Route 94 is somewhere nearby, maybe half a mile away. Over that hill perhaps. Maybe a little closer than a half mile. So? Ignore it. Get used to it.

But it's like getting used to the tiny chunk of unidentifiable brown matter that drops into your glass at the restaurant. It's much too small to make a fuss over, and anyway, the drink already dissolved it. What are you going to do, demand a new drink? Because of something no one can see? Raising your voice at the waiter, while your date eyes you, clutching her purse . . .

You take a sip. It doesn't taste any different. Does it? Maybe it does, a little. Well, but you don't feel any different.

Do you?

Maybe you do, a little. So you don't take a second sip, and you don't ask for another drink, and you have nothing.

The sound of the highway was like that. Something you think you can get used to, but actually you can't. It was like an underground river, undermining the foundations of the property's claim to seclusion, respectability, and permanence.

Everyone has seen and pitied those who live directly on a major interstate highway. The tiny houses, the open yards. You drive past them—the world drives past them—the highway is an element of speed, a conduit of distance—and here are those who have made their dwelling amid endless frenzied motion. The signs of middle-class aspiration—the porches, with metal awnings, the occasional above-ground pools. Tricycles. The small, open, treeless yard twenty feet away from an unending torrent of steel, a river of cold eyes.

The government aluminum chain-link fence between the houses and the road. And sometimes, a second fence. A heartbreaking fence of white pickets laid down three feet from the government fence. The highway breathes through it.

The highway. The ultimate public place of American civilization. Our plaza, our town square, our marketplace, our agora, our forum, our seashore. When we visit a city we pretend we are seeing the public, but the city is a quaint nineteenth-century picture of the public, in a yellowing photo album in an attic.

The Highway is the public's modern presence. Each person enclosed in their speeding shell of plastic and metal, with the stereo and sometimes even the television turned on, insulated from the others. They see only the few shells around them, and they hear them not at all. They are inside the public place, but not of it. A dynamic paradox of our civilization. The members of the public, inside the public place, concentrate exclusively on private affairs.

But what of those *just outside* the public place? Those who live near it? They have no private lives. Their private lives are exploded—the public rushes through their conversations, their thoughts, their pauses, their perceptions.

And you, who are always in the public space or else so far away you can't hear even a whisper of traffic—you who enjoy the expensive illusion of a closed interior, of a Home, you who think *I am in here*, and the People are *out there*, you who imagine that no one can hear another person's thoughts, let alone *drive through them by the thousands*—you think you know what the public sounds like?

No. You can't hear the sound of the American public on TV or the internet. Are you kidding? No one would willingly listen to it. No one can bear it. The sound of the American public is a deafening, monstrous roar, without syllables, without pauses, without increase or decrease. It is the constant bellowing and thrashing of a beast.

The beast is People. The People. Ten thousand times more of them than you can talk to with a megaphone. Forget trying to talk to the People, no one does, no one can. The People can't even see you. You are nothing. The People move at a different speed, occupy a different time. You're like a single frame of a film.

No one can see a single frame of film, not even subliminally.

That's what you are when you live by the highway. You are a single frame of film. You see your nothingness glinting off the scales of the People as they slide by roaring. And when you close your eyes you hear your nothingness as a space the People roar through.

The trees at the back of Mom's property. Nature is a thin crust around the People. The People is the total monster. The People is time. The People are there in your body too.

Sleep is a highway.

Sleep is a public place, it is a highway. Now—standing on Mom's property that very first day and remembering how to listen, catching the knack, hearing the highway inside the wind, it's like riding a bike—I understood. I understood why for me the fear of almost falling asleep always took the form of *the fear of being hit by a speeding car.*

At Mom's house, when the wind stops, you hear what is always there: the sound of the highway. It is very soft. Soon it replaces silence. It becomes what silence is in the richer suburbs: the background of your life, the place from which your breaths arise, and to which they return.

*

Mom's minivan pulled up to her house, and I took the two bags with my pitifully few belongings out of the back—the wind stopped for six seconds, and we stood still, listening, I remembered, I heard it—and then we walked up the brick path and went inside.

Her Russian accent—so strong in my childhood, and strong too in my occasional, brief phone conversations with her over the past two years—seemed to lessen as we talked in the car, until by the time we entered the house, I could hear only a distant trace. It was as if she too were like the highway. She'd gone away into the background.

I had to be careful here.

When we got inside, she turned to me.

"I'm very glad you're back," she said.

Her eyes shone. My chest felt like there was a car stuck in it.

"Me too," I managed.

Then she hugged me. To keep from crying I had to bite my cheek. I kept saying to myself, I am home, this is my family, I am home, this is my mother, I am home.

But I didn't feel any of it. And I remembered what Ty said. That for me, looking at my father or mother was like looking from the outside into the idea of a mother or father.

We stood hugging in the vestibule.

Her smile, her tear-blurred eyes, my thin arms, the back of my head: a thick, cold pane of glass through which I, from somewhere outside, looked in.

Most of them, in fact, have never known
a hearth to come to, and have never lived.

*

My little brother got back an hour later from swim practice. Alex was eleven now. I'd seen him maybe a dozen times over the past couple years. The few times he'd visited Chariot Courts he'd moved like children do at a stranger's house—furtively. He'd sat very straight, not looking from side to side. Now his fluid movements, the untrammeled tone of his voice surprised me.

That night, after a hearty home-cooked dinner—dumplings and beet soup, something I hadn't tasted for two years—Alex and I sat and watched TV in the living room while Mom worked at the kitchen table, figuring out her team's cleaning schedule.

During an ad my attention was drawn to the wall, covered in brown wood paneling (the house had been built in the seventies). There, at the base of the wall, was a small square panel of metal, painted brown. Alex noticed me watching.

"Hey," he said. "Remember this?"

He jumped off the couch and went over to the wall. He crouched down next to it.

"Come here!"

He was grinning. I got off the couch, walked over. The metal panel was approximately four inches tall, three inches wide.

"This is the kind of detail," I said, "that you can't remember."

"It's weird, huh?"

"That's one way of putting it," I said.

I pulled the panel open from the top. There was a surprising amount of resistance, but my fingers remembered, and they applied just the right amount of pressure. The panel popped open.

The roar of the highway filled the room.

Alex began to laugh.

"You still think it's funny," I said.

"It's funny again," he said.

I let the panel snap back and the sound died. It was a vacuum system, built into the house. You hooked up a tube to the panel and you could vacuum without a vacuum cleaner. There were panels at the base of most rooms in the house. Some kind of seventies futuristic living technology that never caught on.

"Do you think," Alex asked, "that the sound is always there? Or does it just turn on when you open the panel?"

He pressed his ear to the wall.

"Do you hear it?" I asked.

He was quiet for a while. His blond head, his blue eyes.

"I think so," he said.

*

After dinner, Alex took me up to show me his room. His ancient stuffed bear—with one eye hanging by a thread—I remembered it from when I used to sit by his bed and read him books, nights when Mom roared—slumped on a low bookshelf, underneath a newish *Sports Illustrated* poster of Michael Jordan. His bed was the same narrow one he'd had since he was six.

"Hey," he said. "Check this out."

He handed me a piece of notebook paper. When I unfolded it, I saw a pair of breasts, drawn carefully, artfully, in purple crayon and black pen. I didn't know what to say. Alex looked at me expectantly.

"The girls your age don't have these," I said eventually.

I looked anxiously at his face. Because now I remembered Keith, on the school bus, with his admiring crowd of nine-year-olds, and I grew suddenly, horribly convinced that Alex was about to say,

I do it with high school girls. I do it doggystyle.

And my eyes got big with the thought—*on the diving board*—I looked back down at the terrible purple breasts to keep from looking at his face.

"They're mountains," he said.

I looked up. He wasn't joking. I looked down at the paper again—*no nipples.* Mountains. Not breasts. Beautiful mountains. I remembered the mountains in Sarah's brother's bedroom, the pictures that seemed to glow, and I said,

"I know, I was just kidding."

He looked at me strangely for a second. Then he led me over behind the bookshelf, to a box with a sheet over it.

"Mom doesn't know about these," he said.

And then he removed the sheet. Two small toads sat on dried grass in the middle of the kind of cage they sell for keeping bunnies. A few beetles and a couple black ants moved along the sides.

"I found them near the back fence," said Alex, staring excitedly at the toads. "You know, where the ground's always wet? I got these bugs for them to eat, but they won't eat them."

He took out a pen from his pocket, poked one of the beetles, pushed it toward the toad. The toad stared at it impassively. The beetle began to crawl sluggishly toward the other side of the cage.

"You think they're ok?" he asked me. "You think they need some other kind of food?"

I looked at the toads.

"I think they eat flies."

And then I said it again,

"They eat flies."

I pulled myself together when I heard myself say that. I looked over at Alex, but he hadn't seemed to notice my mistake.

"I know," he was saying mournfully. "But flies are so hard to catch."

*

That first night, in my old bed, I fell asleep easily. My evening practice had been a little strange. I'd meditated like usual, just like at Chariot Courts. I even used the notebook, which I hadn't done in a while. But I felt I should try it again, in this new environment. And so I wrote, redescribing the afternoon—parts of Mom's house, the property, the highway sound. Everything seemed to work ok. What came out were nice, good, solid, decorative redescriptions. Nothing like the fly tree.

But when I looked down at my notebook, I saw that the words were very close together. They were smaller too. It looked like some force was cramming them together. I examined the blank space at the bottom of the page. It looked like a wind had come out of that blankness, cramming all the words together, making them huddle together, like a crowd of refugees.

That crowded, tiny, close writing looked . . . desperate. I flipped back to earlier pages, to Chariot Courts pages, and compared them. Yes, I wasn't imagining things. The old letters were tall, the cursive expansive, spacious. I flipped back to what I'd just written. Words crammed and crushed together, recoiling from the blank space at the bottom of the page.

And the sound of my thoughts in my head was strange. They felt . . . loose. The thoughts felt very, very slightly looser than they used to.

It was a little unsettling, but it wasn't a problem. I fell asleep fine.

*

It would be wrong, even in those last days, to suggest that every moment was marked by the foreboding of what was to come.

One day, for example, when Ty drove me to Mom's after school—drove me *home*—I saw that the fall had reached its apex.

Multicolored leaves lay tumbled everywhere. The blue sky tinged with gold at the edges. Warm wind sighing through the rolled-down windows. A holiday atmosphere.

I remembered a dream I used to have—I couldn't remember when it started—I must've been very small. When I could still prophesize. An ancient dream. I couldn't recall the last time I'd had it. But now I remembered how in the dream, I went to the supermarket by myself. And when the automatic sliding glass doors opened, I saw sand spilling out of the aisles.

I wandered through the aisles in the dream. There was a glow coming from the little rivulets of sand—a sun color—it made the fluorescence seem unreal. And when I got outside, in the dream, there was sand everywhere. The whole world was turning into a beach. The army of the beach arriving everywhere at once, waving its flag of sand.

It got so bright in the dream it was hard to see, so I closed my eyes. I wasn't surprised in the dream to find that I could see with my eyes shut. Of course I can . . . Through the thin sand-tinted flesh of my eyelids, people and cars and bicycles and dogs moved, slowly, in a thick gold light, with a sound like the crashing of waves . . .

And always at this point in the dream, I had the insight: *This is what I've been doing wrong.* This is my problem, I thought in the dream, I keep my eyes open, that's why I move in such a jerky, awkward way, that's why I talk too fast, why I'm too loud, why it's always too bright. There's no reason to keep my eyes open, I realized in the dream, no one else does, I can see better with my eyes closed . . .

And as I sat in Ty's passenger seat remembering the dream, I felt that now at the warm apex of autumn, phantom lids had come down over my eyes. The whole world seemed to exude the beautiful glow of something you didn't have to open your eyes to see. Something that would be there whether you saw it or not.

When I got to Mom's house, she was in the kitchen. She had tea going, a plate with those little Russian cookies lay in the center of the clean kitchen table. We sat in the high-backed wooden chairs and talked. We talked about school, about Sarah, about the reasons I'd had to leave her house. I'd become unmanageable, she said. I needed a father, she said.

And I thought, She doesn't know either. She has been trying to fix things, to make things better. Just like Dad. Just like me. And I saw her looking at me, at my face and head and chest, and I thought, She too is looking at the idea of a family, looking in from the outside.

She moved her hands in a little futile motion. My eyes filled with tears. I turned away, pretended to cough.

*

When winter came holes of prophecy appeared in my sleep.

If it was going to be snowing the next morning, I could see the snow through the holes.

*

In late November, on a Saturday, I drove myself to the library. I'd passed my driver's test—it was over a year since my sixteenth birthday, but I'd never had any prospect of having a car to drive, so I hadn't bothered. Now a prospect had appeared. One of the women who worked for Mom's little housecleaning business had been deported, and she'd asked Mom to keep her car for her, in the hope that she'd be allowed to come back. If she couldn't return within a year, their agreement went, Mom would sell it and send her the money. Until then, I was allowed to drive it short distances.

It was a little blue Plymouth Horizon. A very small car. It shook a little at forty miles an hour. The windows rolled down manually.

I drove the deported woman's car to the library looking for art. Specifically, the art of the Italian Renaissance. My interest in the artworks of this period was more definite than idle curiosity or a vague desire for self-improvement.

Because I'd stopped writing in my notebook. The redescriptions had definitively failed. My thoughts were too loose, what came out in the writing wasn't good. Half the time it was illegible. The rest of the time it obsessively spiraled over memories of the divorce, of the difficult years of tension between me and Mom, before she'd finally sent me to live with my father. Or of Ian, his Fire Sermon, or of Sarah's poem. In any case, it wasn't helping me sleep.

Sleep was getting very rare, very precious. I waited for a few drops of oblivion to roll down the long, crooked pipe of the nights. Or like a desert plant, that waits all night for the single drop of dew, opalescent, just before dawn, I lay awake feeling the drop of sleep forming on my bare, dry eyes all night.

My writing wasn't working. I needed something stronger. I thought maybe art would help. Art, so I reasoned, represents the effort to turn the resistant substance of the thing world into the substance of thought. My own writing, perhaps, was simply too weak to perform the job adequately. But maybe very high quality, powerful art would open a space in which the looseness of thoughts—a looseness caused, so I thought, by a discomfort with the world of things—would settle. Even for a few moments. I imagined that, if I had access to art of a sufficiently high power, I might even be able to fall asleep, as I had once in the bits of world remade by my redescriptions.

Sarah suggested the Italian Renaissance. I'd driven over to the her house, when her parents were out. We made out a little on the couch in her brother's old room. She'd smoked some pot, then we listened to "More Than a Feeling." She grew nostalgic, reminiscing over the early days.

"I think I need something stronger," I said.

She laughed, held the joint out to me. I shook my head, didn't smile. The sweat of sleeplessness on my back and arms. It had cost me a terrible effort to smile that afternoon, my face actually hurt from it. Most of the time we'd been kissing my eyes were open.

"Something stronger than what?"

Her smile went away while its softness lingered. I never met another woman who could do that. Usually the moment when a person stops smiling a certain coldness comes out. The straight bones of the face. But Sarah could stop a smile, when she wished, and the slight defiance of gravity with which a smile somehow endows a face—it stayed.

Despite the facial softness I could hear her breathing. It sounded very loud in the silence. So I spoke quickly, telling her, furtively, about what I'd been trying to do with my writing, how it hadn't worked, how I didn't share it with her because it wasn't that kind of art, not a sharing art, but an art that was supposed to do something. It wasn't doing it anymore. I needed something stronger.

She looked thoughtful.

"Well," she said. "The strongest art in the world is from the Italian Renaissance. Everyone knows that."

"The *Mona Lisa*," I said. "That kind of shit?"

She laughed. Nodded.

"The word *renaissance*, it means *rebirth*. And what gets reborn is the old gods. The gods of ancient Greece and Rome."

She didn't say "Pan" but she didn't have to.

"They say," she said, "that no one understands Renaissance art. They all feel its power, so they keep it around. It's worth a ton of money. They know it's super powerful but no one understands it. Especially adults can't understand."

"Who says that? That no one understands it?"

Her mouth went flat.

"I mean, I never heard that before is all, when we did the school tour at the Art Institute the—"

"Ian," she said. "Don't be mad at me. Ian said it."

We'd been sitting on the couch, facing each other, her legs curled up under her. Now she straightened, pushed away from me. Stared at the floor.

"I'm afraid," she said softly.

"You helped me with *Salome*," I said.

She shook her head.

"*Salome* was easy. *Salome* was only like a hundred years ago. This is totally different."

"I'll tell you about it," I said. "I promise."

She shook her head. I started to protest but she pushed her hand out, stopping me.

"It's already different," she said. "You know it has been. The time when . . . it could be between us . . . that's . . ."

And I knew what she was about to say, so I started talking fast, to keep her from saying it. And so she didn't, she never actually said it, and I left a little later.

Thinking back, I wonder what I wanted at that moment. Did I really want to stop her from saying, *It's not between us anymore, it can't be between us anymore.* Did I want to stop her from saying it because I wanted to preserve the possibility of contact? Or did I stop her because I didn't want any contact anymore, didn't need any, didn't want any, and even her saying it, even her *referring* to the absence of contact was too much contact, was too close, and . . . it burned. It burned in my mind.

*

I parked the deported woman's blue Plymouth Horizon in the library parking lot. The sky was overcast, for which I was mildly grateful. Open sun had become difficult for me. All surfaces closed up under its torrential glare; the opacity of things inescapable.

The sky was overcast. Inside the library, after wandering around for a bit, I discovered the art section—a single aisle of mostly oversized volumes. The Renaissance collection took up two shelves. After considering, I selected two works. My criteria prioritized size. The larger the number and bigger the size of reproductions of paintings, the better.

One was a book about Giotto. It was a large book with many

full-page color images along with a great deal of writing and scores of black-and-white illustrations. The other was a tall, relatively thin book. But it made up for this by the fact that half of the pages consisted of large, full-page color reproductions of paintings, with the facing page offering what seemed like helpful descriptions of the painting.

The title, to which I paid little attention at the time, was *Bellini*.

18.

Pan

It wasn't until later that night, when—unable to sleep—I turned on the light in my bedroom and dragged the massive Giotto volume out from under my bed—that I began to understand how close I now was to the end.

I'd gotten the book out to verify a sudden intuition or fear or retrospective prophecy that had seized me while lying sleepless, listening for the single drop of oblivion to roll down the pipe into my open eyes.

And now, after switching the light on, I experienced the strange feeling the insomniac undergoes when adding actual physical illumination to the ceaseless awareness that has turned the dark virtually, for all practical purposes except reading, light. There's a sudden shock when one realizes the visibility one has lain suspended in with one's eyes open is not true visibility, is in fact closer to dreams. The colors and textures—and above all the *angles*—revealed by the physical light show one with heartbreaking clarity *I was actually much closer to sleep than I realized, perhaps I was actually sleeping*! There have been nights when actual tears formed at this revelation. But this night I was too intent on verifying my suspicion.

I took out the Giotto book from under my bed. I flipped through the pages impatiently until I found the one I sought.

There.

I rocked back on my haunches staring. The forms, the shapes of the reproduced painting or fresco were of lesser interest—though I noted the unmistakably medieval quality of some of the represented architecture—a tower, a stretch of wall.

What held me was the color.

Red. A very particular red. The red, in fact, of the cover of the Signet Classics edition of *Ivanhoe*.

I rose and went to the bookshelf on which were arrayed the two dozen books I'd brought with me from Dad's, most bought with Ace money, a couple stolen from the high school library. I found the frayed volume I sought, placed it on the wooden floor next to the open Giotto.

It was the identical hue.

*

Perhaps two or three days later, I sat reading in a corner of the living room. Alex was playing Nintendo. All day the snow had been erasing the distances outside the house. School canceled for both of us. Mom was out—her clients didn't recognize snow days.

I had the Bellini book open on my lap. Alex was playing *Ghosts 'n Goblins.* The sound of sword swipes glittered in the dry, heated air.

The third reproduced painting in the book delivered the revelation. The painting was called *The Drunkenness of Noah.*

I looked out the window for a while at veils of white. Then I looked down at the book again.

The figure at the bottom of the composition was very clearly one of the sleepers from the vision created behind my closed eyes by the second movement of Bach's third orchestral suite.

*

A week later—with not more than four or five hours of total sleep between—I sat on the closed toilet seat of the beige tiled bathroom on the second floor of the house—staring at the painting of a head.

The portrait was called *Doge Leonardo Loredan.* From the base of the head—which was posed atop what to a superficial viewer might appear as a body—flowed a silvery cloth of the kind on which John the Baptist's head was delivered to Salome. I suspected that the head—no neck was visible, no inch of body flesh—was set atop a pile of books, over which the cloth had been draped. I might have been wrong. Perhaps it was a manikin's torso, or a broken column. In any case my identification of the inner nature of the image didn't depend on speculation about this detail.

The very first time I turned to the fourth page of *Bellini*, I recognized it. The head from *Salome.* And Sarah's ancient words rolled through my mind:

"Would your head like be suddenly empty? Would I like be sitting

here with you, and suddenly your head would like—roll back—and your tongue would loll out? Would you be in the painting? Would you be out there in the air . . . headless?"

Then, without any effort on my part, my mind called up the closing movement of the List, the final, rising chord of panic symptoms:

11. The fringe of body around my looking getting very bright.
12. Very alien.
13. The feeling that I could come out of my body. My head, in particular.
14. That my looking/thinking could pour or leap out.
15. Wonder where thoughts come from.
16. Wonder what looking is.
17. Afraid of what's next.

The day I first discovered the book, my eyes rested on *Doge Leonardo Loredan* for much less than a second. I turned the page quickly, to some kind of landscape scene, with an innocuous saint, head fully part of his body, standing in the foreground. But it was as if the other head—its terrible shape, the occulted Doge's hat giving it the panic horn, google it! Look at it!—It was as if that profile *bled through* the page. I could see its shape glowing from the trees and rocks.

I put the book down at once. But over the next hours and days I found the head rising in fields of color:

The light blue of the faded paint of the deported woman's car.

Sarah's orange blouse.

Snow.

The wood grain of the kitchen table.

The pale skin of the back of my hand.

And so for several days, and worse nights, the Doge's head with its panic horn rose in any color my eyes fell upon.

That morning, I told Mom I was sick, couldn't go to school. She nodded, looked concerned, asked if I needed her to find her thermometer. Did I feel feverish? I nodded, then shook my head, told her to go, I'd be fine . . .

Alex's bus left. Now, with the house deserted, I carried the tall, slender volume to the tiled bathroom, locked the door. Sat on the closed lid of the toilet.

Prayed to God.

And then I opened the book to *Doge Leonardo Loredan.*

*

As I sat staring at it the buzzing started. At first I actually looked around the bathroom for a fly. But when I moved, the buzzing stopped.

It's winter, I thought. No flies.

And then I sat down again on the closed toilet lid and opened the book, and the buzzing started.

Very, very faint.

Zzzzzz—zzz—zzzzzz.

I remembered the tree spreading in the air—I saw it again in the tile-enclosed column of air at the center of the small bathroom, with its abnormally tall ceiling—saw the fly tree once again. The half hour, or hour, or two hours, or perhaps even a full day of the fly's spasmodic movements collapsed into a moment, time folded into space—the black tree rose in the column of air.

Again I got up and looked for the fly. Again the sound died. I sat once more on the closed toilet lid.

Zzzzzzz—zzz—zzzzzz.

I wasn't hearing it with my ears, but with my body.

And the buzzing, I realized—it wasn't a fly. It was the traffic . . . the torrent of cars, the endless rushing of traffic on the highway a quarter mile away, rumbling through the earth, coming up through the porcelain, rattling its metal fixtures infinitesimally, producing a *buzzing* I heard with my flesh, with my body, which was now completely and utterly a thing no different from the porcelain toilet, the metal handle, the tiled walls.

*

I stared at the head in the picture.

The face stared out of the absolute blue of timelessness, its single horn rising at the back of its skull.

And I felt the *strangeness* of my looking—the looking and thought that was in me—the *strangeness* of it. And that head—it rose against a background of blue in utter strangeness, in the *same strangeness*—and as I stared—I saw the head perched atop its little hill and I thought—Larry's right—the rock stays put—he was right after all—the rock stays put, not the first time, not the second, not the third, but the rock stays put at last . . .

Those words were not mine—they might as well have been

Larry's—they were what was left in my head when I fell out. They stayed running through my head, the ghosts of words, the husks of thoughts, the whole time I was out. Because I fell through my body. The solid world, the thing world opened, the gate opened, and I fell.

When the last part of me came out of the body, it finally happened. At the last moment, I saw something I could keep. I put on a little of His knowledge. As the last part of me exited, just before I stopped knowing anything, I saw and I knew. I saw that time was a part of the body after all, a part of things.

I saw that when you're outside the body, beings that move in time look like trees and the world of beings that move in time resembles a forest.

The calmness and silence of Pan's gaze.

CODA

I believe now that the instances of "prophecy" littered throughout the preceding report are in reality not visions of the future, but mere sensations, registrations of the brute fact that everything has already happened. Anyone who at any point directly experiences the finitude of time will probably feel something not dissimilar, radiating unpredictably forward and backward from the moment of insight.

Acknowledgments

I'd like to thank my editor, Helen Rouner, and my agent, Denise Shannon. I'd also like to thank Lauren Clune, Aaron Kunin, Lorin Stein, Ben Lerner, Jordan Castro, and everyone at Penguin.

Dave, T., S., L.: Je n'ai pas oublie. This book is dedicated to Aislin.

About the Author

Michael Clune is the critically acclaimed author of the memoirs *Gamelife* and *White Out*. The latter was chosen by the *New Yorker* as one of the best books of 2013. Clune's work has appeared in *Harper's*, the *New Yorker*, *Granta* and elsewhere, and he has received fellowships and awards from the John Simon Guggenheim Memorial Foundation, the Mellon Foundation, the Baker-Nord Center for the Humanities and others. He is a professor at the Chase Center at the Ohio State University and lives in Cleveland Heights, Ohio. He was born in Ireland.

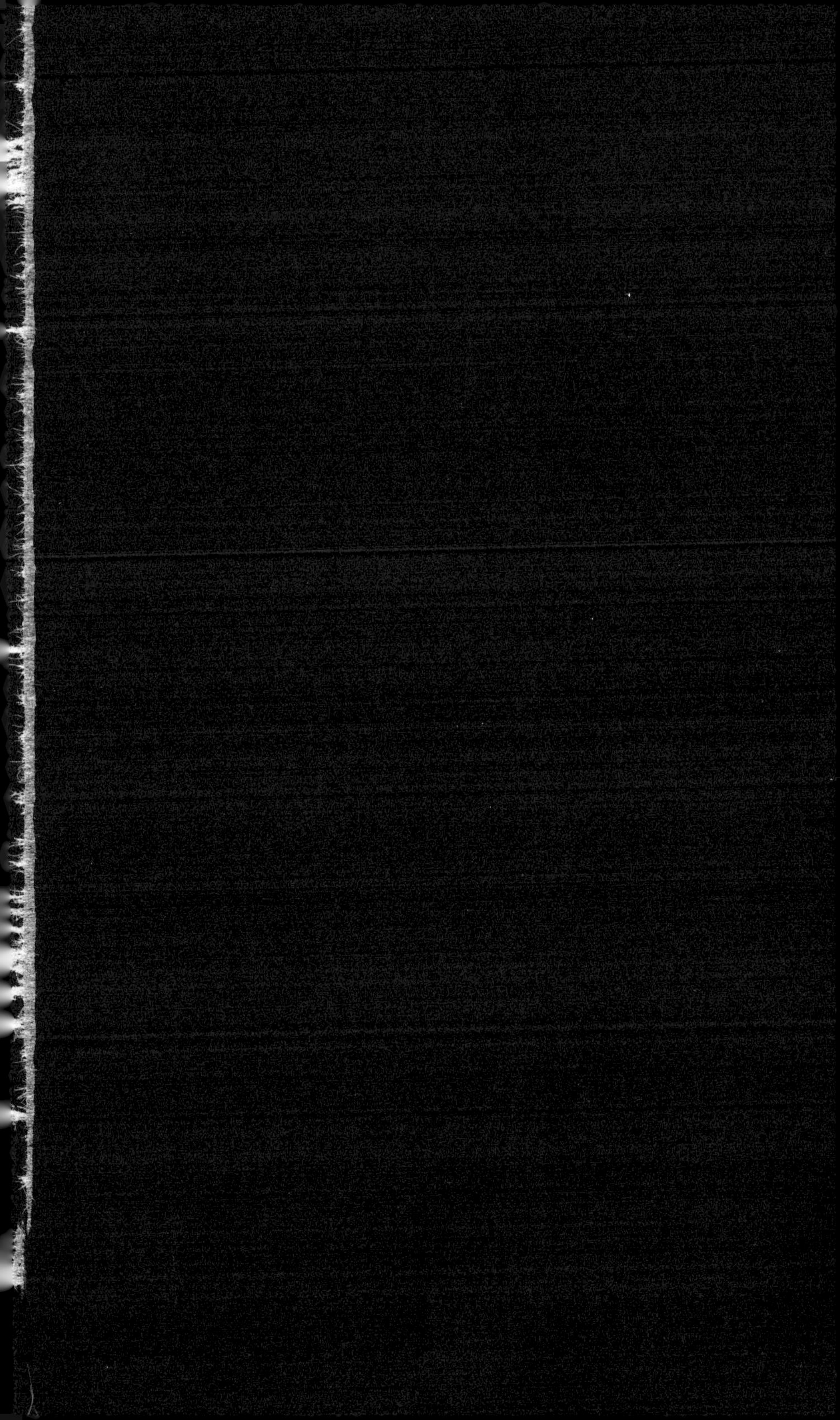